Sundown
Requiem

The MacKenzie Trilogy

❖ MacKenzie's Farewell
❖ God, Guns, and Charter Schools
❖ Sundown Requiem

Also by William Allen Burley
Cardinal Points of View: A Modern Chapbook

Sundown
Requiem

William Allen Burley

SUNDOWN REQUIEM

iUniverse books may be ordered through booksellers or by contacting:

iUniverse
1663 Liberty Drive
Bloomington, IN 47403
www.iuniverse.com
1-800-Authors (1-800-288-4677)

ISBN: 978-1-5320-6266-7 (sc)
ISBN: 978-1-5320-6265-0 (e)

Library of Congress Control Number: 2018914579

Print information available on the last page.

iUniverse rev. date: 12/19/2018

Dedicated to all who have a concern
for the health of the Earth,
who care about social injustices,
and share their lives with someone they love.

❖ Prelude ❖

❖ Invocation ❖

Twenty-five years earlier, on New Year's Eve, 2015, I married Annie Caton. I considered ours a love affair for the ages. It lasted longer than I could have imagined.

In 2040, I saw an advertisement for a new edition of *The Generation Diary.* The product was a compendium of twenty years of headlines, photographs, and news articles spanning U.S. and world events from 2020 to 2040. The contents appeared to be generic in nature, selected by editors to remind a mixed readership of what happened over the past one-fifth century. The advertisement showed up in magazines, as a pop-up on my computer, and played on television as a sponsor of the Exploring Channel and the *History Explained* series.

I finally felt vindicated for my obsessive pursuit. I was pleased that on my own volition I started collecting clippings in 2015. I secretly amassed a trove of headlines, articles, and correspondence that had particular meaning to our lives. Some featured world affairs, others were more personal in nature. I was scrapbooking everything in preparation to give Annie a gift on our silver anniversary.

My plan was to present her with two albums. The first was the completed scrapbook. The second was an empty album ready to be filled with memories from our final years. Then, on July 4, 2039, in Annie's fifty-ninth year, she died. Her passing was six months before our anniversary. Since we were wed on the last day of 2015, news events of 2040 needed to be added to complete the book. I had planned to choose the final entry along with Annie, but I completed the task alone.

I never had a chance to give my wife the scrapbook while she was alive. But I kept my promise and completed the project in 2040. It is my most treasured possession.

2015

Rambling Rockers

Trump Announces Run for Presidency; Is Encumbered with Racist Baggage

• Editorial / Opinion •

19 JUNE 2015

Three days ago, on June 16, 2015, Donald J. Trump announced his candidacy for President of the United States. He entered the race as a Republican. He rode the escalator down to the lobby of the Trump Tower, his headquarters and home, where he made his statement. He was accompanied by family and supporters.

Never in modern political history has a candidate entered the presidential campaign carrying so much overt racist baggage. Trump's actions and words prove him to be a bigot every American should abhor. His vile behavior is well documented in courts of law and on the pages of American newspapers.

The published stories are supported by his very own words. There is no ambiguity in what he says. He considers all people of color or origin who are not white citizens to be inferior or alien. He grouped African Americans, Latinos, and Muslims as perpetrators of crime, violence, and terrorism. His xenophobic rants should be rejected by every American.

Donald Trump's hatreds stem from long-standing family prejudices. His father, Fred, was a white power sympathizer. In 1927, he was arrested during a KKK thousand man march through the streets of Queens. Although there is no record of what happened to Fred Trump immediately after the march, he went on to become a real estate developer in the outer boroughs with a reputation for rejecting black rental applicants.

Donald Trump follows in his father's footsteps. In 1973, he and Fred were sued by the Federal government for racial discrimination regarding blacks seeking rental properties. The Trumps lost, paid a sizeable fine, and agreed to cease their discriminatory practices. But they never apologized.

More recently, Donald Trump publicly called for the execution of the so-called "Central Park Five." In 1989, five black and Latino youths were accused of assaulting and raping a white woman in Central Park. Trump spent $85,000 placing ads in the four NYC daily papers. He called for the return of the death penalty especially to be applied to the accused. Fourteen years later the five were exonerated based on DNA evidence. Nevertheless, Trump doubled down on his insistence they were guilty. He never apologized.

Trump is also the mouthpiece for the "birther" movement. He rejected the legitimacy of President Barack Obama's citizenship, demanding to see Obama's birth certificate. He couldn't accept the fact that a child of an interracial marriage was a citizen. He questioned Obama's college records. He never apologized.

He disparaged President Obama's legislative accomplishments. He has sworn to end Obamacare, not because of its faults and liabilities, but because it was an accomplishment of a black man. He never apologized.

He refused to disavow David Duke, leader of the KKK. He lied saying he didn't know Duke when, in fact, film clips show him talking at length about Duke. He never apologized.

The editorial board of *Rambling Rockers* has never endorsed a candidate for political office. We continue to follow this policy. But we unanimously agree that un-American behavior must be identified and condemned. No conducts are more reprehensible than bigotry and racism. And no candidate is more racially motivated than Donald J. Trump. Honor the men and women who served in the Second World War fighting white supremacy by rejecting Trump's candidacy.

Remember, despite proven guilty of racism and bigotry, candidate Trump continues to lie about his complicity. Donald J. Trump has never apologized.

Maryann Caton, 35 | Robt. MacKenzie, 47 | Jake Canfeld, 9 | World POP: 7.2 billion

---

Annie lay sprawled across the couch scrolling through photos of her friends on her smartphone. She was comfortable with her friends calling her Maryann or Annie. Behind her, in the study alcove, she heard Rob tapping away at the computer. She knew he was preparing a lengthy syllabus for the college course he would be teaching at Western Connecticut State University, slated to begin in a few weeks. Rob was a visiting professor in the Department of Environmental Studies filling the endowed Jane Goodale chair. His preparations were meticulous. Described in his syllabus were the course's philosophy, practical outcomes, teacher responsibilities, and student obligations. A comprehensive bibliography was included.

She re-focused on the phone. A particular photograph caused her to chuckle. "Hey, love," she called into him, "I found our Grant Wood image."

"You mean the one with me holding the empty ice cream cone instead of a pitchfork? Aye, it was very funny."

"You're supposed to eat ice cream quickly before it falls to the ground," she kidded. "Haven't I taught you anything?"

"You have. I've learned to eat ice cream out of a cup."

"The photo's a bit lopsided. Jake needs practice." She tilted the phone a few degrees to make the image vertical.

"If you want to keep it, we'll fix the alignment before consigning it to an album. Do you have an album title in mind?"

"Yes, honey, I've labeled it, 'Summer of Love.'"

"Sounds like a movie title or a romance novel. Still, good choice, lass. Better that than 'Roxbridge Glows in the Dark.'"

"Yes, it is. But maybe Roxbridge won't be selected. The Low Level Nuclear Waste Repository could be destined for either Halyard or Millington."

"Aye, I agree. It could wind up in either of those two towns. We'll learn more at the hearings. But I'd prefer our odds to be much less than one out of three."

Annie studied the image of her and Rob. They were standing in front of the Young Republican table at the Roxbridge Firemen's Carnival. Both had been scooping ice cream in

4

the food service area. Taking a break, they decided to treat themselves to cones, then have Jake photograph them blocking the political table. Assuming poses like the dour couple depicted in Grant Wood's painting, "American Gothic," seemed like a good idea, especially as the presidential races heated up and candidate rhetoric became inflammatory.

It was while lining up for the picture that Rob's scoop of rum raisin hit the ground. Before it could be resurrected, Jake squashed it like a puff-ball. As a result, Rob was left with an empty cone. Never one to let ice cream go uneaten, Annie rapidly finished her scoop and cone. Years of training with Ben and Jerry's made her an expert.

She was pleased with her smartphone image. It showed her wearing a tie-dyed "Hillary" t-shirt. Its colors matched her eyes. But her Three Stooges "Moe-style" mop of hair was totally unlike the farm lady's severe comb-back. Maryann felt her chin. In the photo the cleft was obvious, but the scar on her upper lip caused by a fall on the beach at Lake Erie as a kid was barely noticeable. Finally, the height difference between her 5'3" and Rob's 6'3" was much more dramatic than the height difference between the gothic pair.

She studied the image of the man she was marrying in December. Rob's green shirt had the same effect as her shirt had on her eyes. His became as green as clover. It was the perfect color to accent his Celtic reddish blond hair.

Both were fair skinned, she was reminded, products of their northern European heritage. They applied sunblock SPF 50 daily. Jake had a darker complexion inherited from his father. While Rob and Annie fought to avoid becoming sunburned, Jake tanned.

"No matter that Jake and I have gone to the Roxbridge Firemen's Carnival for three years, I never grow tired of it. You too, Jake?" asked Annie.

Jake was engrossed untangling a length of twine. "Yep, it's cool. Mom, please hold the end while I unravel this mess."

Annie grabbed the loose end. "Did you hose Rob's ice cream off your shoe?"

"Yeah. I hosed off both feet. It's cool to smoosh around in wet sneakers."

"Where are they?" she asked. "Did you leave them outside to dry?"

"They're on the back deck in the sun, like you said." Jake hesitated, then looked at Rob with repentant eyes. "Rob, are you mad at me for squashing your ice cream?"

"Nae, I'm not, laddie. I'm the one who dropped it."

Jake looked relieved. "I thought maybe you did it on purpose . . . ugh . . . rum raisin!"

Rob shrugged and shook his head. "I like that flavor, lad. It's better than the pink muck you eat—what's it called— bubblegum and anchovy?" Rob laughed, as if his made-up flavor could possibly be enjoyed by anyone.

"Okay you two ice cream connoisseurs. Let me get a word in. Rob, dear, did you enjoy your first Roxbridge carnival?"

"Aye, Annie, that I did. I now feel like part of the town. Working side-by-side with others is always a good way to make friends, especially serving ice cream."

Rob looked puzzled by Jake's efforts to untangle the string. "What are you doing, Jake? Why are you spending so much time untangling that knot?"

Jake explained what he thought should be obvious to anyone. "I saw a clown at the carnival that held up his pants with rope.

6

I wanna try it. But I don't have any rope, so I'm using string. I think it'll work. I'll make a good clown."

"Aye, that be true, laddie," agreed Rob winking at Annie. "You'll make a perfect clown. Here, let me help you with that tangle."

"Speaking of clowns, Rob, did you hear that Trump's thrown his hat into the ring? He's going to run for president."

"I know, Annie. I caught his announcement on television. I don't think he usually wears a hat, though. He might mess up his coiffe. A daily dose of lacquer spray seems to be his choice to keep his mane in place."

She snickered. "I remember in March when you compared him with an orangutan. Nothing's changed."

"Aye, he's the same. In fact, he's been the same nasty blowhard for all the years I lived in the city. For the most part, I ignored his shite. I'd see stories about him and his mistresses in the tabloids, but he and I ran in different circles. Needless to say, very different circles! So I never paid much attention to his nonsense." Rob kicked at a clod of grass.

"From time to time his face would scowl out of a bookstore window when another of his ghost written books was published. Why anyone would buy one was a mystery to me. From the reviews I read, they were all empty sets of platitudes. Those boasts lured people into enrolling in his so-called university. What a scam!"

Annie wondered aloud. "How can such a disreputable character be considered a legitimate presidential contender?"

"That's a good question, love. At the risk of generalizing, I'd say our country is loaded with like-minded disreputable characters. Too often these low-lifes are considered high-minded heroes. Take a look at the evangelical ministry."

"Yeah, like Falwell, Graham, and Robertson. I know what you mean."

"Right. You're an American citizen by birth, Annie. Sometimes natives become oblivious to the nastiness around them."

Rob became more reflective. "I'm a naturalized citizen. I turned my back on clan and religious schisms in Scotland. I thought America would be better. I fought in the American army. Yet the longer I live here, I've learned America is just as pitiful as Scotland, maybe worse. The reasons for division here might be different than in Scotland—white versus black, rich versus poor, religious versus secular. But hatreds are hatreds no matter what shape they take or where they thrive."

Annie grimaced with a memory. "If Trump's words and behaviors aren't bad enough, I saw a clip of him engaging in violence at a professional wrestling match. Shouldn't our country elect someone who is mature in both words and actions? Rob, do you think an embarrassment like Trump has a chance to get elected?"

Rob was silent at first. Then he spoke in a hushed voice as if he was giving an eulogy at a funeral. "I don't know, love. Stranger things have happened. Look how long our country tolerated Joe McCarthy and George Wallace. I'd say Trump's chance to be the Republican Party's nominee is a long-shot. My guess is Jeb Bush will emerge as the front-runner. But if Trump survives the primaries, he'll come face to face with a formidable Democrat, maybe Hillary, maybe Sanders, maybe Warren. I think any one of those three would whip his ass. But I could be wrong."

2016

The New York Messenger

"THE SPIRIT OF PUBLIUS"

Brexit and Trump

Protectionism and Xenophobia Find Fertile Soil
in Western Democracies

DECEMBER 11, 2016 $3.00

ANALYSIS: By Charles Eisenrich, NYM Political Staff Writer

London — The year 2016 will be remembered for the stunning U.S. presidential election and the unexpected outcome of the British referendum to leave the EU. In both instances, the results surprised pollsters and analysts who saw the winners as unlikely long-shots.

Ballot issues resembled plebiscites. The economic direction of each country faced radical change. In the end, untested philosophy rode roughshod over long established trade practices, backed by the delusion that national isolationism would improve the lives of working-class citizens.

The votes also unearthed long hidden fears of immigration, distrust of career politicians, and boosted a return to devout nationalism. The very idea of what it meant to be British was in question. Whether hopes of returning to an "English way of life" will be realized or dashed will be determined in the coming months.

Prior to the vote, Britain's cabinet was in favour of remaining in the EU by a 4 to 1 margin (24 remain, 6 exit). Prime Minister David Cameron called for the vote amidst mounting pressure to do so. In retrospect, he was unwise to rapidly accede to the Exit Coalition's pressure. The Exit crowd mounted a rapid and compelling advertising campaign touting future economic benefits. Many inflated boasts claimed the money saved by not contributing Britain's share to the EU would be poured back into the national health care system. At public meetings, Exit politicians made impossible promises or lied about Britain's future prosperity.

Now the island nation has to figure out how to leave the EU and still maintain a semblance of pride. Brussels has made it clear they will not kowtow to English demands. Any imagined leverage the Exit group promised has been erased. Britain is on its own and can only hope EU ministers will open a few doors towards normalcy. The idea that Britain, a small island nation of 65 million, can exert her influence on the world stage is a myth. Britain's strength rests in the combined might of the EU, a partnership of 501 million citizens. This was the lesson that should have been learned in two world wars. England cannot go it alone.

The US presidential election resulted in its own set of surprises. Donald J. Trump gained 306 Electoral College votes compared with 232 for Hillary Clinton despite Clinton's popular vote lead of 2.4 million. British citizens continue to puzzle over the American Electoral College process.

How did it happen? How did a serial womanizer, a documented racist, and a proven liar become the leader of the most powerful nation on Earth? What hocus-pocus, sleight of hand card trick was perpetrated on the American electorate? How were Americans so bamboozled that they risked their nation's standing in the world? How could they have compromised their security by entrusting their nuclear arsenal to a man who asked, "Why not use nuclear weapons"? rather than say, "We must never *again* use nuclear weapons."

Studying Trump's actions and listening to his words affirm he is a troubled man, if not mentally ill. He is boastful without shame. He is an extreme narcissist. He has a thin skin and behaves like a seven-year-old. He threatens or belittles other world leaders or US politicians with bullying tactics more appropriate to the playground. He claims he will "Make America Great Again" despite exhibiting behaviors that promise to degrade America. He claims he's for the everyday worker, but his past business practices show he's only for himself. His record of business failures and bankruptcies belie his boasts of business acumen. Politically, he promises to "drain the swamp" in Washington. Instead, he has cleared a spot for his own reptilian self.

The election results in both the UK and America stem from similar systemic social and economic causes:

- Xenophobic fear of people of color
- Long entrenched racial hatreds
- Little understanding about non-Christian religions

- Stagnant wages and benefits
- The looming decline of the white majority
- Governmental gridlock and corruption
- The power of the military-industrial complex
- Environmental deterioration
- The rich get richer—the poor get poorer
- The squeeze of population growth

Academics and scientists are wrestling with these problems. Often their work gives a glimmer of hope. However, the brainlessness of our leaders undermine the good intentions of honorable men and women.

With apologies to prehistoric hominidae, our two nations have fallen into the grasp of dull humanoids. Britain and America are ruled by two species of great apes: England's fictional "mangani species," (Cheetah in the Tarzan movies), and Trump's orangutan persona emulated by his "monkey see-monkey do" followers in America.

Maryann Caton, 36 | Robt. MacKenzie, 48 | Jake Canfeld, 10 | World POP: 7.33 billion

---

Rob held the seven foot tall Douglas fir vertical, while Annie tightened the T-screws holding it securely in its base. In fact, the tree was not a real tree at all, simply the topped section of a much larger specimen from an evergreen farm in Warren. The original was felled to harvest boughs for wreaths, roping, and other Christmas decorations, as well as a decoration for the MacKenzie living room.

Rob stepped back to analyze their work. Annie remained prone under the branches. Rob tilted his head, circled the tree, and decided it could be made straighter. Jake watched from across the room.

"I'm sorry to say this, love, but it's leaning left. Please undo the screws on the left a few wee turns. I'll pull the the top to the right. Then tighten the screws on the right. It looks like there's more room on the threads. That should do it."

"Ouch!" complained Annie. "The needles are sticking me. Hold on. Which way do I turn them?"

"Loosen, left. Tighten, right."

"Okay, I've got it."

The tree slowly straightened as Annie adjusted the screws. Rob held it until she was done.

"Good job, lass. Now I'll grab your ankles and pull you out." Rob laughed and moved toward her feet.

"Can I help?" asked Jake, flexing his muscles.

"Don't you dare, Rob! You, too, Jake! I'll get myself out." She inched backward, raised to her knees, then stood. "It looks fine and dandy. I'm not getting under there again."

Jake piped up, "I can get under, Mom. We're about the same size."

"No need for either of you," said Rob. "It's perfect! Let's get some holiday grog before we decorate it."

"I bought a six-pack of the Christmas Beer you like, Rob, and there's egg nog for me. Jake, what would you like?"

"I'd like the yellow stuff in the bubble lights," he said, "but I'll settle for Mountain Dew."

Rob chuckled. "A fine choice, lad. They're the same color. At college in North Carolina, we called Mountain Dew 'Appalachian urine.'"

Jake laughed like a donkey. "Cool!" he brayed. "Gimme a glass of piss."

"Enough, you two, settle down!" Maryann glared. "This is the holiday season. Save your nonsense for All Fools' Day."

With refreshments sorted out, they returned to the living room and began decorating the tree. Maryann was in charge. After they arranged the lights, she assigned jobs.

"Rob, you're the only one tall enough to put the bagpipe Santa Claus on top, and I'll give you the smaller decorations to hang up high. Jake, you carefully arrange the wooden ornaments Nana sent. Be careful. They're only glued together. I'll hang the large glass Bohemian balls at the bottom. There's an art to that. Oh, and Jake, when we get to the tinsel, no throwing it on in clumps. We did that in Mars, and I hated it. So sloppy! One strand at a time."

"Aw, Mom . . ."

"That will take forever, love," said Rob. "Why not randomly drizzle it over the branches and let gravity and chaos theory take over."

"This isn't a science experiment, sweetie. This is Yuletide, the prelude to Hogmanay. There'll be no chaos in this household." Annie sounded resolute.

After Jake marched up to bed, Annie and Rob snuggled on the couch. Table lamp lights were off, but the Christmas tree sparkled with color. The bubble lights bubbled, at least those they were able to secure vertically. Conservation minded Annie had turned down the thermostat. The house was cooling as the temperature dropped outside.

"We have two big events coming up in a few weeks, Rob, Christmas and our first anniversary. What do you think we ought to do? How should we celebrate, or do you already have something in mind?"

"I resisted not including you in my plans, love, but I wanted to surprise you. I have planned something. Now's as good a time as any to free the flock. If I don't, you'll learn soon enough, and then it won't be a surprise. There are multiple parts."

"Really?" she asked, both pleased and amazed that her husband had taken the initiative. "Will you tell me, or do I have to guess?"

Rob laughed and pulled Annie close. He arranged his mother's wedding gift, a warm wool throw, over their legs. He kissed the backs of her hands, "Nae, dear, you don't have to guess. As I said, you're gonna know soon enough, when the bills come in . . . so here goes." He held her tightly.

"First, for Christmas, I ordered three mountain bikes at Southtown Chain and Sprocket. Having properly geared machines for these hills will allow us to get around more easily than on the clunkers we brought up from Manhattan. We'll be able to use them to do errands. The cars can stay in the garage. When the bikes come in, we'll transport them home in your SUV. If you want, we can make an even bigger celebration of the day with lunch at the Charcoal Grille in Woodbury."

"What a good idea, honey!" She kissed him on the cheek. "Do you think a new bike's enough of a gift for Jake? I worry about that. His father always gave him a check. He was generous, but I think boxes to open are more fun than an envelope to unseal. Should I get him a few more gifts?"

"That's up to you, Mother Caton. The lad has plenty of stuff, but a lad never grows tired of new underwear or socks. You'll figure it out."

She shrugged. "I guess."

"But for you, Annie, the bike's the big and only Christmas gift from me this year. No jewelry."

She laughed. "That's fine. My wedding ring's the best gift

of all time." She allowed the tree lights to reflect off her band. "Honey, will you let me buy you some extra gifts?"

"Aye, okay, but not much. The bike's a gift to myself. Then, of course, I have you."

"It won't be much, love, just some underwear and socks." She laughed. "I know your size."

They rolled into each other's embrace giggling at their shared intimacy and beautiful passion. If Rob hadn't continued revealing his list of surprises, they would have been hurrying to the bedroom.

"I love kissing you, lass. Your lips are soft and sweet." He looked into her eyes then touched the tip of her nose with a finger, as if he was playing middle C on the piano. "There's more to my madness. It's for Hogmanay, New Year's Eve, our wedding anniversary."

"Tell me, my highlander," Annie anxiously prodded. "What have you planned?"

Rob began to lay out the events. "You know we're invited to the Peters' for a New Year's Eve party. If you haven't done so, let Abby know we're coming."

"Oh, okay," she said with restrained enthusiasm. "It will be nice to celebrate our first anniversary with our friends—folks who attended our wedding. That's thoughtful of you, honey. Good idea."

Rob explained further. "The reason for going to the Peters' is that I couldn't get tickets for January first. There's no show. They're closed on New Year's Day."

Maryann sat bolt upright. "Tickets? What tickets are you talking about?"

"Tickets to *Hamilton*, my love. I couldn't get them for our anniversary, but I did snag a pair for Saturday, January 28." He laughed. "It starts the Chinese New Year."

"How did you get *Hamilton* tickets?" she asked amazed. "Are they genuine? The show's been sold out for a year."

"Aye, they're the real thing. Getting them was complicated. But I didn't break the law snaring them. Let's just say I have a fairy godmother, even though I don't believe in fairies or in God. Chalk it up to ULAR, my version of the Golden Rule."

He kissed her forehead. "We'll take the train in from Brewster on Friday afternoon the 27th and stay at the Columbia Club on East 43rd Street. Carl Leslie, an old piping friend, is putting us up for two evenings. He's the club manager."

"Great! I've never been to the club, even though I'm a Columbia graduate. What fun!"

"True! And to top it off, on Friday evening, like the Penn Club, Columbia's celebrating Rabbie Burns' birthday. We're guests for the weekend. I'm not piping, but I did promise Carl that I'd recite the 'Ode to A Haggis' in Scottish dialect. What do you think?"

"My goodness, Rob! That's all fantastic! Oh, honey, I love you so much for doing this. It will be so special."

"One last thing, Annie. Jake's spending the weekend at the Higgins' while we're gone. It's all set."

"Dear, you've remembered everything. You're so thoughtful."

"We'll see. I hope my think machine's working. I've a lot of remembering to do to get the 'Ode' fixed in my noggin. Let's see, if I recall, the first verse goes . . . *Fair fa' your honest, sonsie face / Great chieftain o the puddin'-race! / Aboon them a' ye tak your place, / Painch, tripe, or thairm: / Weel are ye worthy o' a grace / As lang's my arm.*"

Annie read somewhere that most post-coital behavior

was usually characterized by relaxation and drowsiness. That certainly was the case with Rob. Within minutes after intercourse he was asleep, breathing heavily, a smile on his face. Annie watched him drift away obviously content and fulfilled by their love-making.

Not so for her. When sex was over, the memory of his caresses, tongue, and penetration continued to arouse her beyond the point of sleep. Tonight, she was especially alive thinking about the happy and eventful days that lay ahead. She wanted him to hold her again.

She propped her head on her pillow to see him better. Ambient light filtered into the room from the stars and a crescent moon. He was making clicking sounds as he breathed. She felt his warmth radiating out, spreading under the quilt, defying the December chill. His body seemed to be emitting pheromones, drawing her to him even as he slept. She entered his warm spot and kissed his ear.

At first, he slept on. She tried tickling him with her tongue. Not getting a reaction, she touched his groin. Still nothing. She pinched his nipple. No reaction. Finally, in a fit of impatience, she nudged his shoulder and cooed, "Robbie . . . Robbie . . . c'mon, lad. Wake up. I can't get to sleep. Talk to me, honey. Tell me you love me. What brand of bicycle did you order?" Suddenly, she saw Rob's eyes pop open. "What did you say?" he asked, as if startled. "Something about bicycles?"

She laughed. "No, silly, I was suggesting we go mattress riding again, repeating the trip we just had. You know what I mean. No bicycles are necessary."

He rubbed his eyes and made out her face in the dim light. He sat up. "Okay. I'll be back in a minute. I've got to pee. You know, Appalachian urine—Mountain Dew. Keep my place warm."

"Don't worry, love," she replied coyly, "I'm not going anywhere." She curled into a ball and waited for his return.

By the time he slid back into bed, she saw he was wide awake. He told her that while voiding, he remembered reading in the *New York Messenger* an analysis of Brexit and Trump. He moved closer to her. But he was distracted, she could tell, not responding to her hints and signals, lost instead, somewhere in his head.

"Put your hands on my breasts," she urged.

He cupped her then released them. He propped himself on an elbow.

"What's wrong?" she asked, turning to face him.

"Huh? Wrong? Oh, nothing, lassie. I just can't keep the Brexit business out of mind."

"Can't we talk about it later?" she suggested, amused but also frustrated.

"I may forget it later."

"All right," she sighed, "tell me what you're thinking."

"I saw a BBC newscast laying out the many reasons for the Brexit results and how Scotland might respond. There's movement afoot in Edinburgh to abandon the UK and go it alone as an independent nation. Same for Northern Ireland."

"Mmm," she murmured. "How do you feel about that? Does it bother you? Move closer."

"I don't know what to feel. I've lived apart from Scotland for thirty years, so I've lost touch with what voters think. But I prefer Scotland remain part of the EU. Much of the world's banking is headquartered in Edinburgh, and North Sea oil is driving the economy."

"Mmm . . . driving the economy," she quietly parroted, his blather fading away as she dozed.

"Then there's the long-standing animosities between

England and Scotland. For centuries the Red Coats kept Scots locked in their thumb-screws."

"Mmm . . . thumb screws . . . Hamiltooo . . ."

"I'm thinking it's time for Scotland to break free from any remaining chains of Britannia. It's time for Caledonia to become 'Scotland the Brave.'"

"Mmm . . . mmm . . . mmm . . ."

"What do you think, honey?" he asked to his snoozing partner. "Am I too optimistic? Should Scotland bolt the UK and peg its future on the EU? Honey, are you awake?"

There was no response. He saw she was asleep. He touched her shoulders and gently caressed her neck. Why had he prattled on about Scottish geo-politics, he wondered, when he could again have made love to his beautiful wife, a wee lass from Mars, Pennsylvania.

2017

The Carlsbad Critique

PART OF THE MINUTEMAN TODAY NETWORK

Cavetown brine well collapses-radiation released into air-residents call for DOE investigation

Henry Suarez, The Carlsbad Critique Published 4:22 p.m. MT February 22, 2017

Cavetown residents are calling upon the United States Department of Energy to investigate Friday's collapse of a brine well at WIPP #2. The floor in cavern 45-2Wd suddenly subsided into a heretofore undetected brine well. The integrity of concrete containers holding transuranic wastes from the Tres Cruces Laboratory in Las Niñas, NM, were compromised. The Cavetown facility is Waste Isolation Pilot Plant #2. WIPP #1 is 25 miles east of Carlsbad, 12 miles north of Cavetown. This region is often called the "nuclear corridor."

A history of unexpected emergencies has plagued WIPP sites since their inception. Despite containment caverns 2000 feet below the surface, radiation leaks have been detected from time to time. They are caused by shifting salts that are impossible to detect by seismic monitors.

Industrial mistakes also occur. Four years ago a container exploded releasing americium radiation. Waste water from Barnwell, SC, had been packed with organic cat litter rather than clay-based cat litter. A chemical reaction resulted in a buildup of explosive gases.

Residents are calling on the DOE to review the contract, history, and qualifications of WIPP's operator, SAFE-Nuc Futures Corp. SAFE-Nuc Futures is a subsidiary of Gronk Industries, Inc.

Maryann Caton, 37 | Robt. MacKenzie, 49 | Jake Canfeld, 11 | World POP: 7.43 billion

---

"Did you see the Goontown cartoon in Sunday's paper?" Annie spun the comics section across the breakfast table. "It says exactly what I've been saying since Trump took office."

Rob put down his coffee mug and picked up the paper. He saw Antoine Renault's page-wide cartoon of an insane asylum conference room. Renault's men and women were seated around a long table looking perplexed, knowledgeable, urbane, self-important, and resigned. Diplomas were on the wall. Two windows with bars prevented escape.

The group was in the midst of a discussion about the president's mental health. Opinions and ideas were expressed in bubbles above each participant. The frothy bubbles were like a tornadic halo of doom on the horizon, ready to wrench a neck or suck a victim into its vortex.

"For months I've been saying he's crazy," said a woman peering over half glasses perched on the bridge of her nose.

"But the American Association of Psycho-Babble has prevented us from making assertions about people who are not our patients," said her neighbor.

"Our patients' diagnoses are confidential," said the next in line, a balding man wearing a bowtie. "We can't say anything."

"What if a patient told you he had the nuclear codes and was planning to blow up the world on Halloween. Would you say something then?"

"Yeah," said a woman with doleful eyes. "I'd say, 'Why did I get into this business? My patients are driving *me* crazy.'"

Another expert chimed in, "Look, my fellow shrinks, if nothing else, Trump is unhinged. He exhibits rampant narcissism, Nazi-like racial hatreds, antipathy to Jews, and a desire to own all the gold in the world. He's nuts! Don't be afraid to speak out. His actions define his insanity."

The final expert wondered aloud: "Do you think he'll disavow his daughter and son-in-law? They're Jews."

Annie muted the television and yelled to Rob. "Hey, honey! Did you see the news about New Mexico? Part of a nuclear storage cavern caved in due to a brine well that opened up undetected."

"What station was it on?" he called from the study.

"CNN, but it was first reported in a small newspaper in Carlsbad. When the floor collapsed, waste containers broke open and released radiation. It made its way to the surface and leaked into the air."

Annie put down the TV remote and wandered into the study where Rob sat at the desk. She saw he was wrestling with words trying to compose a poem. He wrote verse to take a break from correcting student papers or from planning lessons.

When he versified, he often looked at some imaginary point in the distance. Sometimes he was successful unearthing a word, sometimes not.

"I'm sorry to interrupt your concentration, dear," she said, "but I want to tell you about Cavetown, New Mexico. It brings back recent memories."

"Give me a minute, Annie. The word I'm searching for is on the tip of my tongue."

"Then I know what it is!" she blurted out, kidding him. "It's bud. You know what I mean—taste bud? The word was in your mouth all along on the tip of your tongue. And it rhymes with plenty of other words—cud, crud, dud, and mud." She laughed at her nonsense.

"Very funny!" he said and meant it. He chuckled, "No, I'm searching for something else. Something more profound."

"What?" she asked. "You think you're the only poet in this house? I'll show you—it's easy." Her eyes scanned the ceiling as if searching for inspiration.

"I've got it," she said. "Here goes: Miracle the pig's in the mud. / He's Jacob Caton's best bud. / Once he tried to stampede / Not knowing he'd need / To chew like a cow with a cud."

She laughed. She felt very clever. "See, Mr. Scotsman-Robert Burns!" she bragged. "I can dream up nonsense limericks, too!" She was pleased with her contribution to the Hellenic world of Calliope, the Greek muse of poetry. In truth, she hadn't thought of Greek mythology since college.

"I like it, Annie," he said approving. "You ought to include it in your collection."

She frowned. "What collection? I don't have a poem collection the way you do. This limerick's my first. But it's a start. I think I'll name it, 'Miracle the Pig.'"

"Too late for that. Jake has dibs on that title. Why not, 'Pig in the Mud' or 'Pig Makes Crud'?"

"Oh well . . . I guess so. I'll think about it. Wait a minute, what were you writing when I came in?"

Rob turned and faced her. "Something to get across the concept of global warming. Something not too academic, not too dark, not too foreboding. I'm trying to create a poem to tell the story. Problem is, everything written about climate change is so dire. I thought I'd try a different strategy."

"If it's finished and you're ready, read it to me."

"Okay, love, if you can bear another one of my allusions. Even better, you read it. I value your opinion, and I'd like to get your reaction." He passed Annie the yellow lined paper that bore his words.

Double	Down
There's no more ice.	There's no more ice,
she said twice.	She said twice,
it's too warm.	It's too warm,
you were warned.	You were warned,
the air's so bad.	The air's so bad,
it makes me sad.	It makes me sad,
don't breathe so deep.	Don't breathe so deep,
your eyes will weep.	Your eyes will weep,
shut the door.	Shut the door,
deny, ignore.	Deny, ignore,
it's too late.	It's too late,
you sealed your fate.	You sealed your fate,
cry at last.	Cry at last,
your time is past.	Your time is past,
you will die.	You will die,
try not to cry.	Try not to cry,

> the Earth will heal.   The Earth will heal,
>   that's for real.   That's the deal.

"Rob, it's good, very good! And I can read it two ways—in a rhyming sing-song pattern or as separate sentences. Very inventive of you." She patted his shoulder.

"I've got to stay one step ahead of the students. It seems every year their attention spans shorten. That means I've got to be creative to keep them focused."

"It's the same story," said Annie looking depressed. "I was involved with Savannah River waste dump litigation before we were married. Remember? It never ends."

Annie and Rob returned to the living room and settled on the couch. Rob was finished with his poem and put the computer to sleep. He had dissected and tweaked his verse over and over. Annie resumed filling him in about what she learned on CNN.

"I'm sure you know where Carlsbad, New Mexico is, Rob. Down near Texas?"

"Aye. I know about it. I'm familiar with the geology of the area—the Permian salt beds."

"That's right. As CNN explained, the beds were the result of the evaporation of an ocean that covered the southwestern continent."

"Aye, it was vast."

"It's amazing! An ocean where now there's desert. CNN said the region's called the nuclear corridor because of the salt."

"True, lass. Carlsbad and its neighbor, Cavetown, are sitting on top of the bed. I read that the salt is 2000 feet below the surface and 600 meters thick."

"Really? That much?"

"Seems so. Unfortunately, someone discovered that salt is good insulation against radioactivity. But there are caveats."

"Like what?"

"You know, when nuclear waste is stored, it creates heat. Heat is a product of a chemical reaction. Wee amounts of water are released. Salt and water unite forming a paste that oozes around containment vessels, then solidifies permanently locking the vessels in place. That's what's supposed to happen, except when it doesn't. Surrounding caves can collapse."

"Jeepers, the alleged magic cure for nuclear waste was right under the feet of Carlsbad and Cavetown, and it backfired."

Annie shrugged her annoyance and continued adding details, contributing to their shared knowledge. Two years prior, before starting her own practice in Connecticut and serving as Roxbridge Town Attorney, she was employed by a Manhattan law firm that dealt with environmental issues. Radioactive waste was her speciality. She had to learn the science.

"The nuclear corridor is accepting high-level waste, Rob. The stuff they're burying is junk contaminated with transuranic elements."

"You know what they are?"

"Sure, artificially made radioactive stuff like plutonium and americium. They have atomic numbers higher than uranium. I had to do some reading to understand what was going on in the waste disposal industry."

"Understanding radioactivity usually requires a degree in physics or chemistry."

"The necessities of my job forced me to learn."

"Och, Annie! You sound like a nuclear physicist. I didn't know you knew all this."

"I had to learn it to understand what was going on in South Carolina. You and I never got into it when the waste dump controversy erupted in Connecticut. The garbage we were faced with was nasty, honey, but not on the same level as transuranic waste."

Rob shook his head in frustration. "Aye, we were lucky. Now Carlsbad and Cavetown have chosen to be our country's hell on earth, or hell in earth in this case. They're the beneficiaries of the Yucca Mountain project being scrubbed."

Annie agreed. "Hanford and Barnwell can't handle any more junk. They're over-loaded as it is. I've heard accidents are happening with more frequency. In South Carolina, radioactivity is seeping into Savannah River tributaries. That story was on *60 Minutes.* Junk that's supposed to be contained in a confined area is starting to escape affecting wider horizons."

She licked her lips. "I'm getting thirsty, honey. Can I get you a glass of tonic or soda water?"

"We're saving the soda water in case there's a spill stain. But, aye, a cold drink would be good to cool me off after talking about a hot topic. Tonic sounds perfect."

Annie returned with two insulated plastic tumblers bubbling with tonic on ice. A section of lime was in each. She rejoined Rob on the couch. He was studying the remote. As smart as he was, he could never remember what all the buttons did and the number combinations for hi-def TV stations.

Annie picked up where she left off. "If you remember, love, here in Connecticut we were faced with the same problem, only concerning low level waste. Connecticut's high level stuff from the Navy and the Millstone power plant was going to New Mexico via Barnwell."

"Aye, I remember. I remember everything except how to use this damn remote." He slid it on the coffee table. "Jake reminds me all the time," he continued, "about us being heroes for keeping the dump out of Roxbridge."

Annie laughed. "I admit, he's a bit over dramatic about all that. But I'm glad we were able to play our parts."

Rob nodded. "We did okay." He sipped his drink. "Nuclear waste is an unsolvable problem, dear. You know that. Humans have created enough nuclear poison to pollute the world for ten-thousand years. There's no effective containment for it. New nuclear power plants that come on line will only add to the problem."

Annie leaned against him. Rob draped an arm around her shoulders. "It seems to me," he said, "that nuclear waste is as good an example as any to illustrate the unsolvable problems we humans have created."

"Too many people consuming and wasting," she added.

"Aye, that's it. As our numbers increase, we demand more and more electricity and material goods like this bloody TV. All these things need power to produce them. Power generation results in toxic waste products whether carbon dioxide or radiation. No safe places exist for industrial waste to be stored without polluting the environment. Waste piles up. We're being consumed by the garbage we create."

"It's very sad," she acknowledged. "In addition to untouchable radioactive by-products, it's everyday refuse like plastics that wind up in the ocean."

Rob became more reflective, his voice lowered. "I don't know what to tell my students when they ask me about this problem. You know? I give them the usual pep talk advocating conservation, reusing, and recycling. Sometimes I advocate limiting family size. But I'm not sure they buy it. If truth be known, in my opinion, there is no answer. Human beings are on a one-way street to a very bleak future."

2018

The Minuteman Sentry

PROTECTING FIRST AMENDMENT RIGHTS

Trump Resignation in Question

OCTOBER 13, 2018

Robert Szmanski, News Editor
@ mmsszmanski.com
The Minuteman Sentry

**NEWS
ANALYSIS**

President Donald J. Trump has hinted his future as 45th president may extend into 2020. He plans to run for reelection. That is the message of many White House observers and political analysts. Even with the House trending toward control by Democrats after the November election, and Republicans left with only a narrow margin in the Senate, whatever support Mr. Trump enjoys with his base is not in danger.

Regardless, Articles of Impeachment quietly are being drawn up by a small group of anti-Trump Democrats. A few Republicans who are embarrassed by the president's bizarre behavior, or angered by Mr. Trump's refusal to consult with Congress about his legislative and foreign policy actions, have hinted they may sign on to the Democrat sponsored impeachment initiative.

Trump usually counterpunches when attacked or imputed. However, with evidence mounting that he has used the presidency for material gain and personal benefit, it is possible he will have to leave before impeachment proceedings are formalized. Those who know the president, understand he will never submit to cross-examining nor accept the judgement that he has committed a crime.

Despite his announcement to run again, speculation about his future has been fueled by numerous recent events, said sources. The Trump Corporation Jetliner is now housed in an out of the way hangar at Ronald Reagan Washington National Airport. The Secret Service is guarding the building. Sources believe a Trump helicopter is also under the same roof.

Ivanka Trump and Jared Kushner are rumored to have listed their D.C. home for sale, although the action has not been confirmed. Their influence in the White House eroded to the point where former advisor Steve Bannon called them "impediments to nationalistic aspirations." It became apparent their youth, naivete´, and inexperience made them unfit to be "senior advisors." Kushner's inability to accurately fill out forms for top-secret clearance became the joke of late night TV comedy.

According to White House sources, Mr. Trump has raged that he will never accept impeachment. He insists the American people will not accept it, either, and will resort to rioting, if the impeachment process gets underway. His disillusionment about his success and his unwillingness to ever admit wrongdoing, have pinned him into a corner with no way out except total rejection of Constitutional law. Psychiatrists believe capitulation is impossible for him. It seems he'll either dig in his heels, or attempt to retreat on his own terms.

A Boston doctor wrote a public letter to Mr. Trump advising him that he could become the greatest president ever to have lived, something Mr. Trump now asserts about himself. The doctor suggested all the president needed to do was eliminate the U.S. stockpile of nuclear weapons and campaign to have them removed world-wide. Trump's response was to order his military to build ten times more H-bombs than the U.S. presently stockpiles.

Finally, after a year and a half, it appears Special Counsel Robert Mueller is about to hand down more indictments regarding Russian interference in the 2016 election. Sources say Jared Kushner, Donald Trump, Jr., confidant Roger Stone, and other staff members are targets. Paul Manafort, the Republican campaign manager, and his associate, Rick Gates, have already been indicted. Gates has admitted guilt and is helping Mueller as part of a plea deal. Manafort refused to help Mueller, was found guilty in a court of law, and now has taken a plea deal to shorten his prison time. Charges include making false statements, conspiracy to launder money, and other actions connected to their effort advising a pro-Russian political party in the Ukraine. Michael Flynn, Trump's short lived National

Security Advisor has pled guilty to four counts of lying about his communication with the Russians.

Trump's ghostwriter, Tony Schwartz, has long predicted Trump will leave office before the end of his first term. CNN reported that Schwartz tweeted: "The circle is closing at blinding speed. Trump is going to resign and declare victory before Mueller and Congress leave him no choice." The results of the 2018 midterm elections will help to affirm or invalidate Schwartz's prediction.

Maryann Caton, 38 | Robt. MacKenzie, 50 | Jake Canfeld, 12 | World POP: 7.50 billion

---

Jake exploded through the side door as if he had just been warned by Paul Revere. Nova was in tow. "Is Rob home? Hey Mom! People say Trump's gonna quit! Can we go out for pizza tonight?"

Annie dried her hands and met her son in the mud room. "Take off your shoes, honey," she ordered, "they're caked with mud. Nova needs to be rinsed off, too."

Jake looked down at his shoes and dog to affirm his mother's assessment. "Yeah, I'm sorry. The snow's melting. The ground's soft. Colorado dirt sticks like glue."

"That's okay. Rinse off in the stationary tub in the basement. But do it before the mud dries. After that, it becomes concrete. And after cleaning Nova, dry her. We don't need a wet dog running around up here."

Jake returned from the basement with Nova nipping at his cuffs. Annie was back in the mud room tidying up.

"What about it, Mom? Can we do pizza tonight? Trump's leaving is cause for celebration."

"No pizza tonight, Jake. When I heard the speculation about Trump's departure, I decided to fix something special— something all three of us like. We're eating at home."

"What is it, Mom? C'mon tell me."

She hung his hat on a peg. "Tacos. I've got all the fixings: ground meat, chiles, fresh tomatoes, guacamole, sour cream. Since moving to Colorado, finding Mexican food has been a cinch."

"I don't know about Rob," Jake admitted, "but I love tacos. Someday I'll have my own place and eat tacos all the time."

"You'll grow tired of them."

"Not on my ranch. It will be a special place. I plan to raise llamas, grow alfalfa, and learn to yodel. I'm calling my spread the 'Okey Doke Corral.'"

They walked into the kitchen. Jake re-rinsed his hands then poured a glass of milk.

"Why Okey Doke Corral? Where did that come from?"

"I saw *Gunfight at the O.K. Corral* at Judd's. It was about Wyatt Burp. That's where I got the idea."

Annie corrected him. "His name was Earp, not Burp."

"I know, but Burp's better. Get it? Burp's better. Burp's better. Cool!"

Annie shooed Jake upstairs to his new bedroom to begin his homework. She called after him, "We'll talk about Trump at dinner when Rob gets home."

Nova stayed in the kitchen near the food. She stretched out gnawing on a rawhide chew. Then she rolled to her back, the chew held in the air between her paws. Annie knelt and scratched Nova's belly. The chew fell to the floor. Nova moaned in pleasure.

"What a silly girl you are," cooed Annie, "but you picked the right family to adopt. We're silly, too. Stay there while I get you a treat."

Since relocating to Boulder in August, 2017, the MacKenzie

clan had been happily making their way. Annie kept a written journal record of their new adventure. Rereading it, she was proud of her family's adaptability and growing activism. She skimmed through the entries.

Rob began his University of Colorado assignment teaching two sections of students the art of clear, uncomplicated science writing. His online tutorial enrolled a small cohort of researchers and fledgling scientists.

Unexpectedly, he was asked by the chancellor to sit on the university's sexual harassment committee. She noted he was immediately faced with two cases. The first involved harassment of a male English instructor by his department chair, a woman. The second case dealt with an alleged rape of a female sophomore by a senior male. Binge drinking was involved. The case had its origin at Get Tanked, a student hangout on the hill.

She wrote about Veteran's Day. Rob drove Jake and her up Flagstaff Mountain Road to witness the lighting of the Boulder Star. They had shared gifts. The occasion solidified their family bonds. Rob now wore a wedding band she gave him that night. It was a symbol overlooked at their marriage in 2015. It was securely at home on his finger.

Her life became complex and challenging. Environmental law and competing interests again locked her in their compelling grips. Because she had knowledge of and previous experience dealing with nuclear waste, her Pine Street law firm, **Pearl 2 Pine,** assigned her the task of resisting efforts by Gronk Industries to open up the Rocky Flats National Wildlife Refuge to fracking. Intuitively she knew the fight would be bitter and long, involving the Nuclear Regulatory Commission, research reports detailing ambient trace radiation, Colorado's carbon extraction laws, and Gronk's immense political clout. Her job was to protect the health interests of the citizens in Broomfield and Golden—maybe beyond.

Gradually, Annie became aware of the homeless problem in Boulder. Despite being an affluent university town filled with entrepreneurial start-ups and designer shops, dozens of people squatted in the parks or hid in back alleys. A large homeless shelter in North Boulder was besieged with clients during the winter. As word of Boulder's largesse spread through the homeless underground, the City Council's good intentions to help the indigent resulted in a growing homeless population.

She recognized the dilemma needed to be humanely fixed. She thought about the problem, but was unable to arrive at any apparent solution. She attended meetings of advocates for the homeless. She returned time and again to hear City Council discussions. Council members began to recognize her. A few spoke with her after meetings. She was determined to help. She believed somewhere there had to be a solution. Maybe she could find it.

The MacKenzies celebrated Thanksgiving with her brother's family. Fred told her he was overjoyed that at last they were all together. A journal entry recorded she was pleased to see Jake absorbed into the large gathering of Lois Caton's relatives, the Murphys from Lafayette. Finally, after years alone, they were amidst a holiday family mob. It was perfect.

Jake thrived in school. He was liked by his classmates and adored by his teachers. They thought a kid from New York and Connecticut would be haughty and stiff. But Jake fooled them. He was funny, had an amusing way of slaughtering the language, and was interested in everything—from sports to the arts. He absorbed his lessons like a sponge. She received encouraging notes from his teachers which she kept with her journal.

In an effort to rapidly learn Spanish, Jake labeled every item and surface in their home with 3x5 cards bearing Spanish words. Even fresh fruit was labeled. It would have been impossible for Rob and her not to have been affected. They were surrounded by vocabulary prompts. It helped refresh her Spanish, something she had not used since an archaeological undergraduate trip to Peru twenty years earlier.

She noted they grew close to their relatives. Jake enjoyed Uncle Fred's tales of the occult. Fred told him ghost stories about the Stanley Hotel in Estes Park. He grew to know his twin cousins, Lindsay and Jeannie. He visited Aunt Lois's custom framing shop in Louisville "I've Been Framed." Annie had a Robert Rauschenberg print matted and framed by Lois.

She connected with Lindsay the way she had connected with Taylor Peters in Roxbridge. Lindsay also wanted to become a lawyer. Lindsay told Aunt Annie she was her role model.

Annie noticed Jeannie following her own path, marching to her own drummer. Her niece had traded her skis for a snowboard. Yet, the sisters continued to travel together to Nederland in the winter to practice their sports.

Annie remembered that in December she, Rob, and Jake drove to the Humane Society on 55th Street to pick out a dog. After the Boulder Star ceremony, Jake had asked if they could have a pup. With a dog-park so close behind their house on Rim Rock Circle, how could she and Rob say no? It would be a good Christmas gift for them all.

Annie had a dog when she was a child. And she knew Rob grew up around Border Collies in Scotland. They both loved canines.

Entering the Humane Society building Annie made one

rule, "Whatever we get, keep it small. Rob," she pleaded, "I know your fascination with wolves, but, please, no Scottish wolfhounds. I don't want a dog that looks like it's walking on stilts."

❖

"I don't get it, Rob. Trump's president. I don't like him, but he's the boss. Why is he threatening to resign?"

Rob swallowed a mouthful of taco and sipped his Dos Equis before responding. "I don't think he's threatening to resign, lad. That's just rumor. He's said he plans to run for reelection in 2020. Hmm, your question is complicated. You're mum's the lawyer. I'll let her explain. But first, why don't you like him?"

"I can't put my finger on it," said Jake. He flipped a piece of taco shell across his plate.

"Don't play with your food, honey," Annie reminded him.

"Okay, sorry. Anyway, something about him makes me uneasy. He hardly smiles. He has squinty eyes like a rat. He yells at the news guys. He makes fun of some of them. And I hate his hair. He looks dangerous."

"Any more shells left, Annie?" asked Rob. "These tacos are muy bueno!"

"Si, Roberto, dos. ¿Y usted, Jacob?"

"No mas, Madre. Estoy lleno."

Rob filled his shell with ingredients. "Ask mamacita about why Señor Trump's might be thinking about quitting, Jake. She knows the details."

"Si, Rob. Well, Mom . . . what gives?"

"Hey, you two, relax. Although I had a course on British constitutional law as an undergraduate, and a required course on the U.S. Constitution in law school, I'm no expert. It's complicated and subject to interpretation."

"That's okay, Mom. I know you can do it."

"Fire away, Annie," said Rob, after swallowing another swig of beer.

"I'll try." She collected her thoughts. "Trump's a shady character, Jake. Up to now, the public didn't know about all his dealings. In fact, they may never know everything. The problem's been made worse because he refused to share his income tax returns. If he was on the up-and-up, he'd have nothing to hide. At this point, he appears to be concealing something, maybe illegal deals."

"What deals are illegal, Mom? How does that work?"

"If he accepted money and didn't list it on his income tax return, he'd be guilty of not paying his fair share of taxes on that money—essentially defrauding the government. That's a crime. Whatever you earn you must report." Annie sipped her sangria.

"Wait a minute!" Jake blurted. "If Trump makes a trillion dollars, how does he get away with not reporting it?"

"Aha, my son! Therein lies the crime. Trump may have created fake businesses, used fake names, hidden money in secretive countries. The money, in this case your trillion dollars, gets funneled through one fake company to another fake company to another fake company. It disappears as if into a corn maze with no clear way out. The crime is called money laundering."

Jake sat stunned. "How does he know how to do it? When I listen to him, he doesn't sound very smart—just loud."

"Lawyers!" barked Rob. "They do it for him!"

"Rob's right, honey. A whole industry exists to cheat people and to cheat the government. Lawyers are the main culprits. As a lawyer, I'm not proud of that."

After a sip of wine, she continued, "Anyway, the Special

Counsel, Robert Mueller, has been investigating whether or not Trump was laundering money, and if he was tied up with Russia. Trump may have committed a crime. It looks to me like Mueller is closing in. That's why Trump may resign after the midterms."

"Can't Trump get away with it by being president?" Jake was puzzled. "Once he bragged he could shoot someone on Fifth Avenue and not get arrested."

"No, dear. A crime's a crime. He'd be arrested and sent to prison if it was proven he committed a crime. But apparently he's talking about resigning. And I'm guessing he might trade his resignation in return for not being arrested and tried. He must know he's guilty but didn't think he'd get caught."

Quiet settled over the dinner table. Each digested the raw truth about the forty-fifth president. They were also digesting tacos. Jake belched. "Sorry, Mom. It was a Wyatt Burp." He laughed.

"Don't stop with your story, Annie," encouraged Rob. "Give Jake the whole picture. You filled the lad in about Trump and Mueller. But there's more. Tell him what Congress might do."

"What, Mom? What else? Rob says there's more."

"That's true, Jake. Trump's been getting squeezed from two sides, like crushing a nut in vice-grips."

"Good allusion," approved Rob with a smile. "I like the nut in vice-grips imagery."

Annie grinned and nodded at Rob. She resumed explaining the situation to Jake. "Do you know about impeachment, Jake? Do you know how it works?"

"A little, Mom. Senators can kick him out."

"It's more complicated than that, but essentially you're right. The Constitution allows presidents to be removed from office if they violate provisions spelled out in the Constitution, or commit crimes listed in the federal criminal codes. For example, if congress agrees with the majority of the president's cabinet that he's mentally unfit, he can be removed from office. The vice president takes over."

"Trump's nuts, Mom! He's insane!"

"Maybe so, but that has to be proven. If not insane, in my opinion he's at least unpredictable. One way is to determine if his actions and words are logical and legal. If not ousted by his cabinet, he still can stand trial in the Senate. The Chief Justice of the Supreme Court presides over the trial."

"Roberts?"

"Yes. The accused is questioned. If he lies under oath, and it can be proven, he's guilty of the crime of perjury. He can be accused of treason. That's why his dealings with the Russians are so problematic. He can be tried for obstruction of justice. That's interfering with an investigation. He's not allowed by the Constitution to earn any money other than his salary. But he has and has bragged about it. Jake, think about all his hotels and golf courses."

"Like Mar a Taco? He crunched a shell.

Annie corrected Jake, "Lago." She chuckled.

"All these actions fall under the broad category of high crimes and misdemeanors. For any one or all of these misdeeds, he can go to jail."

"Boy, that would be good!" said Jake. "From what I've heard, he's done them all."

"But it sounds like he's running again, Jake," Annie reminded him. "If impeached, I'm betting he'll get a free pass out of jail from Mueller and Congress. It's like having a 'Get out of Jail Free' card in *Monopoly.* I'm convinced he'll cut a deal."

"What will happen to him, Mom?"

Rob answered. "When his presidency is done, he'll go back

to cheating people in civilian life. That's all he knows how to do—that and tweet. But remember, lad, once the election is over, the numbers counted, and the winners announced, anything can happen including Trump keeping his job."

2019

The Hartford Courier

SOUTHERN NEW ENGLAND'S HISTORIC BROADSHEET

Millington LLNW Dump Closes—H2O Blamed

By Staff Writers, Leon Daniels, Megan Morgan and
Tulce Torello | THC.com | **NUTMEG NEWS, LLC**

June 19, 2019

Connecticut's Low Level Nuclear Waste Repository in
Millington has been closed. Two years after being chosen to
permanently warehouse the state's home generated waste,
gates were locked on April 16, 2019, by the Nuclear Regulatory
Commission. Millington was named the state's choice for the
facility over the communities of Halyard and Roxbridge.

The closure is attributed to the damaging effects of the mineral
iron sulfide, also known as pyrrhotite. When the mineral comes
in contact with water, its corrosive powers are unleashed and
weaken Portland cement products like concrete foundations,
sidewalks, and containment vessels. Hundreds of structures
across southwestern Rhode Island and northeastern Connecticut

were structurally damaged or compromised as a result of pyrrhotite aggregate that was mined in Millington.

Millington's lock-down came as a result of the union of ground water and pyrrhotite. The resulting chemical reaction attacked the concrete nuclear waste containment bunkers. Despite efforts to separate water and iron sulfide, and to isolate both from the bunkers, engineers have not been able to stop the corrosive infiltration nor discover its source.

Until the problem is solved and the bunkers have been certified safe, Low Level Nuclear Waste will again have to be stored on site by state generators. Connecticut's inclusion in the Atlantic Pact ended when the Millington site opened for business. As a result, the state's former nuclear dump in Barnwell, South Carolina, no longer accepts waste from Connecticut or New Jersey.

Maryann Caton, 39 | Robt. MacKenzie, 51 | Jake Canfeld, 13 | World POP: 7.75 billion

---

Annie and Rob drifted away from the Saturday morning Farmers Market and walked north into Boulder's commercial center. Rob carried two bike saddle bags filled with produce: leaves of kale, a mixed dozen sweet peppers (red, green, and yellow), a bunch of spring carrots, and a freshly baked loaf of cranberry wheat bread from Breadworks. They left their bicycles behind chained in a bike corral off Arapahoe Avenue. Annie figured their produce would be fine for the hour it would take to show Rob the original location of her law firm and the new signage on the building they now occupied.

At the Pearl Street Mall, they headed west. The mall was

showing signs of life as locals meandered out, shopkeepers unrolled awnings, and tourists arrived. In front of the Boulder County courthouse the hat vendor had parked his wagon. What appeared to Annie to be homeless people drifted in and out of the public restrooms. A few shaggy wayfarers reclined against backpacks on the courthouse lawn. A pair of suntanned Boulder policemen began their patrol.

Finally, Annie saw the iconic Haitian contortionist limbering up next to his 3x3 foot plexiglass box. He planned to fold his body into it as the finale of his dexterity performance. In an attempt to draw a crowd he was calling, "Look at me! Look at me!"

Annie passed by him everyday on her way to the office. She knew him by name. "Good morning, JeanPierre." She dropped a bill in his bucket.

"Good morning, Miss Annie," he replied. "Going to the office on a Saturday?"

"No, just taking my husband to see the firm's new sign."

"Okay, Miss Annie."

He nodded to Rob. "Hey mon, you got yourself the pick of the litter with Miss Annie. She's a keeper. Have a good day."

Further on, the maker and seller of nylon hammocks was engrossed in a book, unaffected by the passersby. Trendy outdoor clothing stores advertised lightweight fleece pullovers, down vests, brightly colored running shoes—all at exorbitant prices.

Sleepy-eyed college students pushed through coffee shop doors or sat idly in the shade strumming tuneless guitars. Many were painted with tattoos. Annie was thankful cigarettes were gone from the mall—smoking was prohibited—as well as skateboarding, bike riding, and dog walking. She looked around. Boulder was awake.

They continued walking along the north side of Pearl beyond the mall and entered what was colloquially called the West End. Three doors after crossing 9th Street Annie stopped and pointed at a structure on her right.

"That's where our firm started, Rob. This was our original home, Attorneys on Pearl."

A graceful brick building sat back from the sidewalk allowing for a small garden behind a black iron fence. A patch of lawn survived. The structure was divided in half. Both sides featured covered porches and balconies.

"From up there," Annie pointed, "you can see the Flatirons and part way up Boulder Canyon. We had the right side. It's small, but in the beginning the firm was only the three original partners. If for no other reason, we had to move as we grew larger."

"Did they own the building?" asked Rob.

"No, they rented. Both sides had separate leases."

"Who was on the left side?"

"The Cannabis Research Association. It was before pot was legalized in 2014."

"And . . .? I sense there's more to the story."

"Yes. Three years before you and I moved here, Boulder experienced a multi-day rain event."

"Aye, I remember reading about it."

"Anyway, both basements flooded. In our half, paper files were ruined. Fortunately, we kept electronic backups. We now have a technician whose job is solely dedicated to recording and saving information."

"Smart."

"Yes, as I said, the offices were small, and we learned the foundation leaked."

"I'm not surprised. Old brick is porous."

"But the ultimate cause for moving was what happened in our neighbor's basement. They were illegally growing pot. It got flooded, too. The weed rotted and stank. They may have been an association dedicated to the dissemination of research, but they weren't licensed to conduct research—especially not on Pearl Street. It all prompted our move."

She turned back east. "Let's walk over to Pine Street, and I'll show you the new sign. I'd suggest we eat lunch at the Boulderado, but we need to get home before the veggies wilt and the bread gets toasted."

"Aye. I wouldn't want anything to happen to the kale," Rob muttered.

They retraced their path heading east on the mall, then turned left at 13th Street and continued on for two more blocks. They passed the Hotel Boulderado where Rob stayed while interviewing for his job, and Annie was feted when she landed hers.

On the southwest corner of 13th and Pine stood Annie's law firm. Rob had visited it a number of times since her hiring. The address was 1239 Pine Street, the Canyon Building. Like her firm's previous office, it was housed in one half of a two-part complex. However, different from the previous office, the two-part complex was divided into two structures separated by an alleyway leading to a hidden mews. One office faced 13th Street. Annie's office faced Pine.

Both businesses sported new signage. The 13th Street sign was torch-cut stainless steel.

❖ **ARAPAHOE SECURITY MORTGAGE, LTD.** ❖

The advertisement for Annie's firm read:

❖ PEARL 2 PINE, ATTORNEYS AT LARGE, LTD. ❖
The Earth is our Business

"I like them both," said Rob. "As Jake would say, 'awesome' or 'very cool!' It's urban-rustic-industrial. But your firm's sign is the better of the two in my estimation. The Earth is our Business," he read. "That rings true for me—the earth is everyone's business."

"I'm glad you like it, honey. Everybody seems to be pleased." She kissed his cheek.

"Hey, love," he said. "Let's start heading back. I want to see if JeanPierre has escaped from his box."

Jake returned home with Nova and filled her bowl with fresh water. It had been hot in the treeless dog park, even though a small kiosk offered a bit of shade. Jake heard the rumble of the garage door opening up. From a side door he saw his mother and Rob wheel their bikes inside and park them. Space was tight in the Rim Rock Circle garage. Everything— cars, bikes, lawn mower, garden tools, garbage cans—had a designated spot.

Rob took off his helmet and handed it to Annie who already had removed hers. Then he unhooked the saddlebags. Annie hung the helmets on a pegboard above the workbench. Rob's went on the highest hook, Jake's was lower, Annie's was at the bottom. Rob noticed Annie had switched hooks with Jake. Before taking the vegetables into the kitchen, he corrected the oversight and returned them to their assigned spots.

Everything fit, everything was organized, every space had a purpose. For a tight garage arrangement to work, Rob turned to scientific thinking and observation. He invented a taxonomy of importance for each object in the garage, and planned their storage based on size, frequency of use, and ease of access. To lay out the space he used a CAD program.

Neighbors were amused by Rob's orderliness. They wondered if he had an obsessive-compulsive disorder. Annie assured them that tidiness was only reserved for the garage. "You should see his sock drawer," she said.

"Yo, guys," welcomed Jake, "did you get any peaches?"

"Not until the end of August," said Annie, "but we did get carrots and kale."

Jake shuddered. "Oh, boy! I can hardly wait. How 'bout you, Rob? Kale sandwiches for lunch?"

"Nae. I don't think so, lad. There's plenty of tender dandelion greens in our lawn ripe for the picking."

"You're not serious, are you, Rob? Nova's peed out there. I clean up her poop, but there's nothing I can do about her Appalachian urine."

"Okay, gentleman! Enough!" Maryann always became testy when her two immature males started a scatological discussion featuring excrement and body fluids. Their behavior was stupid, she thought, nothing at all funny about it. It was male nonsense.

"We have farm fresh organic produce to enjoy," she reminded them. "But we'll wait until tonight when Rob grills, and I make a salad. For lunch I bought a loaf of that cranberry wheat bread you like, Jake. Let's have PB&J on toast."

Rob nodded. "Aye, that would be perfect. Kale sandwiches will have to wait. I love you, Annie."

When Maryann disappeared into the pantry to get the toaster, Jake glanced at Rob as if he had lost his ball bearings. He whispered, "Rob, I thought you hated kale."

"I'm not fond of it, laddie, but your mother takes it personally, if I don't relish it. She's compelled to defend kale, as if her best friend was on trial. It's better that I say nice things about the plant. I want to keep your mother happy."

During lunch Jake was full of random information and questions. Cohesion of his thoughts was impossible. He began by describing a new behavior Nova was displaying.

"If we're walking somewhere and I try to turn left and Nova wants to continue straight, she sits down. She won't budge no matter how much I tug, no matter how much I urge, no matter how much I threaten."

"It's all in the tone of voice you use," said Rob.

"That's not it, Rob. I've even tried bribing her with treats. You know how she responds to food. Still, no luck. She stays sitting and staring in the direction we were heading. She won't move an inch. It's almost as if she's following the instructions of her name, Nova."

"What do you mean?" asked Maryann.

"Nova. Her name can be cut in half from n-o-v-a to *no va,* two Spanish words."

Maryann stared blankly.

"It means no go, Mom. Nova means no go. She's living up to her name."

"Then what do you do?" she asked amused. "Did it happen today? If so, how did you get her home?"

"Good news. By chance I found the answer. She's small enough to be carried. Once I pick her up and head in the direction I want to go, she's fine. It's like dialing in a new station on the radio. I put her down and she follows along as if nothing happened. It seems as if suddenly she forgets why she was sitting."

Rob and Annie laughed while Jake described his dog

management skills. Hearing her name, and sensing her people were happy, Nova found her chew and joined them under the table.

"It's a classic case of *ambulatory caninus interruptus*," offered Rob. "That's a mild form of the sickness, *doggone*, and related to the syndrome, *bossy nova*."

Rob waited for the expected accolades he thought he'd receive for his cleverness. Instead, Jake veered wildly into a new thought and changed the conversation.

"Hey, Mom. Would you be upset if I changed my name from Canfeld to MacKenzie?"

Annie saw honest sincerity in her son's eyes. "No, I wouldn't be upset, love. But why now? Is it because your father's gone?"

Jake delayed answering by asking Rob, "Would you mind if I mooched your name?"

Rob grinned broadly. "Nae, laddie. That would be fine with me. But first, answer your mum's questions."

"I started thinking about it last year at the Boulder Star lighting ceremony. I realized Rob's become my father—maybe not my biological father—but you know what I mean."

Annie nodded her understanding.

"So, if I don't have a biological father, I need to get another variety."

Rob laughed again, but was pleased. "I'm honored you'd like to become a MacKenzie, lad. And I'm thrilled you think I'm a good enough variety to be your father. Let's make a deal. I'll find out if I can adopt you and join your mum as legal guardian. I think your name can be changed as a result. Or, when you're older, probably eighteen, you can legally change your name yourself."

"Okay, Rob . . . er . . . Dad. It's a deal! Let's start doing some research."

"I'm going to leave that up to you, lad. If you want it bad enough, you ought to research the laws and decide what's the better option. Your mum can help you get started."

Rob stood and pulled Jake from his chair. Nova danced around their feet. Rob wrapped Jake in a fatherly bear hug. Maryann grinned, air clapped, then blew her nose.

Rob uncapped a bottle of ale and rejoined Annie and his newly minted son at the table. Although unofficial, the new mantle of fatherhood Jake had bestowed upon him felt wonderful. Its weight of responsibility was a burden he never thought he'd enjoy. He was forty-seven when he married Annie. Luckily for him, she had entered their union bearing a remarkable gift—Jake.

He loved Jake without reservation. Now he knew Jake felt the same about him. He wondered what kind of variety Jake meant when describing him, but it didn't make a difference. All that mattered was that a person with free will had chosen him to be his guardian. Jake wasn't his son by fact of birth, but by conscious decision.

Annie broke his trance with news. "Rob, dear, with all our cycling around doing errands yesterday evening and this morning, I forgot to tell you the news. It totally slipped my mind." Annie rose to get more ice for her tea.

"We had kale to buy," said Rob. "Your mind was occupied by healthy green leaves." He chuckled. "All right, what did you learn?" He winked at Jake.

"It came to our office as a fax. The Millington dump's been shuttered."

"In Connecticut?" asked Jake.

"Yes."

"Och! That is news! Really? Why?"

"The concrete containments began to crumble and leak

radiation. They started to degrade as a result of groundwater and pyrrhotite forming a slurry that undermined them. There was fear that might happen. NukeSafe was never able to get groundwater under control."

Jake was listening. "Does that mean they'll put the dump in Roxbridge?"

"I don't think so, sweetie. Granite Hill had its own set of water issues. Rob . . . I mean your father . . . warned of water in the caves, and that the site overlooked the Berkshire River."

"Yeah, I remember Dad talking about it." He fist-bumped Rob. "We explored those tunnels, didn't we, Dad? That's where we found the dead pig."

"Aye, I remember it so well," affirmed Rob, grinning.

Maryann continued. "It's similar to what happened two years ago in New Mexico. One of the salt mines in Cavetown crumbled. Water caused the problem there, too. At first, the salt mines appeared to be a good place to bury high level nuclear waste. But water proved the engineers wrong."

"Was that NukeSafe, too?" asked Jake.

"No. SAFE-Nuc, which is part of Gronk Industries," said Maryann. "But it makes no difference who builds a nuclear dump or where it's built, radioactivity always seems to find a way to get free, like an evil genie escaping a lamp. Coincidentally, Colorado's having to deal with another form of low-level waste—waste from a process that's being resisted in New England."

"What's that, Mom?"

"Fracking. All the fracking that's done in this state results in contaminated rock dust, soils, and slurries. **Pearl 2 Pine** presently is suing three drilling companies. They buried their waste in conventional landfills. That's a no-no. Fortunately, they got caught. Now they face big fines and never-ending scrutiny."

"How does drilling stir up radioactivity?"

Rob answered Jake's question. "There's a bloody lot of radioactive elements in Colorado rock and soil, lad. When boreholes are drilled, the material extracted is mixed with slurry fluid. Radioactivity is concentrated. It reaches the threshold of low-level waste, the same concentrations we dealt with in Connecticut. But the Colorado stuff we're talking about is from the ground, not from hospitals, labs, or power plants. Either way, it must be encapsulated in special concrete containers, then stored in an approved waste repository away from water."

Jake wrinkled his brow. "If it can't be put in a landfill, where will it go?"

"A dump's being constructed in Weld County," said Annie, "up toward Nebraska. A big pit's being excavated. It's lined with a so-called impervious plastic liner and clay soils. Then, when waste is trucked in, the concrete containers are buried. Everything has to be water free. No water can be allowed to get into the pit and erode the containers. And no waste from the pit can be allowed to escape and contaminate groundwater—the water we drink."

"How big's the pit?"

"Big. Acres long and wide."

"How much waste can it hold?"

"Fifteen years worth."

"Then what?"

"Dig a new pit or stop fracking."

"Jeez!" said Jake. "What a mess!"

"Yes," agreed Annie. "We must protect water," she continued. "I'm sure you're aware, honey, that water is essential for life?"

"I know, Mom," said Jake, scowling as if she thought he knew nothing.

"That's why so much effort has been taken to find it on Mars," interrupted Rob.

"Rob's right," she said. "In addition to being necessary for life, water's the mightiest force on Earth. Seventy percent of the planet is covered by water, either in liquid form or as ice. But you know the ice is disappearing."

Jake sighed. "Yep, we talked about it in school."

"That's good, lad. We need water to live, but ironically, it often kills us. We try to harness it, but it has a mind of its own. It's formless, can be bitterly cold or scaldingly hot, and take the form of a solid, liquid, or gas. It's one of the three most destructive forces on Earth."

"Yeah, I've seen what hurricane flooding can do. But if water's one of the forces," Jake asked, "what are the other two?"

"Volcanism," said Rob.

"Human beings," added Annie.

2020

The NEW YORK MESSENGER

"THE SPIRIT OF PUBLIUS"

Iceland Volcano Threatens
Northern Hemisphere

JULY 10, 2020 $3.50

Air traffic may be affected ❖ Mini-Ice Age possible

Opinion: ❖ By Rolf Sjorennson, NYM Correspondent ❖ Reykjavik, ISL

One hundred two years have passed since the Iceland volcano, Katla, erupted in 1918. Iceland has 30 active volcanoes. The last big volcanic event occurred in 2010, when Eyjafjallajokull showed its wrath. Ten million travellers were stranded worldwide as 100,000 airline flights were cancelled. Seismologists have been closely monitoring Katla. Every 99 years or sooner since the 12th Century the volcano has erupted. Her tardiness has experts deeply worried.

"Volcanoes erupt when their systems are gorged with magma, ash, and gas," said Sven Magnusson, a geophysicist at the Reykjavik Seismology Institute. "Unlike animals who release excessive gas pressure from their bung holes, volcanoes get relief by blowing their tops. The more gas in their guts, the more violent the explosion. Ejected is ash, hot gases, and molten rock—magma—which rapidly flows in a pyroclastic surge to the lowest geographic point in the area. Often, the lowest point is the ocean."

The amount of ash that may be spewed into the atmosphere is what worries scientists like Magnusson. A major eruption of Katla could cause an "Icelandic winter" in the northern hemisphere.

Katla's threat is similar to the threat posed by nuclear weapons. Weapons experts have warned that the use of nuclear and thermonuclear devices could result in a nuclear winter. Bombing raids, missile launches, and retaliations could darken the skies with debris, blocking the sun's ability to spur photosynthesis. Darkness could last for months or years. If so, food supplies would dwindle, then disappear. Mass starvation would overtake the entire animal kingdom. Humans would be no less vulnerable than the wolf. Extinction rates would soar, including an extinction event for homosapiens.

The last violent mass extinction occurred 66 million years ago when an asteroid struck what is now Mexico's Yucatan Peninsula. The result was the Cretaceous-Paleocene extinction. Atmospheric dust and particulates kicked up by the collision blocked the sun's regenerative powers for years. Harsh conditions and a loss of food resulted in a 75% extinction event for all species then alive, including large animals.

So far, the world's nuclear nations have shown restraint. Although North Korea continues to threaten with its warhead stockpile, other nations mostly ignore the childish actions and rhetoric of its leader, Kim Jong Un. Hopefully, sane minds will prevail, and the world will not succumb to a nuclear war. Since President Trump's departure, the U.S. government has been low key, while seeking diplomatic solutions to the problem. If a nuclear winter were to occur, it would be man-made and totally unnecessary.

Humans can control their destiny as far as war is concerned. But they have no control over the war-gods in the Earth's core, If the hammer of Thor escapes its volcano hell-hole to wreck havoc, the entire biomass will suffer. In the end, Mother Earth decides whether we live or die. The belief that humans can control and rule everything is a myth. We are fossils in the making.

Maryann Caton, 40 | Robt. MacKenzie, 52 | Jake Canfeld, 14 | World POP: 7.84 billion

---

Reading news articles, Professor MacKenzie became aware of a trend. The proliferation of nuclear weapons had resulted in the public's new-found demand to understand the difference between atomic and thermonuclear devices. Rob was pleased by this shift in attitude. He was sorry interest had been generated by weapons of mass destruction. But, as far as he was concerned, interest in anything scientific was better than no interest at all.

Perhaps people were waking up to the realization that science education was essential to understanding how the world worked. But the new interest was curious. It didn't square with

61

slumping test results, especially in the sciences. The decline mirrored the restrictions on science education that had been imposed by former Education Secretary Betsy DeVos, while she was part of the Trump administration. The failure was slow to recover.

Conservative evangelicals railed against the idea that schools were the appropriate places for children to be mind-washed by scientific theory. Evolution? Let one's faith provide the answer. Global warming? It's cold in January. Gene therapy? A scheme promoted by dark-skinned people from Asia. Nuclear physics? A puzzle only Jews could solve.

Conservatives argued it was better to leave the design of science education to municipal school districts. Local concerns and novice teachers were better prepared to show young students how to plant and irrigate corn, how to repair an internal combustion engine, how to use a rain gauge, and how nitrate fertilizer needed to be gently handled so as not to detonate.

DeVos's effort to limit science education thrilled the religious right. But it gradually took its toll on young people's knowledge. Hence, the sinking test scores.

Unwittingly deprived of the scientific method and of proven scientific facts, an unexpected backlash resulted in the public's desire to learn more about scientific progress, like nuclear chain reactions. Or was the new interest in science the result of something else? Did understanding the difference between fission and fusion really matter, or was it linked to the pleasure of understanding how America could blow other nations off the face of the Earth? MacKenzie thought he knew the answer.

"The bombs, Rob. There's been a lot of stuff in the news

about them with all the craziness over North Korea. What's the difference between the A and the H? How do they work?"

Rob and Jake were patrolling the raised bed gardens that bordered two sides of their home. Produce was growing. There was a row of kale. They were pulling weeds, pinching off sucker shoots, looking for cutworms.

"Aye, laddie, you're right. People are fascinated by them, horrible as they are. Has your general science class studied the atom?"

"Yeah. We learned about the atomic structure—protons and neutrons that make up the nucleus, and electrons that spin around the core. Each atom looks like a miniature solar system."

"Aye, that's right, son. But most people, especially those who've never studied chemistry or physics, have a hard time grasping the idea that every bit of matter is made up by atoms in motion."

Rob pointed to a nail in the garden frame. This piece of metal we used to join the timbers is a compound of atoms. If the nail was pure iron, all the atoms would be identical. But it's likely that to strengthen the nail, some kind of compound was used. Maybe iron, zinc, and molybdenum. Metallic compounds are referred to as alloys. As a result of mixing three separate metals, a new metal alloy can be formed. You with me?"

"So far, Rob. I'm familiar with the periodic table."

"Good. Then you know some elements are inert, very stable, some are more easily excitable, like the gas neon, and some are in a perpetual dither, like uranium. The easily aroused group, the radioactive elements and isotopes, can be manipulated to blow apart. If you put enough fissionable enriched uranium or plutonium in one spot, an atomic reaction will occur—a massive explosion."

"Boom!" exaggerated Jake.

"Aye. when U.S. physicists were first trying to learn how much uranium was needed to make a bomb, they experimented in a laboratory at Columbia University where your mum went to school. They pushed pieces of uranium closer and closer until their geiger counters went crazy, and things started to get hot."

"Wow, they could have blown up New York!"

"True. But they were lucky. Fortunately, for Columbia and New York's upper West Side, the pieces were separated in time, so no explosion happened. That's why the early A-bomb research was called the Manhattan Project."

"But what's the difference between an A-bomb and an H-bomb?" asked Jake, his curiosity piqued. "They weren't doing H-bomb research in New York City . . . were they?"

"No, not in the city. H-bomb research came later in places far removed from populated areas. I'll tell you that story in a minute. But first I want to float a physics idea." Rob uncoiled the hose and began watering the plants.

"I can do that, Dad. I like to water."

"Good lad." Rob twisted the nozzle to a gentle spray, handed over the hose, then followed Jake on his watering rounds. He noticed Jake was as tall as his chin. Jake would never match his height, but he had shot past Annie and was taller than his deceased father had been. Rob guessed Jake was headed to somewhere around five ten. He continued with the physics lesson.

"As I explained, laddie, all matter is composed of atoms. When enough atoms are bonded together they form a molecule. Molecules combine to form tangible substances. If the molecules are all composed of the same atom, the tangible substance is an element, like iron or aluminum."

"Or copper, sulphur, and oxygen."

"Right. When two different atoms combine, the molecules

become compounds like table salt. But not all elements or compounds are solid. Some are gases like hydrogen and, as you mentioned, oxygen. Put enough molecules of hydrogen and oxygen together you have water."

"I know," said Jake. "H2O. Two atoms of hydrogen, one atom of oxygen. That's water."

"Aye, very good, Jake. You have the right idea." Rob pointed to the row of kale. He indicated it needed another drink.

"But here's the thing, son. Something's needed to glue the hydrogen and oxygen atoms together. What do you think that might be?"

Jake was silent a long time. He had moved on from the kale and was soaking the tomato plants before he responded. "I'm not sure, Rob. Is it gravity?"

"That's a good answer, lad, but not exactly. In order to form atoms—in order to split them apart—in order to bind them together—in order to turn them into compounds—in order to make the plants grow in this garden—in order to create life and keep humans alive—the essential ingredient is energy. It can be energy in the form of light, heat, or radio waves. The sun is a gigantic battery. Gravity's a little different—it's a form of magnetic energy. Energy has no atomic structure. Yet it is the force that gives each atom its own structure by holding electrons in their orbits. It's like a magic elixir that glues everything together or sometimes splits things apart."

"Like super glue."

"Stronger."

Rob pointed to another garden patch. "That's enough H2O for the tomatoes, lad. Give the carrots a drink."

Jake was quiet as he flooded the carrots and summer squash. "I get all that, Dad. But what makes the A and H-bombs different?"

"To answer that question you need to accept the fact that atoms are held together by internal energy."

"Sure, I get it. I understand."

"That internal glue is immensely strong, but not unbreakable. Under the right conditions atoms can be torn apart, releasing their energy. Released energy activates the potential energy in other atoms. The cumulative release of energy results in a chain reaction culminating in a massive explosion."

"Like the finale of Fourth of July fireworks?"

"Nae, lad. Not even close. Those explosions are like sucking Pop Rocks by comparison. Nuclear explosions are massive. The energy released when atoms split is like a supernova exploding in a far-away galaxy."

Jake laughed. "Nova's turned out to be a blast to have around, but I wouldn't call her super."

"Aye, true, lad, but she's a sweet dog, even if sometimes she refuses to budge."

"I know," Jake said, laughing. "Okay. I get the picture about the potential for atoms to release energy when they come apart. Is that what happens in an H-bomb blast?"

"Nae, it's more like what happens when an A-bomb detonates. A two-part critical mass of enriched uranium or plutonium is loaded into a bomb casing. A critical mass is an amount that is atomically unstable. The two parts are kept separate until forced together by a conventional explosive. When forced together neutrons are released. They smash into more atoms releasing more neutrons, releasing uncontrollable amounts of energy. It happens in less than a nanosecond. It's called fission."

"How much uranium makes a critical mass?"

"I don't know exactly, son. But not much. It has to fit into a bomb casing or on the nose of a missile."

"Does the same thing happen in an H-bomb?"

"Partly. There are two stages to an H-bomb. The first stage uses a blast which creates a pulse that compresses and fuses small amounts of deuterium and tritium. That's called fusion.

"Neutrons are released generating a chain reaction that amplifies the explosive effect of a jacket of uranium wrapped around the device. The two explosions occur faster than the blink of an eye. The energy released is as powerful as the energy of the sun."

Rob hesitated and appraised Jake's watering efforts. "These weapons," he continued, "are the products of the devil, and, for me, that's saying a lot. You know I don't believe in deities, neither God nor Lucifer." Jake turned off the water and recoiled the hose. "Thanks for explaining it. I wanted to know, but now I'm sorry I do."

"Don't apologize for asking questions, son. To flee the truth would make you as ignorant as the caveman."

"I don't know, Dad. They didn't know this stuff. Maybe they were smarter than we think."

"Let's take a Tour d' Colorado," suggested Annie. "We've lived here for two years but never travelled further than Denver and Carter Lake. There's so much to see. We had no comparable landscapes in the east."

"Aye, and nothing comparable in Scotland, either. There are mountains in the highlands, of course, but nothing like these beasts. Average rainfall in Scotland is about 150 inches; average rainfall in Colorado is 15 inches. We get one tenth the precipitation of Scotland."

"It's dry here, Dad," said Jake. "That's why I have to keep watering the garden."

"Why don't we plan a field trip?" offered Annie. "I want to see the Great Sand Dunes National Park."

"Aye, me, too. And I'd like Jake to see where uranium was mined." Rob unfolded a map. "There's a wee town in the southwest corner of Colorado called Nucla. I've read about it. Only 700 folks live there, and if you decide that's your Garden of Eden and buy property, you're also required by law to own a gun."

"Cool!" said Jake. "The wild west!"

"Aye, but in this case Colorado's west isn't about cattle and rustlers—it's about mining uranium to make bombs."

"Do they still mine?"

"Nae, the pits have been closed. But the Nucla folks would like to see them reopened. Other than mining, there aren't many ways to earn a living in that part of the state. They have no doctor, no dentist, and no hospital closer than two hours away. I don't mind driving through the town, but I don't want to stop and visit."

"Sounds grim to me," said Maryann.

"Aye, I suggest we just pass through. Then we can head to the Colorado National Monument in Grand Junction. Fortunately, Trump's administration left that monument intact. When we head back to Boulder, we should stay in Glenwood Springs. There's an old inactive volcano close by, Dotsero, I want Jake to see. We've been talking about the destructive power of nuclear weapons. I want him to see the destructive power of nature. What happened at Dotsero, I call land rearrangement."

Jake was interested. "Is it active?"

"Nae, lad. It last erupted between 3,800 to 5,500 years ago. But the scars are still there. You can estimate the destructive power of a small volcano compared with the destructive power of a nuclear weapon. When Krakatoa blew its top in 1883, it had four times the destructive power of the largest single H-bomb ever exploded." Rob refolded the map.

"Krakatoa ash reached seventeen miles high and darkened the Earth's skies for years. The world's average temperature in the northern hemisphere dropped by more than two degrees fahrenheit. It became cold in North America and Europe."

"Why are you telling Jake this?" asked Maryann, concerned.

"So he'll understand that if a nuclear war were to happen in Korea, the residue of atomic weapons would cover the planet with dirt, ash, and radiation. We'd enter a nuclear winter. As a result of disease, radiation sickness, and starvation, human existence would be in peril.

"A nuclear attack would be similar to four Krakatoa sized volcanoes erupting at once. I want Jake to understand that fact, so he'll become an advocate for nuclear disarmament. He's old enough to face the truth."

"Where did you learn about all this?" asked Jake.

"Don't forget," chuckled Rob, "I'm a science professor in a large university. We nerds get together and chat."

"Jeepers!" said Maryann. "Don't you ever talk about nice things, like football or women? I thought that's what men do."

"I work with women scientists, too, love. You know that. No, no gender based discussions. Not if we want to keep our jobs."

2021

Jeffersonian Jeffersonian Jeffersonian

SUMMER 2021

World Population Reaches 8 Billion

| by Paul Baker | pbaker.com |

Global population reached 8 billion humans this year. The 7 billion mark occurred in 2011. Human numbers increased by 1 billion in thirteen years. World-wide, 90 million people were added annually to the total.

It's estimated the Earth reached 1 billion by 1804. After 123 years, population in 1927 stood at 2 billion. Thirty-three years later in 1960, the total was 3 billion. Then additional billions were progressively added on a steady basis: 4 billion by 1974; 5 billion by 1987; 6 billion by 1999; 7 billion by 2011. At the present rate of growth, nine billion will be reached in 2033.

Demographers calculate the number of people who have ever lived on Earth to be 106 to 108 billion. It's estimated the population of the United States in 2024 will be 342 million people, an increase of 2.1 million annually. By the end of the

21st Century, our planet's numbers will be between 10 to 13 billion.

Why these totals are cataclysmic

Agriculturists, environmentalists, resource managers, and demographers know the Earth cannot sustain huge numbers. Food and water are now in short supply in many places on the Earth, most notably sub-Saharan Africa. Regional crop failures have become routine. Human generated global warming continues, as the electric power needs of a growing population spur fossil fuel burning. Carbon dioxide and methane gas emissions in the atmosphere are mounting. Warming is hastening the melting of the Earth's glaciers and ice shields, thereby raising sea levels. Greenland's ice will be gone in ten years. Faced with flooding, human migration is underway from coastal areas, forcing people to live in more densely compacted urban communities. High human density has resulted in spreading disease and social conflict. Pandemics and local wars are sprouting in locations heretofore peaceful. The fabric of human existence shows signs of unravelling.

Are solutions available to thwart the impending crisis?

Nations must elect leaders who recognize the impending catastrophe and are sworn to fix it. One way is to revolt against continued carbon extraction by outfitting homes with renewable energy collectors and energy savers. Encourage friends and relatives to lead simpler lives. Lead by example. Campaign for smaller families. Reward childless couples with tax credits. Burden couples bearing more than one child with tax penalties.

These are but a fraction of the steps necessary to keep the Earth habitable. Some appear to be inhumane or draconian. A few challenge assumptions long held by humans since social groups formed. Many people think they are entitled to be free to do what they please—unregulated, unfettered, and unrepentant. If that attitude persists, in fifty years our future as a species is doomed. We will have passed the point of no return. Like a blind herd running in panic, we will spill over the approaching cliff and perish.

Population data courtesy the United Nations Population Fund and the United States Census Bureau.

Maryann Caton, 41 | Robt. MacKenzie, 53 | Jake Canfeld, 15 | World POP: 8.01 billion

---

"I made a big mistake today,"

"What did you do, honey?"

"I decided to drive into work rather than take my bike. It looked like it was about to rain. It was cold, too, so any rain might have changed into snow."

"It did look that way," agreed Annie, "but we could use some precipitation."

"Aye, it's been dry."

"Why was driving to CU a mistake? You have a parking spot."

"The traffic west along Baseline Road was bumper to bumper. Stoplight poles are being replaced at 30th Street. Then, once I made it down to Broadway, cars were backed up heading north."

"Yeah," said Jake. "A lot of kids transfer buses there to go to Fairview. CU and high school kids swarm across that intersection without looking. It's like an ant colony fire drill."

"Aye. If I go by bike, the trip's only twenty minutes. If I take the bus after rush hour, the ride's only ten minutes. Today, during rush hour, it took forty minutes to go three and a half miles."

"Just in the four years we've lived here," said Annie, "I've noticed a difference. I'm sure developing the South Boulder Campus has something to do with it. The new dorm space is allowing the university to accept more students."

"To be sure," agreed Rob. "But the university's not doing it out of a desire to promote learning. A larger university footprint means bigger bragging rights. And more students means more income."

"If I go to CU," Jake asked, "I won't have to pay tuition, right? Because you work there, Dad, don't I get a discount?"

Rob nodded. "That's right, Jake. But you'll still have to buy books, pay for housing, and eat—unless you want to go on a four year fast. Save your money. You like tacos."

"And pizza," added Maryann.

Jake laughed and speared his remaining meatball. "Nah. I plan to keep eating. I've got a bit of money saved up from my inheritance, and I made some do-re-mi working at the rec center."

"You'll need every bit of it, honey."

"Is there any reason I can't live here and commute?"

"That's fine with me," she said, "but most kids want to get away from their parents."

"Yeah, I've considered that. But we get along pretty well. I don't think things will change. But if they do, I'm outta here. Anyway, I've got three years to make up my mind."

"And we've got three years to reconsider," laughed Rob.

He divided the rest of the pasta among the three, ladled out more tomato sauce, then topped off the food with two more mini-meatballs apiece—the kind they liked from SafePath.

"How many people live in Boulder?" asked Jake.

"About 110,000," said Annie. "When the university's in session, it swells to 150,000. Why do you ask?"

"Don't know—just that things seem to be getting more congested."

"It's a good question, lad. Adding to the crowd is a huge influx of people on a daily basis. Folks commute from the Denver and outlying areas. That's why U.S. 36 and Baseline are jammed everyday at rush hour."

"What was it like in Scotland when you were born, Rob? How many people were there?"

"As I recall, in 1968, a little more than five million. Balmaha was tiny—it only had a few hundred residents. It's in the country away from cities like Glasgow. Today, Scotland's numbers are only a wee bit more. There have been years when the population declined. It's a slow growth country. That's what keeps it so attractive."

"What about you, Mom? How many people were in the U.S. when you were born?"

"I don't know, dear. Give me a minute, and I'll look it up." Annie left the table and returned with her touchpad. She googled searching for census information.

"Two hundred twenty-six million."

"Wow! That's way more than Scotland."

"Aye, lad, but Scotland's a much smaller country."

"What about now, Mom? Will that thing tell you today's number?"

"I'm sure. Hold on while I search." She typed in a new data request. "Three hundred twenty-nine million. In the time I've been alive, the U.S. number has grown by 103 million."

"What about me? See what my numbers are."

She checked. "When you were born in 2006, U.S. population was 298 million. I told you what it is now. Do the math to see how it's grown."

Jake quietly calculated in his head. "Yikes! Thirty-one million! No wonder things are getting tight."

"Aye," agreed Rob, "it's a problem."

Jake suddenly lit up, as if remembering the second part of a riddle. "What about the world? How many total people are there?"

Rob answered, "Eight billion."

"Has it grown a lot since you and Mom were born?"

Now Rob took control of the touchpad. "There were 3.5 billion when I was born, 4.2 billion when your mum was born, and 6.6 billion when you started screaming. The numbers average only about a 1.2 % increase per year, but when you have billions of people, 1.2 % growth is huge—about 80 to 90 million additional per year. That's the total after births and deaths have been figured in."

Hearing the statistics appeared to be sobering for Jake. But he got a pencil and paper and jotted down the numbers. "I may use this stuff in a report for school," he said.

The information was equally disturbing for Maryann and deeply vexing for Rob. He had taught science classes about the danger of the population explosion. But the numbers continued to escalate. No matter how he manipulated population statistics, he always came to the same conclusion—humanity was on a crowded path of no return.

2022

Daily Boulder Reporter

Boulder Attorney Knocks Muni Push

WEDNESDAY, FEBRUARY 9, 2022 $2.00

Caton-MacKenzie asserts millions wasted—time to work with Xcel—funds better spent solving homeless problem

By Clevon Perez, Staff Writer

Resident Maryann Caton MacKenzie, an attorney with the **Pearl 2 Pine** law firm, made an impassioned plea last night to the Boulder City Council to bring their Quixote-like municipalization quest to an end, and use funds earmarked for the muni fight to help solve the Boulder homeless problem. In the nine years since the city started pursuing municipalization, more than twenty million dollars has been spent, she alleged, with no resolution in sight. Xcel continues to be Boulder's energy provider.

MacKenzie asserted that the original reason for dumping Xcel was to make Boulder greener, reduce fossil fuel fuel emissions along the Front Range, and be a model for other cities concerned with climate change.

"That argument was forgotten year ago," she said. "Now it's all about costs and rates."

MacKenzie handed out a printed statement:

Altruistic motives tied to municipalization have given away to market pressures, exactly the reason for which Xcel was damned at the start. It's not un-American for investor backed utilities and corporations to make profits. People know my law firm is a strong advocate for environmental issues. But we don't litigate pro bono. We have rent to pay, we have employees to remunerate, and we reward good work with bonuses. It's called capitalism, and when it operates without abusing consumers, it's an economic system worth supporting.

Xcel has enlarged its portfolio of renewables and expects to be free of fossil fuel generation in eight years. The IBM facility off Diagonal Highway is now fully powered by the sun, an Xcel installation worthy of being replicated on the rooftops of the city's highrises. Now is the time for Boulder City to join the utility in its effort. In 2017, when muni pursuit was extended with the approval of an additional 16.5 million dollars, it was expected that the city's Quixote quest would end if progress wasn't made. Negotiations came to a full stop. Even after the 2020 deadline for continuation of the muni pursuit was tabled prior to a city vote, stubborn council members continue to insist a muni is feasible and desirable. It's time for the council to admit it was wrong. We must redirect our tax money to repair infrastructure, add new services, and solve a growing human crisis in our city—homelessness.

MacKenzie pledged to join the homeless cause, saying she planned to align with an advocacy group. She said she hadn't yet selected an organization, but when she did, she would announce her decision.

"I plan to make my pledge come true," she said. "I'm not someone who spouts off, then disappears. That's not my style. Anyone who knows me, understands once I tackle a cause, I see it through to its end."

Maryann Caton, 42 | Robt. MacKenzie, 54 | Jake Canfeld, 16 | World POP: 8.1 billion

---

"To begin our work this semester, we need to visit the basic premise of this course. How can we craft our writing to express complex ideas understood by lay people—the general public— and at the same time, inform professionals—scientists and researchers—of our discoveries?"

Professor MacKenzie opened his lesson from the front of the room, then moved down center between a row of desks. He wanted to be closer to his students. For years he had been aware of research that showed close interaction between teachers and students achieved good results. He wanted to connect with his class. Getting closer to these young men and women, he reasoned, would be more productive than remaining in the front, isolated by an implied barrier. A primary school teacher might sit cross-legged on the floor with second graders. But an intuited level of rigid decorum became ingrained in learners as years mounted, and students grew older and more mature.

"I'm going to write a sentence on the whiteboard," said MacKenzie. "It will express a simple idea. I want you to tell me what the sentence means." He returned to the front and began writing. Puzzled, the class watched him.

At the granular level, you indisputably possess an overabundant plethora of Carver's legume groundnuts, arachis hypogaea.

"Anyone care to risk translating this?" MacKenzie scanned faces. Most were blank. He was sure a few had some idea but were too shy to risk answering incorrectly.

"C'mon, folks," he urged. "You all want to be scientists. Science requires taking chances—sometimes failing—other times succeeding. That's how discoveries are made."

Two hands rose. MacKenzie pointed to one. "Aye, you're Nancy Miller, right?"

"Yes, sir."

"Whoa, stop! I told you all when the semester began to drop the 'sir' and 'professor' nonsense. Remember? Call me Rob or Mac. Dr. Mac's okay. I'm much more comfortable with that." The class laughed.

"I apologize, Mac," said Nancy. "I forgot. You're the only professor I know who allows that informality."

"I'm sure there are other barmy teachers like me. You just haven't met them yet. Now, what about the sentence?"

Nancy began dissecting the words. "Well, the name Carver is mentioned, and I know peanuts are sometimes called groundnuts. So it has something to do with peanuts . . . like maybe you like them?"

"Close enough, lass." To the class he said, "I won't drive you all crazy insisting on a precise translation. It simply means, 'Basically, you have too many peanuts.'" Many laughed.

"So there it is, folks," resumed MacKenzie. "A perfectly good sentence of sixteen words replaced with a sentence of six. Both mean exactly the same thing. But the first is exaggerated with multisyllabic words, at least one redundancy, and a Latin term. Who wants to read junk they can't understand?"

He called on a different student who was waving his hand. "Yes . . . er . . . Jonathan?"

"What's the redundancy?"

"Overabundant and plethora. They mean the same thing. In my opinion, using either is pretentious. A simple 'too many' works fine. Remember, we want the average Joe and Jenny to understand what we write."

MacKenzie saw a few heads nod in understanding. "I have another example for you," he said, trying to control a chuckle. "It's even more egregious than the first. Please pass these to the rear." He handed out computer paper containing a quote. "Read this, folks. Try to determine what it means, and who might have said it."

Called from a retirement which I had supposed to have continued for the residue of my life to fill the chief executive office of this great and free nation, I appear before you, fellow citizens, to take the oaths which the Constitution prescribes as a necessary qualification for the performance of its duties; and in obedience to a custom coeval with our government and what I believe to be your expectations I proceed to present to you a summary of the principles which will govern me in the discharge of the duties which I shall be called upon to perform.

The class read in silence trying to understand the passage. Suddenly, a student at a rear desk burst out laughing.

"Aye, laddie, you're in stitches. Do you know what it's about? You're laughing like a goat that's escaped being neutered."

"I learned about this story in American history class, Mac. It's the introduction to the inaugural speech in 1840 by our fifth president, William Henry Harrison. He gave his speech in pouring rain, got sick within a week, and died after being in office for only thirty-two days. His 8,445 words are the longest inaugural to this day. And he had the shortest presidency."

"Aye, that's it! Good man! You remembered your lesson well. One hundred words of blather to say something very simple." He challenged the class. "While you think about the meaning, I'll write on the whiteboard exactly what Harrison should have said."

I'm the new president. Here's what I have to say.

Everyone again laughed loudly as if a clown had broken his suspenders. "Ten words to convey the meaning of a hundred," said MacKenzie. "It's a wee daft."

The group appeared to be grasping the concept he was trying to make—think clearly—write clearly. Vacuum away words and phrases of little or no import. "Here's a good test of your writing clarity. Would your twelve year old brother or sister be able to understand what you've written? If they're flummoxed, you need to rewrite. Then rewrite again."

He veered in a new direction. "A required text for this class is *The Elements of Style* by William Strunk and E.B. White. I hope you all have a copy. Strunk was an English instructor at Cornell"

"Cornell College in Iowa?" someone asked.

"Nae, Cornell University in Ithaca, New York. In 1919 E.B.White was Strunk's student. Do you know who White was other than a co-author with and former student of Strunk?"

The class laughed again. Someone spoke out. "He wrote children's books. The two I remember are *Charlotte's Web* and *Stuart Little.*"

"Aye, exactly. Both White and Strunk were icons of literature. Their guide to clarity and concision is as relevant to science writing as it is about writing essays or fiction. As you work on your assignments, make use of their guide. Study it. Apply it.

"When you have written something for this class, give it to your roommate. You may have to bribe him or her to read it, but not with beer. You want them to be sober when they tell you it stinks." More laughter.

"If they don't understand what you wrote, rewrite it. Read it out-loud. Delete unnecessary words. Choose simple language rather than over-the-top blather." He saw heads nodding, the class apparently understanding the challenge.

"That's your goal for this semester. When you hand in your work, I'll let you know if you've succeeded or where to improve. For every assignment, you may submit it over and over until it's as close to perfect as you can make it. At that point you'll receive an A, no matter how many times it was submitted. I expect everyone to earn an A in this course. An A-minus will be equivalent to failing." Students glanced at each other in surprise. A grade of A was always a welcome boost to a GPA.

MacKenzie continued. "Brevity is next to godliness, not cleanliness. 'Brevity is the soul of wit.' The second is a quote from Hamlet. You must strive for brevity in your writing without sacrificing meaning. That's a challenge in science articles because so much of our reporting requires referencing data and statistics, or, in chemistry, complex formulae. That's where charts, graphs, and spreadsheets can be used as addended references."

MacKenzie's lesson took another surprising turn. "Perhaps the most famous speech ever delivered by a president was given by Abraham Lincoln, our sixteenth, in 1863. It was at the dedication of a soldiers' cemetery in Pennsylvania. You all know it as *The Gettysburg Address.* At that time, it had no title.

"If you haven't done so, I urge you to read it. If you have read it, read it again. Some of you may have memorized it as part of your early schooling experience. Feel the emotion Lincoln was able to convey in 272 eloquent words. Then apply that technique to your writing."

MacKenzie hesitated to allow the class to wrestle with the idea that a war memorial speech could somehow have relevance to writing about chemical reactions or nuclear medicine.

"Here's your assignment for next time. Invent a report where you announce you have discovered that table salt is composed of chlorine and sodium. You've discovered that the compound can affect animal health. You made your discovery working at a university or in a commercial lab. It doesn't matter. It all will be fiction. Pick a current journal that would likely publish your report. Find out their submission requirements and length limitations.

"Figure out a catchy title. Does the heading, *Sodium Chloride (NaCl) Linked to Hypertension in Erethizontidae Population with High Probability of Consuming Urine Soaked Latrine Fixtures* sound enticing? Or, is *Porcupines Suffer High Blood Pressure After Chewing on Outhouse Toilet Seats* the better choice? You decide."

As the class filed out at the end of the period, MacKenzie overheard one student whisper to another, "I love this guy. He's better than late night comedy. He makes me laugh."

"I'm going to attend the City Council meeting tonight, Rob. Do you want to join me? The meeting starts at 5:45."

"Nae, not tonight, dear. I've got a bunch of papers to read. I'll see how my students dealt with porcupines and pee."

Annie chuckled. "That ought to be fun. What were they supposed to write?"

"I'll tell you when you get home. By then I'll have a better idea of how they did."

He put down his pencil, stood, and hugged his wife. "I love you, Annie. Drive safely. Enjoy the meeting."

"I'm taking the bus. I know the time the last one heads back here. If I miss it, I'll phone."

"Okay, lass, then off with you to a civics lesson in action."

She had the last word. "There's a tofu and kale casserole in the fridge that can be heated for you and Jake."

On the bus into town, Annie had time to think about two issues that seemed to have captured Boulder's attention for years. At least, that's what newspaper headlines and letters-to-the-editor implied.

One was the on-going and never-ending debate over whether Boulder should form a municipal agency to provide electric power to the city. Voters first approved the idea in 2013, via a ballot measure. The plan was approved with a total debt ceiling limit of $240 million by the time the first switch would be thrown. Upwards of seven million was necessary to begin the process. Costs would include hiring municipalization specialists, attorney fees, and staff time. As of 2017, five years ago, the start-up costs had exceeded ten million. And the overall estimates had skyrocketed to more than half a billion, when the takeover would be complete.

Overlooked at the time by the novice and naive council members was the added expense of stranded costs. These were the value of tangible assets owned or installed by the utility, Xcel Energy, that would be made useless by municipalization.

The estimated value of those assets was $300 million. When added to the updated takeover cost of $300 million, the total bill would be $600 million—$360 million more than originally approved by the voters.

Maryann read about the new numbers in the local newspaper. Despite the thinnest margin of approval in a 2017 referendum, the year of her arrival in Boulder, the council plunged forward as if on a religious mission. Millions continued to be spent each year chasing a dream that now no one clearly remembered.

Originally, the plan was an altruistic effort to reduce carbon emissions and show the rest of the country that Boulder's muni plan was a model for other small cities to follow. Egos were at stake. Smug "green city" arrogance clouded logical thinking.

The utility was accused of disingenuous lobbying. The notion that an investor backed utility was unscrupulously overcharging Boulder was advanced by Xcel's opponents. The fact that Xcel spent money to argue its case and sway voters was seen as evil. In fact, Xcel was engaged in business no different than Walmart, Costco, or any of the small businesses that lined the Pearl Street Mall. Although Maryann's law firm enjoined battles to defeat polluting gas, oil extraction, and coal mining abuses, they didn't work for free. Salaries, benefits, rents, and bonuses were accepted as a normal part of business.

A second concern found its way under Annie's skin like a splinter working in deeper and deeper. Years ago, residing in New York City, she had passed beggars and panhandlers loitering on the street. She assumed they were homeless or lived in shelters. Quite likely, they were addicts, unable or unwilling to find work. Many appeared to be mentally unstable.

She remembered Rob telling her about an incident that occurred one winter. An indigent man was sprawled on the sidewalk in Times Square. He was shoeless. A concerned street cop took pity and purchased a pair of boots for him. The officer spent his own money.

On his rounds the next evening, the cop found the man again shoeless. In twenty-four hours the boots were gone and for what? A meal? Drugs? Sex? The whole episode was filmed by a local TV crew reporting on the plight of the homeless. The reporter was at a loss of words trying to make the unexplainable understandable.

Manhattan begging became so routine for Maryann that she barely noticed. The epidemic included a teenage cohort. She had heard that subway tunnels contained hidden niches where runaways could hide. At night she ignored bodies wrapped in cardboard boxes sleeping over steam vents. She averted her eyes from malformed humans squatting next to luxury high-rises. On the subway she moved away from the unwashed.

She remembered never questioning her indifference and motives during those years. Avoiding the homeless was an accepted part of living in a huge city. In New York a certain amount of homelessness seemed natural, a part of the complex fabric of metropolitan life.

Moving to Connecticut hadn't changed her indifference. In fact, rural life made homelessness easy to forget. In Roxbridge there were no homeless. If any resident had been in serious financial or marital trouble, somehow the town would help. It may take a village to raise a child, she had thought, but it also takes a village to help one another in times of distress.

Things changed for Maryann when she, Jake, and Rob moved to Boulder. She loved the small city for its down-home prairie feel, populated with upscale intellectuals and artists. It was a liberal town. It had a vibrant art and music scene. A university enriched its culture with college opportunities and scores of young people. There were times, at the age of forty-two, when she felt ancient.

Other than the municipalization boondoggle that had been dragging on for years costing the city millions chasing an unfulfilled quest, Maryann was shocked by the number of homeless souls she encountered. She now defined them as souls rather than ciphers. Some begged on street corners or on medians at intersections pleading for money with cardboard signs. Some asked for spare change on the Pearl Street Mall. Many hunkered down at night in bedrolls hiding under park shrubbery. A few camped in roofed-over grottoes down quiet alleyways. Churches or outreach shelters were full at night, especially in the winter when Boulder weather could be harsh.

She wondered how an enlightened city like Boulder could have allowed so much homelessness to mount up. And in the five years of her residency, Annie thought the numbers had increased.

Being a logical thinker and meticulous planner, she decided to find the answers to her questions by visiting Boulder's seat of power—the City Council. She needed to learn first hand what the city's policy was, if any, toward the homeless. What plans were in the works? How could she become involved? She hoped to learn by listening to the public comments at the meeting and watching the council respond. Maybe she could help.

"Cheers, lass. Good you're home. How did the meeting go?"

"Okay, Rob. It was interesting. But first, how did you and Jake make out with dinner?"

Rob hesitated, then murmured, "Hmm . . . we both got enough to eat." He wrinkled his brow. "I read a report today in the newspaper. A group of 10,000 Brits was evaluated for depressive behavior. I've always thought the bloody English were depressing, but I digress. Anyway, the researchers wanted to learn if there was a correlation between diet and mood. As it turns out, there is! Vegetarians are much more likely to suffer depression than those on traditional diets containing meat, fish, as well as veggies."

"What are you telling me, Rob?" Annie's face grew stern. "Because I left you with a kale and tofu casserole, you and Jake are ready to commit suicide?"

"Nae, nae, love! The meal was very . . . nutritious. But if I had to eat like that on a regular basis, I might go into depression."

"Poor baby!" sympathized Annie. "But you survived! If I go to another meeting and leave you two thugs at home, what would you like me to fix? I don't mind putting something together. Or you and Jake could go to a restaurant. Better yet, you and the lad could prepare your own meals."

"He'd opt for peanut butter and jelly," said Rob, resigned to reality. "Lassie, I really appreciate you caring for us. I really do." He hugged her. "But once in awhile, out of the goodness of your beautiful heart, please make Scottish pizza."

She grinned but looked puzzled. "What the heck is that?"

"Shepherd's Pie. You know what it is—ground meat, peas, corn, diced carrots, a dash of HP Sauce, a jigger of broth, and a coating of baked clapshot."

Annie chuckled. "You and your clapshot. Won't mashed tatties be sufficient?"

"Aye, Annie my love, perfect!" He kissed her. "Now, tell me about the meeting. I'll heat up the casserole. There's plenty left." He glanced at her hoping he wasn't digging a hole for himself. Before she could become annoyed at his disparagement of her food choice, he set a glass of chilled pinot grigio in front of her. He dished out her food.

Annie sipped her wine and took a deep breath, glad to be home. It was time to relax and unwind after a busy day. Talking with Rob about the day's events was more than therapeutic. It was love making through shared ideas. She told him what she had learned at the City Council meeting.

"They're still wrapped up with municipalization, Rob. Despite chasing the dream for nine years and drawing no closer, they persist in pursuing an idea that's become redundant. Their dream has been eclipsed by the progress the utility's made."

"What do you mean?" Rob joined her at the table with his own glass of wine.

"At this point, Xcel Energy's renewables portfolio is exactly what Boulder was seeking in 2013. And Xcel's adding additional renewables as we speak. They've just brought online a massive solar farm in central Wyoming. A portion of that generation is going to Boulder. As far as I can figure, Boulder is now consuming power sixty percent generated through renewables."

Rob offered an additional insight into Xcel's value. "And there's something else."

"What have I missed?"

"When the U.S. is hit by monster storms resulting in millions being without power, utilities from all over America rush crews to help repair the damage. Remember the long line of Xcel trucks heading to Florida after Hurricane Michael?"

"Yes. It was encouraging."

"I wonder whether little Boulder would have the resources to assist elsewhere. Our city champions causes like Sister Cities and Sanctuary Cities, but would Boulder have enough resources to allow a convoy of muni trucks go to . . . say . . . New Orleans, if it gets whacked again?"

"I hadn't thought of that," admitted Annie. "It's one more reason for the town fathers and mothers to face reality. Municipalization makes no sense."

She stopped to savor her meal. "Mmm . . . this casserole is delish. I don't know what you and Jake were complaining about." She smacked her lips, then took a big swig of wine.

"Where is he?" she asked.

"Upstairs trying to decipher the instructions for his new camera. It was a good sixteenth birthday gift."

"I think so, honey. The images he's gotten with his smartphone and point and shoot are quite good. I think he has a talent for photography."

"Aye, love. The lad's a natural." Rob lifted his wine glass for a taste. "When I was about his age in Scotland, I saw a photography exhibit by Robert Mapplethorpe. It was in the school where Mum had been a student and my father a teacher."

"You told me about it."

"Aye, that I did." He sipped. "Mapplethorpe's subject matter was offensive to me, but I admit, his skill with a camera was solid."

"I agree," said Annie. "I know about Mapplethorpe. A few of his images were occasionally on display at the Guggenheim. None the day we met, though. Let's hope Jake sticks to bodies of water rather than to bodies of men."

Rob laughed and again sipped his wine. "What did you learn about Boulder's homeless situation?"

His wife collected her thoughts. "I was surprised. Some of my notions were jumbled. First of all, there are two Boulders. Seems evident now, but not so at first. There's Boulder County and the City of Boulder. They're not always distinguishable in newspaper articles. I feel stupid."

"Nae, Annie. That's an honest mistake. We've been in town

for only five years. Speaking for myself, I haven't been focused on local politics. I have too many needy students to help."

"Okay, I'm not stupid. Thanks for reminding me." She chuckled, then nibbled at her meal while continuing to relate what she learned.

"The county collects a five cent tax on every hundred dollars spent. It's hard to believe, Rob, but those nickels add up to a tidy sum year after year. Through a funding initiative called Worthy Cause, the county awards up to fifty percent of capital expense projects proposed by non-profit agencies. So, for example, if Meals on Wheels wanted to construct a centralized kitchen—maybe in Longmont—they can apply for funding."

"Interesting. That really does sound like a worthy cause."

"You bet. The county awards millions each year. Small agencies that deal with hunger, homelessness, transportation of the handicapped, early-childhood education, and the elderly are benefactors. Worthy Cause seems to me to be a successful initiative."

"Sounds like it," agreed Rob. "But it needs the wee tax to keep it alive, right? Is the taxation a permanent levy or is the plan periodically renewed?"

"Every ten years voters get to decide. It's now Worthy Cause IV as of this year, 2022. Additional authorization will be by ballot in six years. So far, the plan has easily won reapproval. Citizens are pleased with the work of the county. The taxation rate remains at .05%."

"What's the city up to as far as homelessness is concerned?" Rob pressed.

"As far as I can tell, not too much. A strategy is listed on its website. But the six goals are nothing but empty platitudes. At least that's how I read them. Whether any of the ideas are tied to action is a guess."

"What do you mean? Give me an example." Rob was struggling to understand Annie's pessimism.

"Their first goal is, 'Expand pathways to permanent housing and retention.' What the hell does that mean, Rob? Are they widening the sidewalks? How do they define permanent housing? What's retention? It's all feel-good nonsense. The other goals are similarly worded.

"They budget about $300,000 a year to keep families housed in rental units. But in a city where average home prices are approaching $1,100,000, it's chump-change. Moreover, the number of available affordable units diminishes each year, as real estate prices sky-rocket."

"Aye, I see your point. In the five years we've been in Boulder, our home's value has almost doubled."

"Honey, you and I know the only way to achieve a goal is to state it precisely, then tag on benchmarks to measure success based on hard data. The town could pass ordinances requiring developers to purchase land for future homeless housing. Maybe the city could alter its domicile requirements allowing tiny stand-alone units to be built."

"Aye, and in my opinion it's time for auxiliary apartments to be allowed in houses where there's extra space."

She agreed. "The only thing that's getting in the way of progress is narrow thinking."

"What are you going to do about it, dear? Will you get involved? You're a smart lass. Maybe you could spur new ideas. Personally, I don't think the homelessness problem will ever be 100% solved, but a big part of it might be. If you decide to get involved, I know you can be a catalyst for change. The folks of Boulder don't know that yet, but I do." He kissed her hand.

"Thank you for supporting me, Rob. At this point, I'm not sure what I'll do. And I'm unclear what the fixes might be. I'll have to think about it. But one thing I know, I'm heading back to more City Council meetings. I can't erase homelessness from my mind.

2023

The Crown Heights Shofar

OFFICIAL NEWSLETTER OF THE CROWN
HEIGHTS JEWISH COMMUNITY CENTER

1 January 2023

"L'Chaim . . . to life! Mazel Tov . . . good luck! You'll
need a schmear of the second to make it through
the mahalak of the first." - Brucie Greene, 1954

The Plight of Women

by ShoShona Dinkelstern, Gr 9, Shul Baruch HaShem

**As an orthodox Jew, I risk being shunned by my friends and
neighbors for writing this essay. Nevertheless, it's time for
women of all faiths, liberal and conservative, to take up the
fight for freedom of expression.**

**For centuries men have dominated religious thought and
custom. Women have been shrouded in dress and stripped
of ideas. With the Earth's average temperatures rising by
degrees per decade, women, not men, should determine how**

they dress and look. No woman should die from extreme temperatures. No benevolent God would decree that women were subject to the archaic demands of men.

Many Catholic religious orders have banished the wimple. Shia Islam is relaxing laws regarding head scarves. The burqa is no longer required in some Sunni countries. Bans on face coverings in the United States and much of Europe have gradually been accepted by Sunnis, as much for health reasons as for political gains.

I'm calling on all conservative and orthodox Jewish groups in Brooklyn to allow women to dress as they please. This includes Hasidic sects like the Satmars and Bobovs. Enough already. It's time to set women free!

Maryann Caton, 43 | Robt. MacKenzie, 55 | Jake
Canfeld, 17 | World POP: 8.21 billion

John Jay Hall

Dear Annie, Jan 21, 2023

It's been six years since Rob, Jake, and you moved to Colorado. I've been remiss not writing sooner. You helped me so much through my middle and high school years to understand what was happening in the world around me. Remember the gun range controversy? You counseled me that improving its safety could be achieved through peaceful protest. It turned out you were right. I miss you and your family, and hope you all are happy and healthy.

Annie, in many ways you acted as my mentor. It's long overdue for me to catch you up with what I've been up to. It's fair to say the decisions I've made to now were influenced by your example. Again, thank you.

Perhaps you've heard from Roxbridge friends that I am a fresh-woman at Columbia. I was always impressed by how your experience here seemed to be so happy. Like you, I am involved with intercollegiate sports but not as a diver, as you were. I'm a member of the Columbia women's national championship archery team. The team has two components, compound bows and recurve bows. I'm a "recurve bow-woman." As a beginner, I'm on the frosh squad. Within the last month, to my coach's relief, I've starting hitting the target with regularity. Unlike New Milford's gun range, our facility is enclosed on all sides. There's no danger of errant arrows skewering students on College Walk.

So I'm a Lion! Roar, Lion, Roar! I share a room in John Jay Hall with a girl from Colorado. What a coincidence! So far we've hit it off well. In fact, this is my second year in the same room. I'll try to explain.

If I had entered Columbia immediately after high school, I'd now be a sophomore. I'm nineteen. Instead, I deferred my entry by one year. The college has a new program. After being admitted, if I agreed to work one year in the city's public school system as an intern, I could get my room free for that year before starting classes. I've considered teaching as a career, so this plan made sense to me. I still had to pay for food and city transportation, but summer work covered that. For a year, kale, tofu, and raman were big parts of my diet.

I told you about archery. You must remember all the running I did as a teener. You got me started, but I found it hard to keep it up living in NYC, especially after I began my intern job.

I chose to work at Evander Childs High School on Gun Hill Road in the Bronx. It was a long commute, but only required one transfer. I took Broadway #1 to 96th Street, then changed trains to the #2 heading uptown. You probably remember the spaghetti map of subway lines.

The population at EC is 98% students of color. Some are children of immigrants from the Caribbean, most are African-American, many are hispanic in origin. A bunch of different languages are spoken at EC.

I assisted in the Social Studies Department. My job was to tutor small groups of ninth graders about the U.S. Constitution. I'm not a legal scholar, but you and Dr. Livingstone in HS civics taught me a lot. And Columbia had an indoctrination week, when I arrived in the city. I attended seminars in the law school. I'll never be an Elena Kagan, but I know enough law to help. And, as I look at my next three years of coursework, that knowledge will come in handy.

My classes this year are probably similar to what you took when you were here. I have a foreign language (Spanish), contemporary civilization, literature humanities, art and music humanities, science and math.

I have an English composition class. The professor constantly refers to *The Elements of Style,* the little book Rob was always praising. And I have one elective course each semester. This term I'm taking Gender Studies.

Along with my way-too-long letter, I've enclosed a copy of a newsletter from a community center in Brooklyn. It features an opinion piece by an orthodox Jewish girl. It was handed out in Gender Studies as a translation, since the original piece is in Hebrew. It's a ninth grade student's take on women's rights. The handout was to spark debate about restrictive religious customs, and how they disproportionately affect women. It seems to me there has been plenty written and debated about it, but rarely do women in ultra-orthodox religions dare to speak out. Anyway,

I'd appreciate your thoughts on the matter and, of course, what Rob thinks.

Phew! My letter has been all about me. How's my buddy, Jake doing? As I recall, he'll start college in a year. What are his plans? Do you and Rob ever return east? If so, please make time to see me. I'm back in Roxbridge in the summer working for my dad. Or we could meet in NYC in the winter.

I love you all.

Your friend,

Taylor

1 Rim Rock Circle
Boulder, CO
Feb. 14, 2023

Dear Taylor,

What a surprise! It was absolutely wonderful receiving your letter! It sounds like you discovered the perfect place to keep learning. Columbia was just right for me, and by what you wrote, sounds ideal for you, too. When your four years are over, I'm sure you'll fully appreciate the meaning of Columbia College's Alma Mater, *Sans Souci.*

My swim team had its own special song. A student I knew wrote the lyrics. Maybe the 2023 archery team might like to adopt it, although I don't know whether the other Ivies are into bows and arrows.

Brown! Harvard! Yale! Sing Lion daughters.
Give all three the French salute!
Have Princeton meet its fate,

Kick Cornell back upstate,
Give Penn and Dartmouth both the royal boot!

I read your letter to Rob and Jake. Neither were surprised by your activism and willingness to engage in a new college program. We knew years ago that you were inquisitive and bold. If teaching's in your future, go for it, girl! But no matter what you choose to do, tackle it so you'll have "no regrets."

Jake's in his senior year at Boulder High School. He's doing well. His test scores and academic profile would allow him to apply to an eastern school—maybe on the Ivy league level. However, he loves living in Boulder. Besides, Rob's job with the university means Jake can get a free ride.

He continued playing soccer in Boulder after arriving from Roxbridge. But by the time he was in high school, all his extracurricular interests turned to the mountains. His school sponsors a wilderness-conservation club. As a member, he's stood on top of twelve of Colorado's 14,000' peaks. He volunteers improving trails within the Boulder Open Space and Mountain Park system. His club is an active group of young folks. He always has a camera with him. Maybe Jake will become the next Ansel Adams.

Rob started a new program in the university's science department. He's working to improve the writing skills of fledgling researchers. He has two classes each week and an online tutorial operation. Young scientists and researchers from other parts of the country can log in and take the course through the cloud. Oh yes—he requires students to use *The Elements of Style*. Last year Rob was promoted to the rank of associate professor.

As far as I'm concerned—I'm with a law firm **Pearl 2 Pine.** We do environmental work. Environmentalism's been my focus since I graduated from Columbia Law School almost twenty years ago. I'm also getting involved in the homeless situation in Boulder. It might be hard for you to believe, but we have homelessness here, too. Most people think it's only a problem of big cities. Sadly, it's nationwide.

Getting back to the issue of women's rights as implied in the newsletter piece you sent— we discussed it at dinner a number of times, exploring the pros and cons from all angles. Here, in no order of importance, is what we came up with:

1. All women, regardless of religious persuasion, should be able to decide for themselves what to do, say, believe, and wear. Our family's credo (or religion, if you prefer) is ULAR, the Universal Law of Reciprocity. In a nutshell it means "Leave me alone, and in return, I'll leave you alone." Another way of phrasing it is "If you help me, I'll help you." You know it as the Golden Rule. ULAR requires no belief in deities, no adherence to a set of arbitrary rules, and no requirement to dress or function in any way other than to fulfill ULAR.

2. The practice of male domination over women isn't based on intellectual superiority, only on muscle mass and testosterone.

3. With our ability to cryo-freeze human semen, men have become redundant. (This is Rob's idea—Jake disagrees.)

4. Religious clothing is a vestigial remnant of the dark ages.

5. It's healthy to wear breathable, comfortable clothing. Torso binding and concealing wraps and dresses are no different than wearing straight jackets.

Taylor, dear, I'm sure there are other equally logical reasons to allow women to decide for themselves how to live. I watched

you when you were twelve and thirteen seek out books telling
the stories of women who defied tradition and male dictates.
Future choices are yours to make, not some guy's. I know you
will shine in whatever work you choose, whether it's a teacher
or be it a doctor, lawyer, or chief executive. Maybe politics are
in your future.

Rob and I may travel east again this year. We were in NYC
three weeks ago to celebrate the birthday of the Scottish poet,
Robert Burns. The gala was at the Columbia Club. I'm sorry we
missed you. Someday, when you're earning enough money, you
ought to join. It's a good place to make business connections,
and they have good hamburgers.

We're thinking of driving east this summer to see what
remains of our nation's natural resources. We want to go before
the roads become more crowded. The growing U.S. population
is overwhelming everything. Stopping by in Roxbridge to say
hello to the Road Rats would be fun. I'll let you know our plans.

Keep up the good work. Rob and I are proud of you, as I'm
sure your mom and dad are. Jake says the next time the two of
you play *Monopoly*, he'll let you use the wheelbarrow token. He
constantly reminds us that it's good for taking home lots of loot.

With deep affection,

Love,
Annie

"Good evening. My name is Maryann MacKenzie. I live at 1
Rim Rock Circle. I've been a resident of Boulder for almost six
years. Some of you know me through my work as an attorney
at **Pearl 2 Pine**. My legal career has focused on nuclear waste

legislation, waste repository issues, and bringing nuclear waste sequestration violators to justice.

"However, I'm here tonight on another matter. Like other citizens, I've become alarmed by the growing homeless problem in Boulder. The fact that destitute people are in our city should come as no surprise. Homelessness is a nationwide epidemic.

"What concerns me are the bland superficialities expressed in Boulder's Homeless Strategy Vision. It begins: 'Boulder residents, including families and individuals, have opportunities to achieve and maintain a safe, stable home in the community.'

"That's a laudable vision, but we all know that it's a hollow statement. There are virtually no opportunities for the homeless to acquire permanent housing, at least not for a significantly large cohort. The city persists in warehousing people in the North Boulder shelter and relying on charitable or faith based groups to open their doors during especially bad weather.

"The vision statement is weakly supported by six goals. Because of my time limitation, I'll only mention the first: 'Expand pathways to permanent housing and retention.'

"Ladies and gentlemen of the Council, you are all educated people and Boulder caretakers. But, I ask you, what the dickens does this goal mean? Are sidewalks scheduled for widening? Is there a plan for permanent housing that includes many and not just a few? And what is meant by the word, 'retention'?

"The vision as stated and the six goals purported to achieve the vision are mindless nonsense. If you truly want to make a dent in the homeless crisis, I suggest you begin by stating goals with measurable outcomes. I'll give you two examples, but they're only examples. Don't hold me to them . . . yet:

1. By July 1, 2024, Boulder will have completed two censuses of the homeless. Because of the transitory

nature of the homeless, names, ages, and other identifying characteristics will be computerized to eliminate duplication.

2. By December 31, 2024, Boulder will publish a specific plan to provide home ownership to one hundred families and individuals beyond the 160 temporary beds in the North Boulder homeless shelter.

"At the end of the year, I plan to return to the Council and lay out a precise action plan. By then I hope to have formed a committee of citizens committed to solving the homeless crisis, or at least reducing it. A thorough census of our homeless citizens is the necessary first step to determine which candidates are sincere in trying to climb out of the homeless pit. Only then will we know with some assurance how to proceed.

"I will contact the city manager and request a longer block of time for a presentation. I assume that courtesy will be afforded me. Good evening."

Rob recognized the signs of his wife's commitment. As spring turned into summer, Maryann attended City Council meetings more frequently. It wasn't to make statements—just to listen. She told him that by showing up regularly, she was working to cultivate a cordial relationship. Additionally, she was trying to glean which members had the most influence, who had knowledge of the issues being discussed, who was liberal, who was conservative.

Identifying middle-of-the-road members from a predominantly liberal council was tricky. Opinions frequently changed. But as they changed, so did trends become apparent. She learned that within a liberal, progressive council, there were some conservative voices, some practical thinkers, and some resistors to constant tax increases for a never-ending stream of social programs. Middle income citizens were being squeezed hard by escalating property taxes. She learned the extent of citizen's displeasure by reading letters to the editor.

Maryann had promised that she would become engaged in a campaign to solve Boulder's homelessness. Early in her efforts, however, she realized she needed help. She told Rob she was attempting to seek assistance by arranging meetings with a variety of organizations: Boulder Democrats, Boulder Republicans, the Green Party, the Boulder Conservative Caucus, the county and city homeless agencies, churches, and nonprofits like the Salvation Army and the Red Cross. She even tested the waters in the Boulder County School System, knowing they had to deal with children from homeless families. Some children were living in cars or campers.

As it turned out, setting up meetings took time and patience. No one was immediately eager to meet at the request of a new resident, someone with no apparent political clout. She was an unknown factor, despite her being an associate attorney at **Pearl 2 Pine,** a highly respected law firm.

Nevertheless, she persevered, as Rob knew she would. She was on a new mission. He was certain nothing would detract her until she either succeeded or failed. She would see it through to the end. She was tenacious. He was reminded that in high school she was called "the bulldog."

2024

University of Colorado

INDIGENOUS SURVIVAL REPORT

National Report on the Welfare of North America's Native People

December, 2024 / US$7/ CAN$9

Colorado tribes block roadway to summit of Mount Evans—Demand it be renamed "Mount Arapaho"

By Daniel Bearclaw Addison

In an eternal struggle to regain recognition as the rightful heirs to Colorado's pre-European landscape, eight tribal nations have filed suit to rename 14,265 foot Mount Evans to Mount Arapaho. The road to the summit has been blockaded by a coalition of tribes who vow to stay through the winter into the next tourist season or longer, if necessary.

Colorado hosts 58 fourteen thousand foot peaks. The tribes plan to pick off contenders one by one until all European based names have been erased. Each peak will be named for a tribe. Thereafter, when all Colorado tribes have been honored, additional peaks will be named for tribal leaders. If leader names run short, in the Indian tradition, native animals and natural phenomena may be featured.

Indigenous language names may be considered. For example, Pikes Peak could become "Mount Heey-otoyoo," meaning "long mountain." As a result, Longs Peak and Mt. Meeker would be coupled with one name, Mt. Neniis-otoyou'u, meaning "there are two mountains."

It's now accepted that at any one time, 50 million native people lived in pre-Columbian North America from Central America to Alaska. In 2024, eight million remain.

The arrival of Europeans quickly decimated indigenous people through murder and disease. Treaties were conveniently ignored, even if committed to paper. White men's promises meant nothing—they were lies. Tribes were overrun, confined to reservations of dwindling area, then moved again. Native peoples were considered animals and barbarians. Often it was more efficient to kill Indians in mass executions than to attempt rapprochement.

Coincidental to native peoples being slaughtered, so was their food source, especially for western tribes. At the time of Columbus's arrival, 50 million bison roamed the great plains. In 1830, the mass destruction of the great herds ensued as a demand for hides began. In 1844, The Hudson Bay Company alone sold 75,000 bison robes to trading posts in Canada.

In 1870, two million bison were killed on the southern plains. By 1872, an average of 5000 animals were killed each day. Ten thousand white hunters poured into the great plains. If a Native American was shot in the process, it was an added bonus.

In 1880, slaughter of the northern herds began with similar results to what had happened in the south. By mid-year 1883, virtually all bison in the United States were gone.

The white man's greed, hatred, and stupidity reaped horrendous results. The pales became the rulers of the west, but a west susceptible to their ignorance. With meat sources gone, fur bearing animals disappearing, and water in short supply, the usurpers with stone heads and stone hearts tore up the prairie to sow plants unsuitable for the climate. Crops failed. Wind storms picked up soil once locked in place by prairie grasses. The white men created their own hell on earth—the Great Dust Bowl.

Colorado tribes pow-wowed in 2023 and formed a political action committee (PAC). All resources, both financial and spiritual, were centralized. Seventy thousand tribal members pledged to vote as a bloc to elect Coloradans who supported Indian interests. A not-for-profit tribal lobbying cadre was registered with the Colorado Secretary of State.

Leadership of the new coalition will be rotated among the eight tribes every two years. One tribal council will supplant eight. Separate interests of each tribe will be addressed by the larger council.

In a peaceful and well organized plebiscite, the new organization was named Reborn Each Day (RED). Ninety-eight percent of those old enough to vote on the union did so. In place of tobacco pipes celebrating a grand occasion, hundreds of people shook hands and embraced. It was a great day to be a Native American in Colorado.

Maryann Caton, 44 | Robt. MacKenzie, 56 | Jake MacKenzie, 18 | World POP: 8.29 billion

---

"I know you've been wondering what happened to Colorado's indigenous people, Jake. You've mentioned Chief Left Hand a few times, especially when we cycle up Left Hand Canyon to Jamestown."

Jake nodded. "Yeah, Rob. I know there were tribes around here and out on the plains. In Boulder we have streets named for them like Arapahoe Avenue and Sioux Drive. But I'm unclear how they lost their lands to the whites."

"Books abound on the subject, laddie. And I bet you can get a pretty good history from Wikipedia. But most of the stories are written from a white person's viewpoint—the viewpoint of the conquerors. Winners get to write history, even if the winners were cruel and avaricious. Ironically, sometimes the losers refuse to accept reality."

"What do you mean?"

"An example is southern confederate apologists insisting the Civil War was about states rights. In a way that's true. But the argument is cloaked in deceit and rationalization. They argue states had the right to maintain slavery. They wanted slavery to be extended into the west. No matter how you twist the truth, Jake, the cause of the Civil War was the cruelty of slavery, pure and simple."

"I understand that, Rob. But the Indian dilemma puzzles

me. That painting we saw in the Denver Art Museum sticks in my mind."

"Which one, honey?" Maryann was listening in on the conversation.

"The one depicting a small band of mounted Indians with loaded pack horses moving away from a wagon train visible in the distance. It was a beautiful but sad painting."

"Aye," agreed Rob. "I remember. It's called, *In the Enemy's Country.* The painting depicts the whites as the enemy overrunning Indian lands. The Indians were fleeing from what was once their home. Too many illustrations and movies depict Indians as the bad guys and the poor settlers as the victims. We now know how distorted that image is."

"We've lived in Boulder for seven years," said Annie. "I think each of us would benefit from learning about Colorado Indians. Rob," she asked, "do you know any experts at the university who could give us a brief history? I'll see if I can round up some neighbors to join us. And Fred, Lois, and the girls might come, too."

"Good idea. I'll contact the Center for Native American and Indigenous Studies. I'm sure they have speakers."

"What building are they in?"

"They have a cottage on Grandview Avenue."

"I know where that place is," said Jake. "It's only five blocks from Boulder High."

Rob introduced Ursa Bent to the small group of friends and family gathered in their Rim Rock Circle living room. Bent was an assistant professor of indigenous studies at CU.

"Good evening, folks," said Bent smiling. "Thanks for inviting me. It's always a pleasure teaching a group who wants to learn, rather than a bunch of kids taking Indian history simply for two credits." His demeanor relaxed the group. They chuckled, admiring his honesty.

Maryann was unable to tell to what race Bent belonged. He was of medium height, had European facial features, and a long braid of black hair. A small piece of silver and turquoise jewelry hung around his neck. It reminded her of the Spirit Woman necklace Rob had given her in 2015, before he left for a trip to Turkey. Spirit Woman was upstairs in her jewelry box. *I ought to wear it more often,* she thought.

"As you can see," continued Bent, "even though I'm still sunburnt from the summer, I'm not an Indian. I'm a white."

Jake signaled he had something to say. He was sitting between his two cousins, Lindsay and Jeannie. "Excuse me for interrupting, Professor Bent. My name's Jake, and I'm a freshman at CU. I have a bad habit of butting in on discussions. It goes back to elementary school."

Rob and Annie vigorously nodded agreeing with Jake's honesty.

Jake looked at his parents, shrugged his shoulders a *mea culpa*, then asked a question. "How do the indigenous people want to be referenced? Should whites say 'Indians'?—'Native Americans'?—'Indigenous people'?"

"Good question, Jake. You ought to take a course in Indian history while you're at CU. To answer your question, though, it's up to the individual Indian being addressed or referenced. Native people often say Indian. Others refer to their tribe saying, I'm an Apache, or I'm a Cheyenne. When you're a member of a group, you can call yourself whatever you want. Personally, I use the term many of my Indian friends use, People, as in 'I am one of the People.' 'We are the People.'"

Jake added a point. "Indian names have been attached to

many things. Sometimes they seem hurtful like Washington Redskins."

Bent agreed, then gave his opinion. "I have no trouble with teams being named Braves, or Chiefs, or Indians. Those names are fine, almost heroic. But Redskins is different. It's a pejorative term for a racial cohort. The name is a white invention. The Cleveland Browns are a color named team, but it doesn't reference people of color. The team was named for Paul Brown, their first coach. Same for the Cincinnati Reds. Their name has nothing to do with the People. Originally, they were the Red Stockings." Bent sipped water while the group chuckled and joked about the losing record of the Boston Red Sox in the last five years.

"However, the term Redskins," continued Bent, "is derogatory in connotation, at least to some of the People. Indigenous skin color is no more red than African-Americans are black. Skin color varies widely among all groups. I'm caucasian by race, but as you can see, I'm as brown as an autumn acorn."

As Bent spoke about skin color, the MacKenzie guests looked at the backs of their hands wondering what color adjective might define them. Or did it really matter?

"I'm sorry I got diverted," said Bent. "Please feel free to interrupt, if you have questions. Or save them for after my talk." He winked at Jake.

"You want to know what happened to the indigenous Colorado People. I'm asked that a lot. It's a complicated story involving love and deceit, promises and lies. It ended in a massacre. I'll give you some highlights, but you can read the full account in the book, *Bury My Heart at Wounded Knee.* Ironically, the story was written by a white librarian, but told from the People's point of view. They approve of his honesty.

"By 1860, all tribes from the east coast through the plains had been forced to abandon their traditional lands. The expanding white population pushed them west. Along with a belief in the superiority of their European heritage, white westward migration was promoted by the federal government through the concept of eminent domain—land and resources belonged to whomever claimed them. The People's claim meant nothing."

"Like the 1862 Homestead Act?" asked Lindsay Caton.

"Exactly," said Bent. He hesitated to check if his audience was with him. After another sip of water, he continued. "It's estimated that at the start of the white's immigration to the new world, 50 million indigenous Peoples were scattered through Central and North America. That's from Panama to Alaska and all of Canada. Conflict was inevitable. The white's hunger for land, gold, and other resources was insatiable."

"Do you include bison as resource?" someone asked.

"Right . . . and furs and pelts, lumber, and coal. Population growth in the east forced whites to move west seeking a greater share of the land. Predictably, the two cultures were bound to clash.

"I'm frequently asked what made the whites so ruthless in their pursuits. As I mentioned, it was perceived white superiority. It was the same ethos they reserved for all non-whites—hatred and loathing. White inhumanity in the south took the form of slavery. Slavery was a form of servitude economy. If the south hadn't had slaves, the region would have remained a backwater. In many ways, it still is." Bent took another sip, then resumed.

"Like black slaves, the People were not immune from white hatreds—or maybe it was white fear of the People. Today, that attitude is sometimes given a vanilla definition—ethnophobia.

No matter how Indian loathing is defined, it's hatred fueled by ignorance.

"It's not important for you to know every troop movement, every white claim on the land, every mass migration by the People here in Colorado. What you need to understand is that the Cheyenne, Arapaho, and a small band of Dakota Sioux attempted to make peace with Colorado's territorial governor, John Evans. The governor's military assets were under the control of one Colonel John Chivington, a former Methodist minister. But Chivington possessed none of the Christian virtues associated with a man of the cloth.

"Chivington advocated the extermination of the People. After killing Indians, he urged his troops to mutilate the dead, take scalps, cut off genitals. He wanted these atrocious acts to be done to men, women, and children. They're 'nits and lice,' he declared in a public speech in Denver, referring to the People as vermin."

"How do you know these things were said?" asked Jake.

"Scribes and translators attended treaty meetings. And in Denver there was *The Rocky Mountain News*, a daily newspaper.

"All-in-all, the People wanted peace despite being forced off their lands and being restricted from hunting bison. They foolishly trusted white leaders to a fault. In meeting after meeting, truce after truce, the whites promised much but delivered nothing except warnings and orders. Often white demands were confusing to the People or impossible to meet. Tribal leaders who had traveled to Washington believed the ceremonial flags they had been given, letters of safe passage, and medals awarded them by Lincoln would protect them from bloodthirsty troopers bent on murder on the plains."

Ursa Bent took a deep breath and wetted his mouth.

Maryann saw he was becoming emotional by the horror story he was telling. She could hear an occasional catch in his voice.

"In November, 1864," he went on, "a mixed contingent of Arapaho, Cheyenne, and Sioux encamped on the plains in eastern Colorado. They were composed mostly of women, children, and old men. Young warriors were north in search of bison or had joined bands of Cheyenne Dog Soldiers attacking outposts along the Platte River. The families left behind camped along Sand Creek abiding the orders of Governor Evans. In doing so, Evans promised they would be safe from the cavalry.

"Early on November 29, a six hundred seventy-five man force of Colorado U.S. Volunteer Cavalry, ignoring Evan's words, attacked the sleeping village. Soldiers went on a blood-lust rampage killing, raping, and disemboweling men, women, and children. Scalps were taken. Genitals were hacked off. The atrocities equalled the worst ever perpetrated by humans on other humans up to then. John Chivington, the former Methodist preacher led the raid and exhorted his men to mutilate as well as kill.

"Although some surviving People headed south below the Arkansas River, and others escaped north to Wyoming, in essence the People's influence and life on the plains was finished. The backs of two tribes were broken. Today, the Arapaho live in the Wind River Reservation in Wyoming. The Cheyenne reservation is in southeast Montana. Of course, some of my brothers and sisters live independently in Colorado, off reservations. But the tribal life of the nomadic plains People is long gone, never to be replicated.

"From 1851 to 1867, four peace treaties were signed by the whites and the People. All four guaranteed safety and access to tribal lands. Each treaty was subsequently ignored by the whites. The next treaty always included greater restrictions, such as a reduction of available land for the People. These, too, were broken. For the whites, the word 'treaty' meant nothing—just hollow promises. For the People, the first treaties promised peace and a way of life. Gradually, the word treaty meant nothing to either side. All that mattered was 'might makes right.'"

The MacKenzie guests were silent. Some appeared to be shocked, others deeply saddened. Lindsay Caton asked a question. "Professor Bent, how do historians know what was said a hundred sixty years ago?"

"As I indicated earlier, young lady, meeting notes were kept. A man named John Smith translated."

"How did you get involved with Indian culture?" asked Jake. "You said you are white."

"I am a descendent of William Bent, a trader and friend of the Cheyenne. Before he married a mixed race woman near the end of his life, he became a member of the Cheyenne tribe and had three indigenous wives, Owl Woman, Yellow Woman, and Island. His last wife was Adeline Harvey. She had one son. That son was my grandfather. I am a direct descendant of the union of William Bent and Adeline Harvey." Bent wiped his brow with a bandana.

"William Bent was a white who became one of the People in fact as well as in spirit. He admired and trusted the People. He tried to navigate them through the white's rapaciousness. In the end he failed.

"It's my mission to tell how the People were betrayed. I offer my support and promise to help the People of 2024 as they seek to reclaim some of the spirit of their heritage by erasing white names from mountain tops."

"My son, you've been reborn! Jacob Canfeld MacKenzie! Imagine!" Annie hugged Jake.

"Welcome to the MacKenzie clan, laddie. Sláinthe! You're a fine specimen of a Scot." Rob grinned broadly, then shook hands with his stepson. "You know the clan motto, lad," Rob continued. "Let's ring it out together, so all can hear."

Father and son pumped their fists in the air as they bellowed: "Tulloch Ard! Tulloch Ard! Tulloch Ard!"

Annie laughed. "Goodness! My men of the high hill," she said. She shook her head in amazement and pleasure.

"I apologize for waiting so long, Rob. When I became your adopted son five years ago, I decided not to change from Canfeld to MacKenzie right away."

"Aye. I remember. It was fine with me."

"I wanted to wait until I could legally do it myself. Thanks for taking me under your wing. You and mum have been my biggest fans. Name change or not, you've been my father, and a very good one, at that."

"The best!" added Annie. She reached for her husband's hand, looked him in the eyes, then kissed him on the cheek.

"You can smack me on the lips, Annie. I'll bend down."

Witnessing his parent's love gave Jake immense pleasure. His mum had unqualified love for Robert MacKenzie. And Robert MacKenzie showered his mum with love and devotion. He thought their marriage was a union written in the stars. The Boulder Star popped into his mind.

Jake recalled the surprisingly brief nine month courtship his parents had enjoyed. Even though he was only nine years old at the time, he was aware of their growing passion. Some Roxbridge friends wondered whether it was too much, too fast. But now, nine years later, all doubts had been erased from his mind.

Watching his parents shared dedication made him wonder. Would he ever have a partner to love as much as his parents loved each other? His mind briefly flipped to an image of Elena, a female friend. *What was she doing at this moment?* he thought.

Later in his bedroom, Jake practiced writing a new signature. What was the best combination of names and initials? He penned samples before finally settling on one.

Jacob. C. MacKenzie	Jake MacKenzie
	Jakob MacKenzie
J. Canfeld MacKenzie	**J. C. MacKenzie**

"I'm glad the election's over. As the incumbent, I was positive Makepeace would be reelected, but you can never be sure."

"Aye, right you are, Annie. Clinton appeared to have won the presidency in 2016. Every prediction proved as wrong as a right shoe worn on the left foot."

Annie chuckled. "Well, thankfully the dotard's long gone . . . jeez, I loved that name! Kim Jong Un was evil as hell, but he sure accurately described Trump. Remember?"

"That he did," agreed Rob. "A round Asian teapot calling a brass samovar old and leaky. The two of them—priceless! A 'doddering old fool' and a 'wee child fool.' The world has had to survive too many despots. Any pejorative used to skewer former forty-five is, in my opinion, insufficient to fully describe the oaf. My personal favorite was 'president bone spur.'"

Annie nodded. "Some pundits thought Pence would have an easy time of it, after filling in when Trump was gone."

"Aye, but I think people were weary of bullying,

saber-rattling, and the right's disdain for lower and middle wage earners. Pretty-boy Pence was nothing more than the vacuous mouthpiece for big money and conservative evangelical interests. I kept asking myself—how could anyone be against affordable health care for all? That's cruel. Makepeace was a breath of fresh air."

"She sure was," agreed Annie. "Her calming rhetoric was what the country badly needed. Even Clinton's 'basket of deplorables' were tired of Trump and Pence. Trump never fulfilled any of his major promises to them. Everything he did was for one purpose only—to promote the Trump brand."

Rob refilled their coffee, while Annie finished the daily crossword. "The public's exhaustion," continued Rob again sitting at the table, "was shown by how quickly and enthusiastically they applauded our reentry into the Paris Climate Accord."

"Yep, I agree," said Annie. She pondered for a moment. "Remind me, love. Six letters for grass bristle."

"Arista."

"I don't know why I keep forgetting it. I've got 'awn' fixed in my mind, but 'arista' is locked out."

"Lass, you've got to pull out weeds to make room for flowers to grow." He sipped his coffee. "That reminds me. I've got to tidy up the raised beds before the snows come."

"If it warms up today, honey, I'll help you." Annie pushed aside the completed puzzle and reflected for a moment. "Glorietta Makepeace," she said. "What a beautiful name for the forty-seventh president of the United States."

Maryann pulled the last weed from the garden. It was a long reddish blade sprouting from a small clump of bluestem, a wild grass equally at home on the Colorado plains or in a backyard garden. "Arista, Rob," she called. "Here's a sample."

"Aye, a sneaky invasive in with the chives. It pretends it's good to eat."

"Certainly good for cattle," Annie replied. She was smiling at the pleasure of working alongside her husband on a Colorado picture-perfect postcard day. The late November weather was cool and crisp, no ozone alert necessary. A soft sun warmed their backs. A ruffling breeze was having no effect dislodging brown oak leaves the trees refused to shed.

To the west, the Flatirons looked like a painted backdrop for a horse opera, grey slabs of granite dramatically etched against a cerulean sky. She could see teams of young soccer players spread out on the lined fields behind their house. Shouts and cheers drifted on the wind. Never in her life had she been happier than this, she thought, although her wedding nine years earlier on New Year's Eve equaled today's joy.

"You started telling me about a harassment case you're hearing, Rob. Then we got sidetracked discussing the election. Fill me in on the rest of the details."

"I can't tell you everything, love. It's like client-attorney privilege. While a case is being heard, the committee is sworn to secrecy. We can't divulge anything. But I can share the basic issues in the case without being specific. Besides, I'd like to hear what you think."

"I understand if you don't want to say much, honey. But by now, you know you can trust me."

"Lass, I'd trust you with the nuclear codes, if I had them."

"Mum's the word, dear. My lips are sealed with . . ."

". . . a kiss," he said, dropping his trowel and embracing her.

"Rob, careful," she giggled. "The kids will see us."

"Let them. They ought to see love in action."

"They can get plenty of that on the internet." she countered.

But her resistance was swept away by his tight embrace and tender lips. When he released her, she glanced at the field. The players had paid them no attention. The teenagers were focused on soccer offense and defense, not adult romance.

Rob told Annie about the case his committee was considering. He turned over soil as he spoke. "I told you there are two cases, love. One was settled out of court, so to speak. I think a cash award and the firing of a staff member solved that one.

"The second you might anticipate—a male student accused of assaulting a female student. The facts are clear, but the underlying causes are troublesome."

"What do you mean?"

"There's no doubt the female was sexually assaulted. The boy admitted it. But he contends he was led on by the girl."

"Was alcohol involved?"

"Aye, it played a big part. The girl was blind drunk and flirting with the boy."

"Just flirting?"

"I can't tell you more. But, according to the boy, she implied she wanted to . . . well, you know."

"Yep, I can guess."

"He took her to his room. He undressed her. He fondled her. She fondled him. Then, at the point of . . . you know . . ."

"Yes, I know."

"She refused, but he persisted. She has no memory of the evening, she says, except when she said 'no.' She claims she was raped."

He hesitated to let Annie consider the facts. "What do you think, Annie? When does rape begin? Aren't both parties guilty for allowing things to get to a point of no return?"

"Oh, boy, sweetie! You've got a tough one. I'm torn by conflicting ideas. When I was growing up, my mother always warned me not to get into compromising situations. Some boys think if a girl's blotto they're 'asking for it.' Suggestive clothing, makeup, and drinking are signals to boys. At least that's what they think. But girls have to realize their behavior can be interpreted many ways. A girl who wants to look stylish, often looks sluttish to a boy.

"I suggest you read Jon Krakauer's book: *Missoula: Rape and the Justice System in a College Town.*"

"Aye, Krakauer's first rate."

"Yep. You once told me to read *Under the Banner of Heaven* when I was trying to understand odd religious groups. It was good advice. I'm sure you can get the book at the Meadows Library, or they can order it through the county system."

"Good idea. As Jake MacKenzie would say, 'It's cool to live in the same town as the author of *Eiger Dreams*.'" Annie nodded and smiled.

"When Jake's not dangling on the end of a rope," Rob went on, "he likes to read about doing it. Krakauer's a good resource."

"Thanks for letting me use the car, Mom."

"You're welcome Jake . . . er . . . JC. There was no way I was going to let you cycle up and down Flagstaff this time of year. It's dangerous enough during daylight, but after the lighting ceremony the road's pitch black. Besides, you were with a friend."

"Yeah. I know Elena has a bike, but cycling up from Broadway to Chautauqua's bad enough. Then you've got the next really steep part to the lookout. The only way I could take her up was by car."

"Did she enjoy it?"

"Yes, as usual it was like magic."

"Did you sing to her?"

JC laughed. "No way, Mom. Since my voice changed, I sound like a frog. That would have ended a good friendship."

Jake's eighteenth year had been filled with notable events: high school graduation; matriculating at CU; getting a driver's license bearing a new last name; having a girlfriend with a sweet smile and a sharp wit; changing his moniker from Jake to JC. "JC MacKenzie." It had a bonny ring to it.

At the age of eighteen, JC MacKenzie had emerged from the chrysalis of youth into a butterfly. He wasn't as regal as a Monarch nor as colorful as a Painted Lady. Common Ringlet might better define him—easy going, approachable, with eyespots on its wings. JC saw everything around him, considered its meaning, then stored away an opinion for future reference. Like the Common Ringlet whose simple diet was grass, JC's needs were few and his outlook on life uncomplicated. Years spent listening to Rob promote ULAR, the Universal Law of Reciprocity, had made JC tolerant, compassionate, and forgiving.

A social scientist would have been hard pressed to assign JC to any one generation. He had characteristics attributed to both boomers and millennials. He was born at the genesis of a new generation, yet to be defined and named. Pundits were beginning to coin new terms for those born after the turn of the 21st Century. These people were faced with bewildering dilemmas, from understanding middle eastern hatreds toward colonial powers, to environmental degradation, to skewed wealth distribution, to overpopulation. Gaining traction was the term, "Cusp Generation," as if the young were precariously balanced on the edge of a yawning pit, its bottom out of sight. What was down there? Hell? Heaven? Something cataclysmic? Nobody was brave enough to risk a guess.

"I'm sorry Rob and I couldn't join you on the hill this evening. This is the first year since moving to Boulder we missed it. He was downtown at a dinner honoring a retiring colleague, and I was on Mapleton Avenue meeting with some folks. Thank goodness bus 225 now runs later. The last bus out of Boulder to Broomfield leaves at 9:20. No more getting stranded with a four mile walk home."

"I'm glad the connections were good, Mom. The new schedule works for me, too. I can spend a wee bit more time in the library."

"*A wee bit*," mimicked Annie. "Now that you're a MacKenzie, you're starting to talk like a Scot." She smiled at her son. "Does Elena study in the library?"

"Aye."

"I figured." As far as Annie knew, the relationship her son had formed with a young woman was his initial infatuation. Elena was his first girlfriend. For that reason, it was special. "Is she going home for Thanksgiving?"

JC shook his head. "I don't think so. It's a long week but the airfares are high. I think they jack them up on purpose."

"You're right. Say, honey, why don't you invite her here? Rob and I would like to meet her. For that matter, she can stay overnight. The guest room has hardly been used."

"Really? Cool! She's nice, Mom. You'll love her. She has a great sense of humor. She cracks me up. And I'm sure Rob will want to talk with her about her dad's work at WHOI."

"What does he do?"

"He studies ocean salinity. It's another way to measure rising sea levels."

"How?"

"The more glacial melt, the less salty the seas become. It requires precise measurements taken from thousands of sensors from around the globe."

"That will be right up Rob's alley. Does she eat meat? We'll be having turkey."

"Are you kidding, Mom? Her home's only thirty minutes away from Plymouth. That's where Thanksgiving was invented."

After returning from her meeting, Maryann poured a glass of wine, and plopped onto the couch. In less than a minute the mudroom door opened. She heard Rob unleash Nova, then the sound of the dog lapping water. Rob came into the living room his cheeks ruddy from the cold air.

"Hi, lass. It's good to see you're home safe. I was keeping an eye on the house. Nova needed her evening walk. Now she's filling her tanks again."

"I hear her." She patted the couch. "Sit down and I'll tell you about the meeting." She took a sip. "Where's JC? Walking Nova's supposed to be his job."

"At the CU library studying, I think. I'll bet Elena's there, too. He said he'd be home by ten."

Satisfied with knowing where her family was for the moment, she pointed at her feet.

"Look, laddie, my socks are still on." Annie's feet were on Rob's lap.

"Why wouldn't they be, love? You haven't undressed for bed."

"I was surprised by the reception I received from the

Compassionate Conservatives. They were so welcoming! I thought my socks would be knocked off."

Rob laughed. "These can't be knocked off. They're too long." He peeled off her knee-highs, then gave her feet a gentle massage. "So your meeting went well, I take it."

"Oh my gosh, yes! After being politely sent packing by other groups, I figured the Compassionate Conservatives would be the last bunch to encourage me, other than staid Republicans and intractable Libertarians, of course."

"Aye, I get what you mean. Do you want me to rub your ankles?"

"Yes, I'd love it and flex them, too. The left one is still stiff after my sprain."

He nodded. "A loose rock in the trail. It happens a lot." He guided her left ankle through an imaginary cursive alphabet. "You were up on Mapleton Hill, right?"

Annie slid lower on the couch. She was fully relaxed after a long day and now under the therapeutic touch of Rob's hands and the spell of wine.

"Correct. The meeting was in one of those large old homes. I figured folks who could afford to live there had lots of money. It turned out I was right."

"So they lowered their guards and let a ragamuffin in. That was brave of them. What happened?" Rob guided Annie's right ankle through the same exercise, but switched from cursive to block letters.

"After refreshments—by the way the Breadworks makes the best cran-apple pie—we sat in a circle in the living room. I counted fourteen people. It's a big room, Rob. There was space for a grand piano. And guess what?"

"Now you'd like your legs rubbed?"

"Yes . . . but . . . no, silly! An original Rauschenberg was on a wall along with other modern works. Those folks are well off."

"So the poor little match girl wasn't left out in the cold. They sound like decent folks."

"They are. When I started my pitch, they were attentive. I thought they'd dismiss me as another do-gooder."

"Were you able to give them your reasons why reducing homelessness makes sense?"

"I did. I tied it into what I thought were their concerns: vagrancy in the parks, public defecation, smoking and littering, begging, and Pearl Street Mall loitering. In my opinion, all those behaviors have economic consequences. When it gets out of hand, property values decline, and the quality of life suffers. I argued that homelessness was affecting their wallets. I didn't say it quite that bluntly, but that was my message."

"Did your talk ring a bell?"

"I think it did. I honestly believe they want to do something positive. Their questions certainly mirrored conservative values, but comments also echoed compassion for the less fortunate."

"What do you mean? Give me an example."

"A lovely lady complained about transients filtering into their neighborhood. It was to find sheltered places to sleep, she said. Some hide in garden sheds, on porches, or in protected alleyways. Unlocked cars are a target, Rob. Security's a big concern. But then another person rightly pointed out that their dilemma was the result of the city having limited overnight housing for the homeless, and virtually no permanent housing."

"Did they talk about the shelter in North Boulder?" He changed subjects. "Are your feet feeling better? My hands are tired."

"Yes, my feet are very happy. Thank you, love. You can skip

my legs." She folded them under her. That was a signal for Nova to join them on the couch. Nova curled into a ball.

"They're aware two management approaches have been tried at the shelter. They were critical of both. Remember, honey, these folks own businesses or are in charge of large organizations. They have experience."

"What are the two management schemes, love? I've been so busy with my tutorials, I haven't kept up with town politics."

"The first was to give homeless clients a bed for the night plus an evening meal and breakfast. The shelter was built in 2003. It operated under that plan for fifteen years. That was the practice when we moved to Boulder."

"Aye, I do remember now. You volunteered twice a month for a few years serving evening meals."

"I did and enjoyed it. But after the clients slept the night, the next morning they had to leave and fend for themselves on the streets. Some idled their days away, but others were able to find jobs at minimum wage. The trick to keeping a low-paying job—maybe any job—is to show up on time each day clean and tidy. Opportunities are out there—admittedly some ambition helps. The shelter encouraged that to happen. Then, at the end of the day the sheltering procedure started all over again."

"It was a revolving door plan, as I see it," said Rob.

"Yes. A permanent solution was never in sight. Everyone always returned."

"It's like a self-fulling prophecy," he offered. "'I'm homeless, and I'm destined to remain homeless.'"

"That's about it. And that's what the Mapleton Hill group saw, so they were encouraged when the city began a new management plan in 2018."

"Refresh my memory. What was that?"

"The plan consists of three pieces. It's still in operation.

First, in both Longmont and Boulder, help was centralized. It was an attempt to coordinate services from two command centers. Second, fifty centrally located low-income housing units were constructed near the Google building. They filled rapidly. Third, the North Boulder shelter changed tactics. Instead of emptying the facility each day after breakfast, the plan allowed clients to remain inside. Sobriety no longer was required. In effect it became a permanent dormitory."

"Och! Number three makes no sense to me. It's as if the shelter was enabling homelessness."

"I agree, as did the folks at the meeting."

"What are you going to do? What are they going to do?"

"They asked me to return with an action plan." She reflected then laughed. "You know I'm all in favor of that, honey. We talk about problems too much rather than biting the bullet and doing something about them. They gave me a copy of their vision statement. That ought to help me think this through. We're meeting in a month. I promised I'd have something ready. I may need your help in writing it." She laughed again. "You're mister *Elements of Style,* so I'll need to be concise."

"Concision, precision, and decision are my specialties, lass. Count me in. Let me see what they gave you."

Annie handed over the document.

BOULDER ASSOCIATION OF
COMPASSIONATE CONSERVATIVES
Compassion for the needy coupled with fiscal responsibility

Introduction

The Boulder Association of Compassionate Conservatives was formed to promote the idea that restrained political values and fiscal principles can be woven into the fabric of social justice and progressive governance. We acknowledge the inequities that have rent our nation. We believe, however, that by applying conservative fiscal policies and economic theory, we can mend our country while helping the less fortunate, the homeless, the mentally ill, and the drug dependent.

Those in need should not be held captive by hollow promises. Those in need should not be ensnared in a swollen bureaucracy entrenched in generalities. Fact producing research ought to be the foundation for social service programs. Programs ought to be managed with fiscal restraint and accountability. Meeting measurable benchmarks and adhering to tight timeframes are essential. **BACC** does not support open-ended programs. All initiatives must have measurable outcomes and conclusive results.

<u>Guiding Principles</u>

- Progressive social help should be funded by public taxation. Precise planning and budgeting must list exact costs for any project proposed. Cost overruns will be borne by contractors. Progressive social initiatives must be clearly described, outcome based, and fully funded before approval.
- Private funding for voter approved projects is welcomed and encouraged.
- A society that assists the downtrodden and less fortunate results in a community of growing wealth—in real property valuation, consumer spending, and tax revenues.
- A prosperous community spawns new business, motivates entrepreneurship, and promotes social wellbeing.
- Municipal debt should never exceed 2.5 % of the assessed value of assessable property.
- Voters should re-approve or disapprove all social programs annually. Program success should be measured based on meeting budget limitations, adhering to a written timeframe, and evaluating management and contractor performance.

BACC Manifesto

- We believe in universal health care, not as a constitutional right, but as "the right thing to do." Research has proven that affordable health care is less expensive to society than no health care.
- We welcome migrant labor to plant, tend, and harvest Colorado's crops. We urge them to make Colorado their permanent home.
- We believe in the science of climate change.
- We accept the fact that Colorado's population growth has reduced available farmland, affected water supplies, increased urban congestion, and resulted in mounting air pollution.
- We expect government assistance to the needy to be repaid through active citizenship, crime-free residency, freedom from drug dependency, and where economically feasible, the payment of local, state, and federal taxes.
- We support Boulder County's "Worthy Cause" program.

BACC Quid Pro Quo

In exchange for supporting progressive social programs, **BACC** stipulates the following three conditions:

1. Property taxes shall increase no more than .015% per annum.
2. All tax monies received and spent shall be audited by at least two entities—one governmental—one from the private sector. If any discrepancies arise out of the two separate audits, further taxation shall cease until the discrepancies are corrected.
3. Civil discourse in debating government programs and finances shall be the norm. Neither conservative nor liberal theories shall be pilloried. Both ideologies contain

worthy and specious theories. Other ideologies also contain worthwhile initiatives to consider when planning social help programs.

Summary

The conservative approach to governance is one of restraint—encourage free markets with a minimum of government interference. We contend that small government is more efficient than large government. Money in the pockets of consumers is more valuable than taxes in the hands of bureaucrats.

We recognize, however, that our city, state, and nation are enormously complex institutions. When carefully managed, they provide security, sound infrastructure, social welfare, and disaster recovery. A nation nearing a population of 400 million can never return to the halcyon days of post World War II 20th Century. Conservative beliefs must comport with 21st Century realities.

A successful nation cannot afford to squander its human, natural, and fiscal resources. Compassionate conservatism is a political and social philosophy that supports reasoned approaches to complex problems through research, political discourse, and prudent action.

"Okay, lass." Rob handed the **BACC** position paper back to Annie. "It's well written and a lot less strident than other conservative screeds I've read. This will help you frame your action plan."

"That's what I thought, honey. Now all I have to do is get busy."

"Aye, that's the next step."

The TV monitors darkened. Nine City Council members turned their attention to the front. Maryann Caton MacKenzie was standing behind the visitor lectern. The council had just watched a media presentation prepared by Maryann acting as spokesperson for the Boulder Association of Compassionate Conservatives. "BACC," she had called them. The presentation was a draft proposal for the total overhaul of Boulder's homeless policies and practices. Its scope was broad, its implications damning. The draft proposal called for a totally new approach to dealing with the homeless crisis that was threatening to overwhelm the city.

"Thank you for your presentation, Ms Caton," said Mayor James. "It was impressive and informative." The mayor glanced right and left looking for nods affirming her opinion.

Councilman Burke was the first to ask a question. "Ms Caton, given the scope of your proposal, if it was adopted by the city, how long do you think it would it take to be fully implemented?"

"That depends on the priority you give it, Mr. Burke. If you think my report accurately depicts Boulder's homeless situation and accept the recommendations it lists, I think it could be fully implemented in two years—at least the city's part. The county's part may take longer since the other seven county towns will have to figure out how best to meet their obligations. Look at page three of my report for a list of recommended county requirements. You can see substantial infrastructure improvements will need to be made."

Page 3

Draft Proposal

Boulder County Master Plan for
Homeless Housing and Services

- All Boulder County towns must share the burden of providing shelter and services to the homeless.

- Available shelter beds will be based on the ratio of one bed per 500 town residents.
- Based on a survey of the homeless, each town must develop a designated and managed camping area providing clean water, shower facilities, and lavatories.
- All towns must have a centrally located shower room, laundry, and lockers for use on a per diem basis. This does not include the camping area.
- Clients from unincorporated Boulder County are not eligible for town services.
- Shelters will provide safe storage for bicycles.
- All towns must have a counseling center offering the homeless help in the following areas:
  ○ Mental health issues.
  ○ Drug, alcohol, marijuana, and tobacco dependency.
  ○ Money management.
  ○ Job training.

Note: all county towns must modify their zoning laws to allow "tiny town" communities on undersized or nonconforming lots.

"I suspect not all communities will be happy with these recommendations," said Maryann. "There may be voter rebellion."

"I agree," said Burke. "Under this plan each town has to provide a shelter. Am I reading this correctly, Ms Caton?"

"That's correct, sir. But look at it this way. For twenty-five years the City of Boulder has shouldered the weight of the county's homelessness. In some ways, that was to be expected. We were the largest municipality while the towns to the north and east of us were sleepy farming communities growing at a snail's pace. That's all changed. Longmont, Louisville, Lafayette, and Erie are growing at almost 5% per year. That's where housing developments are paving over the plains. Ninety per cent of Boulder's buildable land is already under roof. It's all a factor of the population growth along the Front Range."

Councilwoman Mendez jumped in. "I, too, thank you for your report, Ms Caton. I see it calls for specific steps to be taken, rather than a list of generalities to follow. As I recall, you called for specificity a year or two ago at one of our meetings."

"I did," affirmed Maryann.

"Then you still think our current homeless plan is hollow?"

"I do. That's why so much of this report advocates outcomes that are measurable. For example, if you look at page four, you'll see a table listing exactly the number of beds each town must provide under this plan. It's based on projected 2025 census figures and the ratio of one bed per 500 residents. I've given you data and statistics."

Mendez quickly found the table and studied it.

Page 4
Recommended Homeless Beds per Boulder County Towns

Municipality	Population	Required Beds	Goal
Jamestown	320	0	2
Nederland	1736	4	6
Lyons	2722	6	8
Louisville	27,588	54	60
Erie	32,119	64	70
Lafayette	35,320	70	75
Longmont	102,786	204	201
Boulder	116,025	*232	235
Totals	**318,616**	**634**	**666**

* Boulder has 450 available beds when the services of all providers—municipal, faith based, secular—are combined.

"The table's helpful, Ms. Caton. Thanks for pointing it out. So, if I read between the lines, you and BACC think Boulder City is meeting its bed count obligation, but the present shelter plan is a mess."

"We do. Some of the problems can be attributed to the continual demand for beds and occasional short-falls. The suggested distribution of beds throughout the county as shown on page four ought to resolve that. But in the ten years I've lived in Boulder, the city's tried two shelter management philosophies. The one being followed now was set up in 2017. Both appear to have failed. Homelessness has increased and vagrancy is tormenting homeowners in North Boulder." Maryann scanned the council for signs they were with her.

"The other county towns are not pulling their own weight," she continued. "They expect our city to bear an unfair burden. Our plan argues the homeless problem is also the county government's problem to fix, not solely the city's. However, you may have to force the county's hand by refusing to accept referrals from other towns, unincorporated areas, and agencies. At first, that might sound like a harsh position to take. But the homeless in Erie must stay in Erie and receive services and shelter there. The homeless in Longmont must be serviced in Longmont. It's the same for every town."

A fourth council member, Chip Scotto, spoke up. "If we adopt all or part of your proposal, Ms Caton, should we expect our Human Services Department staff to follow it?"

"You folks on the council set policy. The town manager applies it. Staff not on board risk losing their jobs. But before it ever gets to that, everyone involved—from the City Council—to the administrative staff—to the shelter manager—to homeless representatives—all should be part of the discussion. A good place to start might be to consider the requirements for tiny house ownership. They're on page 5."

Page 5
Fifteen Requirements to Qualify for Tiny Home Lottery

As tiny homes become available, candidates who meet the requirements listed below will qualify for the lottery process of distribution. Those not chosen will remain on a waiting list for two years.

<u>General Qualifying Requirements</u>

- **Photo ID—police check—SS#—DNA or fingerprints.**
- **Proof of Boulder County residency.**
- **Free from drug, alcohol, and tobacco dependency. Agree to yearly drug testing.**
- **Documented effort to find employment.**
- **Attendance at counseling sessions: money management, kicking harmful addictions, anger management.**
- **Meet accepted healthy hygiene practices regarding cleanliness of body and clothing.**
- **No record of violent crimes or sexual offenses.**
- **Ability and willingness to volunteer in tiny home community.**
- **Agree to abide by the occupancy limit set for each unit.**
- **Agree to use public transportation or bicycle. Tiny home communities will be automobile and motorcycle free.**
- **Keep domicile clean, neat, repaired.**
- **Abide by noise restrictions.**
- **If appropriate, have connection with Veterans Administration and VA hospital.**
- **Establish a health care savings account or qualify for federal health insurance.**
- **If employed, agree to pay 5% of wages toward ownership of tiny home.**

Maryann continued. "I know staff has vested interests in the present plan as well emotional ties to it. They're all good people who want to make a difference. But their effort is not working. It's time to consider other options. Adding tiny homes to the portfolio of services is one possibility."

"Maybe we should have a homeless summit," suggested Scotto. "Solicit input, consider present shelter practices, entertain ideas that are new and fresh. I'm certain folks working day-to-day on the problem will want to be included."

"You mean *insist* on them being included," interrupted Maryann. She heard clapping behind her.

"Yes, insist," agreed the councilman. "You're right." He smiled then relinquished the floor.

"When all's said and done," Maryann continued, "I suggest putting this new plan up for a vote as a referendum. Our fellow friends and neighbors ought to decide what path to follow."

The council was silent for a minute. They thumbed through the report's pages. No one appeared ready to ask more questions.

Mayor James brought the presentation to a close. "Your report was helpful, Ms Caton. There's a lot here for us to digest. If undertaken, this is a big project with many steps to complete. Obviously, it needs careful consideration." She hesitated a second, then asked Maryann, "Is there anything else you'd like to add?"

"Yes, Mayor, two things. First, BACC has received pledges totalling three point seven million dollars to purchase land for tiny home communities as advocated in this report. They expect that amount to grow, especially as council progress is made." Behind her, Maryann heard polite applause and a few gasps of surprise.

"Second, BACC is action oriented," she added. "Money pledges are not for eternity. These folks want to see movement.

That's why earlier I urged you not to delay your discussions. I suggest you finalize a decision no later than a year from now. Don't kick the can down the road. The city's been fumbling with homelessness for twenty-five years."

Two council members winced as if they had just been indicted for inefficiency. The mayor shrugged, then nodded.

"Thank you for your patience," Maryann concluded. "You know I can be reached at **Pearl 2 Pine.** Happily, my firm is supporting this initiative. Good evening."

She stepped away from the lectern and turned toward the audience. She was awarded with applause. With the meeting concluded, people rose to leave. Then suddenly she was face-to-face with JC and Elena.

"Mom, you were great!" said JC.

"What are you doing here?" Maryann was surprised but pleased to see him. "I thought you were at the library."

"I remembered this was your big night. So Elena and I decided to come to the municipal building and be your cheering section."

"Hi, Elena. Thanks for coming."

"Hi, Annie. Your report was amazing. I didn't know anything about the homeless problem other than what I see of their encampments along Boulder Creek. It's pretty extensive."

"That's part of the problem, Elena, the homeless are often out of sight while being in plain sight. It's as if they are invisible. We fortunate folks don't want to see them."

"I know you wrote the report," said JC. "But I detected some of Rob's influences—especially the charts, lists, and tables."

"Yep. The laddie got his two cents in. I need to thank him when we get home."

2025

The Clarion Call of the Mountains
The Denver Hitchin' Post

HIGH PLAINS AQUIFER RUNNING DRY—FARMS AND
RANCHES IN PERIL NATION'S FOOD SUPPLY IMPACTED

WEDNESDAY, September 24, 2025 ☁ **ISOLATED STORMS**
▲ **82°** ▼**52°** • © **TDHP $2.50**

Lyle Thompson
@ lthompson.com
THE DENVER HITCHIN' POST

NEWS

The most valuable resource in eastern Colorado is disappearing at an astonishing rate. Water will soon become extinct. Ninety years after the plains were plowed, native grasses disappeared, and the Dust Bowl blackened skies, a second man-made catastrophe is underway. The High Plains Aquifer is about to run dry.

Evidence of the draw-down can be seen by the disappearance of flowing water in creeks and river beds. Streams are being parched dry at a rate of six miles per year. Based on a 1942 compact, water that remains in the Arikaree, Republican, Arkansas, and Platte Rivers must be proportionally shared with Nebraska, Kansas, and Oklahoma. Since river water is out of play for Colorado farmers, deep well irrigation is necessary. Since 1950, it is estimated the amount of water pumped out of the High Plains Aquifer equals 70% of the volume of Lake Erie.

Louis Pratt, 80, who lives east of Sage has seen his wells run dry. As a result he and his wife of 52 years are moving to Denver. "That farm's been in my family since before the big dust-up," he said. "We survived because we figured out how to irrigate from wells using pumps. But each year the wells had to be dug deeper and deeper. Now even that water's gone. Soon eastern Colorado and the surrounding states will become the 'Great American Desert.'"

It is estimated that drought induced crop losses in the midwest equal $35 billion a year. The affected area is America's breadbasket. The plains are where wheat, oats, corn, and cover crops are grown. The worth of these commodities per unit weight is increasing as yields decline. Consumers can expect higher food prices with no ceiling on how high prices might climb.

The desertification of middle America is no different than what is happening in South Asia, North Africa, and Australia. Droughts are increasing in length and severity as evidenced in California and Portugal. With changing weather patterns affecting rainfall events, the recharging of aquifers will take hundreds, if not thousands of years. The Ogallala Aquifer is the result of melting at the end of the last great Ice Age.

Agriculturists and demographers are pessimistic about the future. Hale Meade, Professor of Natural Sciences at Colorado State University, is explicit in his understanding of the problem: "There are too many people. Our planet cannot sustain these numbers. In eight years there will be nine billion of us. We've exceeded the tipping point. A population thinning pandemic or a nice big extermination event would help. And I'm not kidding."

Maryann Caton, 45 | Robt. MacKenzie, 57 | Jake MacKenzie, 19 | World POP: 8.38 billion

---

The cell phone trumpeted. Annie answered it. "Hello?"

"Is this Ms Caton?"

"Yes, I'm Annie."

"I hope I'm not interrupting anything. My name's Joyce Cochrane. I live in North Boulder on Plymouth Street."

"Hi, Ms . . . or is it Mrs. Cochrane? How can I help you?"

"It's Mrs., but please call me Joyce."

Annie laughed. "Okay, Joyce, then I'm Annie."

"Fine," said Joyce, "that gets the formalities out of the way. The reason I phoned is that I read an article about you in the *Daily Boulder Reporter.* It was about your homeless proposal to the City Council."

"Yes, lots of people have commented on it," said Annie. "Have you read the letters-to-the-editor?"

"I have. You must feel encouraged by all the positive responses."

"I do. But they show more work needs to be done. Those who view the plan to be draconian and mean-spirited . . . well . . . if they had to live with homeless folks invading their garages and gardens, they might think differently. What about you, Joyce? Obviously you phoned to say something about my presentation. Are you in favor of a change in direction, or do you think my proposal is too harsh?"

"No! It's not too harsh! Frankly, it's totally fair to expect the other county towns do their share. It's unfair to the City of Boulder to have to shoulder almost the entire homeless burden. And in North Boulder near the shelter, we have to endure 90% of the city's load."

"Endure?"

"Yes, endure. Despite periodic changes in philosophy and management, our community continues to be a target for homeless vagrancy."

"Really! How bad is is?"

"Everyday our pocket parks draw groups of homeless men who monopolize the benches, smoke, litter, and act as if they own the place. I'm guessing drugs are being sold. I'm nervous about bringing my children to the playground."

"I understand. I can tell you it's occurring elsewhere, too."

"I know that. But what has me especially agitated is the number of men who are sex offenders. They've been assigned by the courts to live at the shelter. Obviously, they can't be tattooed with an SO on their foreheads, but it's disconcerting not to know who they are."

"Yeah, it's a big problem. How can I help? My plan's already in the hands of the City Council."

"You seem to have the council's ear. Please! Urge them to get moving. Things are getting worse up here. We don't need more foot-dragging."

Annie became defensive. "I've made my pitch to them, Joyce. At this point, there's not much more I can do except attend meetings and look impatient."

"Is there anything I can do, Annie?"

"Sure. You and your friends ought to attend council meetings. Hold signs that say you want action to occur on the homeless crisis. Play it up to the media. Start a writing campaign. Send letters to the newspaper and to council members. Post emails, tweets, and use Facebook. Demand that our leaders get busy. It's almost certain my plan won't be adopted in its entirety. But that's okay. What I want and what you want is to make improvements. We want the council to begin tomorrow, not next week—certainly not next year."

"Oh, Annie, I agree with you so much! Hey, listen, I have a group of friends I'm sure could be organized. We're not a formal group like BACC, but we do have opinions."

"Opinions are good." Annie chuckled remembering Jake's fifth grade teacher telling him to express his opinions more often. Since then, he had become a waterfall of opinions.

"Would you be willing to come to North Boulder to meet with us?"

"Of course."

"I think hearing from you would help get my friends into a political state of mind."

"Jeepers, you don't want me to do that!" Annie laughed. "You'll have a bunch of mindless know-nothings and do-nothings who will accomplish nothing at all."

Joyce giggled. "Nothing ventured, nothing gained. Thanks for hearing me out, Ms Caton."

"I'm Annie," she reminded Joyce.

"Now they've got me involved with the ABC," said Rob, as he entered the living room having returned with Nova from her evening walk. "You were on the phone when I came in, so I decided to give the dog a little exercise. She seems to be slowing down. She may be older than we thought when we adopted her."

Nova wandered over to Annie for an ear scratch. "I know, honey, I've noticed that, too. You just mentioned something about ABC," she said, curious. "You urge simplicity in writing, but do your students need to relearn the alphabet?"

Rob laughed at his wife's interpretation of ABC. "Nae, lass, not the alphabet. Och! I can see how I confused you. ABC is a university committee. I guess they thought I did so well on the sexual harassment case, they could load me up with something else to do."

"What does ABC mean?"

"Anti-Bullying Committee. Fortunately, we're not charged with hearing cases. It's too early for that. We've been given the task of developing an anti-bullying policy."

"That sounds interesting. Will you be able to fit it in with everything else you're doing?"

"Aye, I think so. I may have to cut my eight hours of sleep back to six. But if I follow what Uncle Willie said, I should be able to manage."

Maryann grinned at the idea that another Uncle Willie-ism was about to come out of hiding. "Okay, love, what did Willie say this time?"

"If you give a busy man more work to do, he has two choices: He can do the work and become cranky, or he can assign the work to someone else, take a nap, and wake up refreshed as a lamb."

Annie laughed. Rob's deceased uncle continued to offer wisdom from the grave. "Just make sure you give the work to someone you know will get it done," she said, "like a woman."

"Aye, lassie." Rob smiled. Her wisdom was equal to that of

Uncle Willie. He shrugged. "Who were you talking with earlier on the phone?"

"A lady from North Boulder. She filled me in on the homeless situation up there. In her opinion it's getting worse."

"Why did she call you?"

"She knew I made a presentation to the City Council. She thought I had some influence over them. She's in favor of my proposal and wants them to get cracking and do something. They have a long history of tabling proposals for further study."

"What did you say?"

"I told her to organize her buddies and attend council meetings. Make their impatience known. Start a letter writing campaign. You know, dear, get involved in the issue. Don't mumble and grumble—decide it's time to rumble."

Rob couldn't contain his urge to rhyme words. "But don't stumble and tumble," he added.

Annie, however, was waiting to ambush him with the ending. "If you remain humble you're less likely to fumble." She and Rob bumped fists and had a healthy belly laugh. For them both, laughter added so much happiness to their marriage.

Annie patted the couch inviting Rob to join her. He sat and kissed her cheek. "If I could guess," she said, "I'm pretty sure I could list bullying issues your committee will consider."

"Okay, my lyrical lassie. What do you guess?"

"Certainly, face to face bullying—someone or some group not liking someone else for any number of reasons."

"Aye, that's true."

"Hate bullying based on religion or skin color. Someone flirts with someone else's sweetheart. And I almost forgot cyber-bullying. Nastiness doesn't have to be face to face."

"Aye, all that's true. And now a whole new category of bullying has arisen. It's about sexuality and oddness. Bullying homosexuals has been around for a long time. Remember Matthew Shepard at the University of Wyoming? His case seems like it happened only yesterday, but it occurred twenty-seven years ago."

"Really? That long?"

"Aye. Now other sexuality based biases are enticing bullies out of hiding, like rats out of a sewer. Gay women are out and have become targets. Transgenders and transsexuals undergoing transitioning are vulnerable. Crossdressers beware. And students that act, dress, or flaunt their oddness in any way are also targets. We're in a culture that is becoming less welcoming, less tolerant."

"I agree, honey," she nodded. "Some of it's a holdover from the Trump disaster, but much of it continues to come from the religious right. Imagine! Jerry Falwell once blamed hurricanes and fires on the scourge of homosexuality! How can someone say that? It's outrageous!"

"Aye, and climate change is a hoax. It's all wrapped up together, love. Too many of us are following false prophets and charlatans. Remember the Apple Church?"

"Yes, the Pippinites."

"We moved to Boulder partially to get away from that nonsense. But I'm afraid stupidity is all around us. We need to keep speaking truth to fools." He pulled Annie closer. "No matter what, my bride, I love you unconditionally. If you want to dress like a clown, that's fine with me. I'll be the jester, Rigoletto, and you can be the clown, Pagliacci."

"That may not work out, Rob. Remember, I can't carry a tune."

❖

"Hi, JC. You're home early. I thought you'd be at the library. Have you eaten?"

"No, but that's okay, Mom. I'm not very hungry."

Maryann could see JC looked glum, perhaps sad. For the moment his usual high spirits had disappeared. "Are you feeling well?" she asked. "You look like you just lost your best friend." Suddenly, she realized she may have guessed the truth.

"I'm okay, Mom. I'm down because Elena is leaving school. She's on her way home to Massachusetts."

"Oh, that too bad! What happened? Is she coming back?"

"I don't know, but I don't think so. Her dad lost his funding, so money's tight. At least that's what she told me."

"What a shame! I really liked her. She seemed to be as smart as a whip."

"Yeah, she is. She was going to major in astrophysics. I'm changing from earth science to the arts, while she picked one of the hardest majors."

"Honey, you don't have to apologize for studying art. Your skill with a camera is art itself. You have design and composition skills that will bloom the more you learn. I think you're making the right choice." Maryann hesitated a moment thinking about how she might help her son deal with the departure of Elena. "Are you going to stay in touch with her? With Facebook and Skype you can talk to each other."

"I know. We discussed that. It may work out, but it's a long way from Boulder to Falmouth. I really like her, Mom." He headed to his room.

JC appeared to have brightened when he returned home after taking Nova for a walk to the dog park. Maryann understood the close relationship he had with his pet. So what he said next about Nova surprised her.

"I can see what you and Rob said about Nova slowing down. And today her head was tilted way left. I wonder what that means?"

"Maybe she had a stroke."

"Will that kill her?"

"I don't know, honey. There's no way to tell what's going on inside her unless we have the vet run tests. The trouble is, often those tests create pain. Sometimes they show nothing. Sometimes they show false positives. Do you know what that is?"

"Yes, a false positive shows a problem that turns out not to be a problem." He considered his pet's condition. "You and Rob think Nova's older than we thought, right?"

"It's a possibility."

"Then she may die soon."

"Probably not, honey. But if that did happen, will you be okay with it?"

"I'll deal with it, Mom. Sure, I'll be sad. But when you have a pet, you have to accept the fact that someday it will die."

"This has been a hard couple of weeks for you, my son. First, you lose Elena. Then you see Nova going down hill. Are you going to be okay?"

"Sure, Mom. I've got you and Rob, and there are more homeless animals at the Humane Society."

"You'd get another dog if Nova dies?"

"I don't think so. Next time around, if it was okay with you and Rob, I'd adopt a cat— maybe two."

Maryann laughed trying to lighten the moment. "I'll have to ask Rob about that," she said. "Rob says cats spook him sometimes. He thinks they have second sight and can read his mind."

❖

"Hey, Rob, a few weeks ago we talked about an article in the Denver paper. Do you remember? It was about water shortages in eastern Colorado." JC pushed his peas into his mashed potatoes. Maryann had to resist telling him not to fool with his food. He was nineteen years old.

"Aye, lad. It was a thorough, well-researched report. Nothing's changed since then. Water is a scarce and valuable commodity."

"I know," agreed JC. "Did you see the letter to the editor in today's Boulder paper? A student praised the report, but his professor told him to check the facts and calculations for accuracy."

"The professor told him the right thing to do."

"The student found a minor discrepancy in the rate stream beds are drying. It didn't change the overall fact that we're running out of water, just that it might not be happening as fast as researchers thought. The student praised his teacher for requiring his class to double-check numbers, and question so-called facts. I doubt I'll get that kind of advice in the art department."

"Don't be too sure, lad. You might. You may be surprised."

Maryann was listening to the conversation. She asked Rob a question. "Do you have any idea who the professor is? It sounds like he's in one of the science departments. Who was the student referring to?"

Rob shrugged apologetically. "Aye, I know who the lad was referring to. It was was me."

Rob entered the kitchen, his face drawn and sad. Maryann immediately knew Nova had passed. The wee dog had not barged through Rob's legs as usual into the kitchen looking for a treat.

"Where is she?" asked Annie.

"In the mudroom. I've wrapped her in towels."

"How did it happen? Did she suffer?"

"We were on the sidewalk over by the rec center. She appeared to be listing to port even more. She stopped walking then fell on her side. I immediately knew she was dead. I don't think she suffered. It happened quickly."

"Oh, poor Nova!" Maryann grieved. "Oh, poor you, Rob! You had to carry her home after seeing her life end. That must have been hard."

"Aye, it was sad. But before bringing her back here, I had to clean up her mess. All her muscles must have fully relaxed. She emptied her bladder and bowels. There wasn't much of either, but fortunately I had my plastic bag." He washed his hands. "Is JC home?"

"Yes, love. He's on his computer Skyping with Elena. I'll go up and tell him."

2026

Daily Boulder Reporter

BOULDER CITY COUNCIL

Hoovertowns Proposed

Wednesday, June 24, 2026 $2.50

Local activist urges creation of communities for homeless—tiny house villages on horizon

By Taffy Adams, Staff Writer

Homeless advocate Maryann Caton tonight rolled out plans and blueprints for the first of four tiny home communities proposed for Boulder. Tiny home communities are part of a sweeping change being advocated as part of the City of Boulder's homeless strategy. It was Caton's second lengthy and detailed presentation before the City Council. She is supported by the Boulder Association of Compassionate Conservatives (BACC).

Caton reminded the council that the biggest part of the proposed plan involved the county. No longer should homeless clients automatically be referred to the City of Boulder. Under the new plan, each county town has to bear a proportional burden for homeless sheltering. Caton acknowledged there has been pushback from neighboring towns. She urged the council to remain resolute in its refusal to accommodate referrals originating outside city boundaries.

Caton told the council BACC has received $5.1 million in pledges to acquire land parcels up to ¾ an acre. It may be unnecessary for the city to annex land as the project moves forward. An offer of $800,000 has been made and accepted on a parcel in East Boulder on 55th Street. Closing is contingent on zoning approval of a nonconforming lot. Boulder's Zoning Commission is in the final stages of amending regulations. When complete, amendments will go to the City Council for approval.

Some residents have expressed resistance to the tiny home concept. Skeptics have referred to the proposed clusters as Hoovertowns, a pejorative term associated with the shanty towns thrown together during the Great Depression.

Caton addressed that complaint. She presented twelve different floor plans and exterior designs. Square footage ranges from 300 to 500 per unit. There are a dozen exterior design schemes from which to choose. Each community will look different than the others.

Based on a design competition, BACC has hired a young architect from Denver, Alison Balfour. Responding to a council question, Caton said no Boulder architects submitted proposals. Caton said Balfour was a visionary, willing to try new materials as well as use leading edge construction techniques. Balfour will also be the on-site construction manager as the project gets underway.

If the City Council approves the zoning changes within the next month, construction of foundations could begin before the first snow flies. Units will be constructed under roof in a Gunbarrel factory and trucked to sites. BACC is aiming for occupancy by late spring. The council was urged to move quickly.

Caton reminded the council that there are strict requirements housing applicants must meet. A crime-free history, willingness to hold a job or income from Veterans Affairs, and the use of bicycles or public transportation are some of the obligations. Additionally, residents will be expected to take part in the upkeep and maintenance of their community.

Maryann Caton, 46 | Robt. MacKenzie, 58 | Jake MacKenzie, 20 | World POP: 8.50 billion

---

Construction ended early on Saturday afternoon. Autumn's encroaching darkness and chilly temperatures convinced the crew chief to send the volunteers home with his thanks. Completing the shiplap siding on the Habitat for Humanity house on 9th Street would have to wait until the sun rose over the eastern plains and bathed the structure with morning warmth. Hammering a thumb was painful anytime, but doing so in cold weather was unbearable.

JC had passed on attending the Colorado v. Arizona football game. The student section in Folsom Field faced west, so he would have been comfortable in the afternoon sunlight, unless of course, he succumbed to the urge to be bare-chested along with dozens of other nitwits wearing fake fur hats with plastic bison horns. Besides, he had reasoned, why sit through one more penalty riddled game played by a mediocre team firmly on the road to nowhere. The cheerleaders were cute, though, he admitted.

Maryann heard JC drop his tool belt on the floor in the mud room. He set it in the space where Nova's bowls once rested. He removed his boots, hung up his carpenter's jacket, and entered the kitchen. At once, he was drawn to a slow-cooker on the counter. The aroma and a peek under the lid confirmed his suspicion: split pea soup was simmering. He knew it contained a hambone. It always did. That was the way his mother made it.

"How did it go today, honey?" asked Maryann. She saw his ruddy cheeks and red hands and knew it had been a challenge for him to stay warm. "Any whacked fingers?"

JC grinned. "No, I escaped my own blunders. Actually, we got a lot done. We're about two feet short of the soffit trim. In another half-day the siding will be complete."

"I'm proud you got involved with Habitat. Their efforts are part of the overall homeless strategy I've been squawking about."

"It's cool, Mom. I've met a lot of nice people. And I've learned about construction techniques. Now I know a sill plate from a header, a rafter from a joist." He lifted the cooker's lid again and looked at the soup.

"We'll be eating soon, honey, when Rob gets home from the rec center. I think he's on a rowing machine. Until then, let me get you some hot tea to warm you up."

"Thanks, Mom, that would be good. He hesitated then added, "Guess what?"

"Oh boy! Here we go," she laughed. "Okay, what?"

"I met a girl today. She's working on the project, too, helping with interior wiring."

"Really? A female electrician? That's rare, I bet."

"She's not a licensed electrician, Mom, she's only helping. But when I asked her about it, she said it was interesting work. She said she might take some classes and look for a job as an apprentice."

"So, she's not a CU student?"

"No, she works at Pedal or Push. She's a bike technician. She actually knows how to adjust front and rear derailleurs." He shrugged. "I only know how to pump up tires."

Maryann laughed at her son's self-deprecation. "You have other skills, love. Don't forget your camera."

"You're right. I think I'll take it along tomorrow to get some pictures of the project."

"Good idea." Annie hesitated a moment before asking JC a delicate question. "You met a woman with unusual talents. Did you get her name?"

"Yeah," he said wistfully. "Sandy Simmons. We're meeting tomorrow morning at 8:30 for breakfast at Le Chanticleer. After that we're going back to work at Habitat."

"When I was on that bloody rowing machine, I tried to think of all the reasons a person might become homeless. It helped keep me from thinking about the ghost miles I was amassing. It's sculling to nowhere." Rob buttered a wedge of cornbread and popped it in his mouth. He stirred the steaming rich soup in his bowl and prepared to swallow another spoonful.

"Did you keep track," asked Annie, "or did you lose count?"

"Rob can walk and spit at the same time, Mom. He's

ambidextrous. Remember in Roxbridge, when we were hiking in the woods?"

She laughed. "I remember. It was ten years ago. That's when I realized he was a special guy." She blew Rob a kiss.

"Hold on lad," corrected Rob. "Ambidextrous means able to use either hand well. You know that. I'm a temporal and physical manifestation of bifurcation."

"Whatever," said Jake, unimpressed. "I know what ambidextrous means."

Annie laughed. "What nonsense, Rob! Forget about bifurcation. You're Scottish-American. That's bad enough."

She warned her son, "Don't fall for his pseudo-science malarkey, JC. Rob can shovel it pretty good sometimes."

Rob grinned and nodded, "Aye. Uncle Willie told me, 'If you insist on twisting the truth, do it enough so a pig's tail will uncoil and stand out straight.'"

Annie and JC frowned then burst out laughing. "Willy was daft," declared Annie.

"I wish Willie was still alive," said Jake. "He sounds cool."

"He's living under a patch of thistles," said Rob "That way no one will plunder his grave."

They tucked into their meals until Annie again asked Rob about the homeless. "While working out, you said you were thinking about the homeless issue, honey. What did you come up with?"

"It's like a corn maze, lass. There's no one path to homelessness and no one simple way out."

"What do you mean?"

"It seems to me the underlying cause for much of it is mental illness—the inability or unwillingness for some people to cope with reality. That's way too simplistic an answer, of course, but I think coping is a sign of mental health."

Annie nodded. "I agree. That's one of the things we talk about at BACC meetings. Do you think we can get a handle on homelessness in Boulder, or are we spinning our wheels?"

"Good question. I don't think the problem will ever be wrapped up neat and tidy. Homeless folks have been around forever." He chuckled. "Remember, the Apple Church in Roxbridge owes its origin to the wanderings of Johnny Appleseed. John Chapman was homeless—a man without a roof—only a pot on his head."

"C'mon, Rob," scoffed JC, "that image is from a movie cartoon."

"Aye, you're right, lad. You should know. You're the cartoon expert around here."

Maryann interrupted, amused. "But rather than sit around unmotivated not doing anything, at least Chapman shuttled through the midwest with his seeds."

"Aye, he was on a mission."

Maryann suddenly remembered another itinerant wanderer. "And don't forget the Leatherman. Years ago he passed through our part of Connecticut on a regular circuit."

"I have a Leatherman multi-tool," nodded JC.

"The homeless situation we're now talking about is more complicated than historical characters," said Rob. "Some are hobos who enjoy being on the road. Some are vets suffering from PTSD. Some are addicts. In Colorado, some are here for the pot. Some have lost their homes due to fires, hurricanes, or foreclosures. Some are mentally ill. The reasons for homelessness are endless."

"What's your opinion, professor?" asked Annie. "Am I and the BACC on a hopeless quest?"

"Nae, lass. I'm confident that among Boulder's homeless

community there are good people waiting for a second chance. Your group's doing the right thing."

"It's sorta like ULAR," said JC. "You're not required to help them, but it's a good thing if you do."

Maryann smiled at her son. "Yes, honey. Like you volunteering at Habitat for Humanity."

Maryann was often reminded of the happiness she felt upon arriving in Colorado, connecting with her brother, Fred, his wife, Lois, and their twin daughters. She was again part of large family gatherings during holidays. That hadn't happened since she was in high school in Pennsylvania. Moreover, now JC had cousins nearby, and Rob had been warmly welcomed into the Caton-Murphy clan.

Listening to JC talk about his cousins tickled Maryann. He clearly was amused by Jeannie, a mop-topped nonconformist with a mind of her own. He admired Lindsay, too, but for different reasons. She was reliable, solid as a rock, although quite opinionated. But unlike Jeannie, who made pronouncements without a shred of supporting evidence, Lindsay measured her conversation, and was unlikely to get into any philosophical or political discussions unless armed with facts. Jeannie was "fake news," Lindsay was balanced reporting. Jeannie relished hanging out on the Pearl Street Mall, Lindsay talked about attending law school. Maryann wasn't surprised she was drawn to Lindsay. She and her niece had "can do—will do" personalities. And the fact that Lindsay was considering law for a career was compelling.

On her daily walk to work across the Pearl Street Mall, Maryann noticed a busy sandwich/ice cream shop. It was diagonally across the street from a Ben and Jerry's store.

Maryann had mapped all the ice cream joints in the midtown area.

One day she decided to take her nieces to lunch. She agreed on a date and time to meet Lindsay. As it turned out, Jeannie was busy that day.

"Hi, Aunt Annie. Am I late?"

"No, honey. Your timing is perfect. How was the ride?"

"Fine. Taking the bus in from Lewisville makes more sense than driving in. The traffic's heavy this time of day and parking in Boulder's a nightmare."

"You're right. That's why I commute by bus."

They walked north on 14th Street away from the depot toward the mall. Then they turned west, heading toward Broadway. Across Broadway on the southwest corner was Lindsay's Boulder Deli.

"I couldn't resist, honey," said Maryann, when it became obvious the deli was their lunchtime destination. "When I saw the name of this place, I knew I needed to bring you here."

Lindsay laughed. She and Annie crossed Broadway dodging the midday crowd. "I've been here twice, Aunt Annie, both times when I was younger. Dad took us. I think Jeannie was annoyed because there were no restaurants with her name. Anyway, we had sandwiches and Hagen Daz. If you don't like the day's featured flavors, there's always Ben and Jerry's across the street."

"I know," said Maryann with a nod and a smile. "I've got all the ice cream stores mapped out."

They ordered. Their sandwiches were brought to their table. When finished eating, they exited with cones. Maryann quizzed Lindsay about school, then asked about Jeannie. "What's your sister planning? Has she said what she wants to do in the future?"

"Frankly, Aunt Annie, I don't know. Sometimes I think she's in a dreamworld. She never mentions school. A good day for her is a day spent somewhere here in mid-Boulder, hanging with friends, strumming on guitars, or spinning hula hoops. I'm sure they're doing dope. She has mom and dad fit to be tied."

"Does she show up at home for meals?"

"Once in awhile at night. I usually see her at breakfast. Then she's gone."

"How does she get by?"

"I don't know. Certainly my parents aren't bankrolling her life style. Maybe she has a job, but I just don't know."

Maryann tried to comprehend Jeannie's actions, but had no concept of it. She had always been focused and motivated. She was surprised by how little Lindsay knew about her sister.

"Does she ever *not* come home at night?" Maryann asked. She was afraid of what the answer might be.

"Sometimes. She says she crashes at a friend's apartment. I don't know where it is or who is her friend. As far as I know, she phones mom and dad telling them when she won't be home. Naturally, they're always upset, but at least they've heard from her."

Annie checked her watch. She had to get back to work at **Pearl 2 Pine**. She accompanied Lindsay back to the depot, then said good-bye. Before Lindsay boarded the bus, they made plans to get together again.

Walking back to work, Annie thought about Jeannie's situation. For no apparent reason, her niece was adrift. She wondered whether homelessness started that way—no ambition, no plans, no future. She grimaced thinking that Jeannie someday might wind up permanently on the street. She vowed to talk to her brother about it.

❖

Daily Boulder Reporter—Art and Culture Review
By Phong Ciao, Critic

Upon entering the Dairy Center for the Arts, the reviewer was immediately bombarded with color, light, and variety. This came as no surprise since the exhibit showcases the best work by CU students selected by their teachers. The exhibit titled *Winter, Wonder, What the . . .?* features paintings, soft sculptures, ceramics, and photography.

Having ascended the ramp to the exhibit hall, the reviewer was faced with the traditional dilemma of gallery habitués—where do I begin? Do I circumnavigate the space clockwise or counterclockwise? This time, the reviewer chose to turn right and was immediately confronted by a series of numbered paintings depicting Boulder's iconic Flatirons. These granite slabs are, perhaps, the most frequently rendered landscape by Boulder artists. In this show, senior Amy Battles jacked the Flatirons from their natural tilt of 55 degrees to stand erect at a perfect 90 degrees. The transition creates a sense of impregnability between the eastern plains and the mountains beyond. No wagon train could ever have breached that barrier.

Moving on, the reviewer had the opportunity to mingle with four free-standing soft-sculptures, each resembling a bison in various stages of spring molt. The artist, Wing Pang, used fake fur (or pelts). He was heavy handed with barber shears to convey the randomness of the molting process. Clumps of shorn "hair" littered the floor.

Beyond the bison herd, the reviewer confronted hard sculptures— assemblages of glazed earthenware shapes miraculously entwined with fragile glass pipettes. The combination is pleasing to the eye, but the delicacy of the forms raised the question—how many thousands of foam peanuts would be necessary to ensure safe transport?

Photo art was located at the far end of the gallery, where a labyrinth of small walls is kind to photographers. Again, the Flatirons made an appearance, their sentinel-like bearing hardened or softened by the time of day the image was recorded. Green and yellow lichens popped in morning sunlight, valleys and crevasses brooded darkly as afternoon shadows melted into secret spaces.

The reviewer was pleasantly surprised to happen upon the work of JC MacKenzie, son of homeless advocate, Maryann Caton. Young MacKenzie's work was of two concept extremes: photos from exposed lookouts catching the sunrise over Kansas, and night photos of hidden grottoes, painted with light from filtered flashlights and other tools the reviewer could not determine. MacKenzie's images recorded from aeries are breathtaking because of the risk and danger inherent in taking them. He does not use drones. But his night photos are mysterious and sublime. The reviewer was left with one fundamental question— how were these images created?

Winter, Wonder, What the . . . ? will run at the Dairy Center until the end of February.

2027

Daily Boulder Reporter

CHAUTAUQUA PARK

UC Student, 20, Falls to His Death on First Flatiron

Tuesday, February 9, 2027 $3.00

Experienced rock climber slips while taking photos

By Arno Anderson, Staff Writer

Rescuers located the body of twenty year old Jacob C. MacKenzie at the base of the First Flatiron at 10 a.m. on Monday morning, February 8. He sustained life-ending injuries as the result of a fall. Jake is the son of Maryann Caton MacKenzie, a Boulder attorney, and Prof. Robert MacKenzie, head of the Science Writing Project at CU.

According to witnesses who were on side trails, MacKenzie was climbing the First Flatiron early in the day alone and without protection. They recall seeing him stop and photograph the skies over the plains to the east. Unusual cloud formations were building and being lit by the eastern sunrise. The unseasonably mild weather made the climbing route ice free.

Rescuers attempted to revive MacKenzie, but he had stopped breathing by the time they located him. EMTs said he had serious head trauma, although he was wearing a helmet.

MacKenzie was an experienced climber and promising photographer-artist. His surreal night photographs of the mountains have been featured in local galleries. An exhibit of his work is currently on display until the end of February in Boulder at The Dairy Center for the Arts on Walnut Street.

Maryann Caton, 47 | Robt. MacKenzie, 59 | Jake MacKenzie, 20 | World POP: 8.59 billion

---

"They're all inside, Annie, you can go right in."

Despite knowing she was a crackerjack lawyer who had received accolades and healthy bonuses, Maryann was anxious about the call to the board room. Through the frosted glass door she saw three shapes sitting at the big table. She affected a smile, then entered.

"Annie, come in. Sit next to us, not down there at the end." The greeting was by Archie Dillard, one of the three vested partners in **Pearl 2 Pine**. All three rose when she entered.

Sitting again, Dillard continued. "Jim, Lucas, and I have been thinking about this for a long time. If you accept, we are offering you full managing partnership. Four of us will decide the firm's future, not three. What do you say? Will you join us?"

Annie was caught off guard. She thought the "brain trust" might have wanted to discuss the class action suit they had filed to prohibit fracking in the Rocky Flats Wildlife Refuge. The firm's investigators found scores of radioactive pockets on the land, which was the old location for the assembly of nuclear weapons triggers. Or her meeting might have been about the firm's support for the homeless campaign she was spearheading. But the meeting was about neither issue. She was being promoted.

Her anxiety was replaced by calmness. "What an honor!" she said. "I accept. But I want to see my present cases through to the end. That's important to me."

"Of course," said Lucas. "If you hadn't, we would have been disappointed. Your tenacity and perseverance are your assets, and by extension, assets to the firm."

The door opened and coffee was brought in. Archie told her a contract was ready for her to sign. He said the stipulations and remuneration package was identical for all of them. They raised their mugs. "Here's to Annie MacKenzie, our new partner," said Archie. "Coffee this morning, whiskey this afternoon." They toasted.

Annie felt her cheeks flush with warmth. It wasn't from the coffee. It was from knowing she was valued.

"Archie and Lucas are hesitant to say this," said Jim, "but often we need a woman's point of view. However, in your case, Annie, it's much more than that. You're a hell of a lawyer."

Annie laughed. "I'm not sure how much my womanness will help, but I'll dole it out, if asked."

The door opened and a paralegal interrupted. "I'm sorry to interrupt," he said. There's an urgent phone call for Mrs. MacKenzie."

"Can't I call back?"

"I don't think you'd want to wait. It's important."

Annie flew through the door to the emergency room at Boulder Community Hospital. She immediately saw Rob standing at admitting station #1. He rushed forward and wrapped her in his arms. *Why were his eyes red?* she wondered. *Was it that bad?*

"Where's Jake?" she asked urgently. "Is he okay? I want to see him."

Rob refused to release her. He guided her to a hidden corner. "Jake's gone, love," he whispered.

"What do you mean?" she asked, looking at him dumbfounded.

"He's dead. Didn't anyone tell you?"

"Dead? Are you serious? He's injured! Oh my God! Please say it's not true!" She broke down and wailed.

He felt her crumple in his arms. She sobbed uncontrollably. He couldn't console her. He, too, was reeling from shock and sadness. Jake was the joy of both their lives. He didn't know what to do except hold her close. He had experienced death in his family and lost a young wife years earlier. But none of the pain then could compare with the anguish he felt now.

Through her tears she asked if she could see him. Her request was now less urgent knowing what she just learned. "I was told he was rock climbing," she wept. "I assumed he was hurt, but not this! Is he in one piece, Rob? Will I recognize him?"

"Aye, my love. You can see him. He's in the fourth cubicle on the right in the trauma center. I'll go in with you."

"Is he badly broken?" She gulped.

"Nae, he's in one piece. He's Jake. He's on his back. He looks like he's asleep. You'll have to pull back the sheet."

"Please come with me, Rob. I don't think I can bear doing this alone."

"Of course, love. Let's check with the resident on duty."

Rob left Annie alone with her son to say goodbye and ministrate his spirit as only a mother can do for a dead child. He waited in the hallway. Fred barged through the trauma center door, saw Rob and demanded, "Where's my sister?"

"She's alone with him in there, Fred. She's shattered, but she needs to say goodbye in her own way. For the moment she needs privacy. A consultation area's down the hall. Let's go there. You tell me what you learned. I'll tell you what I know." Rob rubbed eyes and wiped his nose. Fred followed him into the visitor alcove.

"What can I say, Rob? It's fucking madness! It's unfair! Look at these things. An EMT gave them to me. His helmet split in half protecting his skull. He apparently broke his neck. Why's his camera's in one piece? How can things like this happen?"

Rob became angry. "What in Christ's name was he doing up there this morning?" he asked. "I don't think the weather was forecast to do anything special. Why was he taking pictures?"

"I don't know, Rob. Maybe what's in the camera will tell us."

Annie emerged from the patient cubicle. No longer was she sobbing, but tears continued to stream down. She was ashen and to Rob appeared smaller in stature. She saw her brother.

"Oh, Fred! What am I going to do? I've lost my baby!" They cried into each other's shoulders. Rob resisted joining them. He knew blood relatives had a special bond that needed to be respected. He turned away to deal with his own sorrow.

❖

Two weeks after Jake's death, Annie and Rob were sitting side-by-side in the living room. Annie was reading a legal brief. Since becoming a partner at **Pearl 2 Pine** and Jake's death, she had thrown herself into her work. It was a way to numb the sadness she felt. At home she was quiet and withdrawn. Rob respected her need for grieving on her terms by giving her space.

"Lass, I've downloaded the photos from Jake's camera. They're on my laptop. Do you want to see them?"

She looked up from her work and stared blankly at him. "Huh? His photos? Oh, my, I'm not sure that's a good idea."

"I don't know if it is either, love. But you'll see what he saw before his fall."

"Oh, dear," she hesitated. "The last thing my baby saw…" Her curiosity overcame her fear. She slid closer to Rob. He began to scroll through the images.

"Most of them are routine," he explained, "nothing out of the ordinary. This one's looking down about fifty feet from above ground. You can see how dark it is at the base. I'm guessing it was snapped around 7:30 a.m. This next group is of forest vegetation on the side of the slab." When Annie was finished studying the forest downloads, he scrolled to the next photo.

"Now look at the color in this image! Greys and dusky greens have been replaced by garnet red. It's as if the rock face above him was painted with tomato soup. It's so red—crimson even!"

Maryann looked closer. "What caused it, Rob?"

"Jake's final photo answers that." He scrolled to the last frame.

Annie stared at the image. Her brow furrowed. Rob knew

she was trying to make sense of what she saw. "What is it, Rob? I've never seen anything like it. It looks like a UFO."

"Aye, but it's not alien. It's an altocumulus lenticularis, a lenticular cloud. Sometimes they form into the shape of a single lens, like this one, sometimes they're stacked in layers."

"What causes them?"

"Moist air speeding over lofty places like the Front Range. We never saw them in Connecticut. It was too flat."

"How did it get so red? And the edges look like they've been trimmed with pink and gold."

"The morning's early sun was exactly at the right angle for the light to be refracted by the cloud into the red spectrum. It acted like a prism. The phenomenon doesn't happen often, but when it does, it can produce some amazing shapes. They're not always colorful, either. The conditions have to be perfect to get something like this. If you have a camera at the time one of these forms, you're lucky."

Maryann pondered Rob's words and gulped. "Or in Jake's case, having a camera was very unlucky."

Fifty-two people leaned into the steep hill clustering around Fred Caton as he prepared to say final words remembering his nephew, Jacob MacKenzie. Relatives, friends, and acquaintances were assembled under the guy wires of the Boulder Star on a warm spring morning. No one appeared to resent having been made to trek up the treacherous slope to the site. Down Flagstaff Road to the east, Boulder City was spread out on the plains. When all were assembled and had caught their breaths, Fred signaled for them to move closer.

"Good morning, folks. Thank you all for hiking up here to pay tribute to Jake. It's a steep climb. Dig your feet in. Get solid footing." He waited until the guests were comfortable. "Down by the stonehouse, did you see the two mule deer in the field?"

A few nodded and smiled indicating they had been lucky.

"They have the most soulful eyes," continued Fred. "We have a lovely print of one taken by Jake. He was nose to nose with it." He scanned the hill. "Keep your eyes out on the way back down to your cars," he added. "We might have awakened other critters hiding in the rocks." People glanced at the slope.

He continued. "You all came to know Jake in a variety of ways. Habitat for Humanity folks . . . thank you for coming today. Jake loved working on your projects. You kids from the art department knew Jake well, although he began calling himself JC when he was eighteen. JC is how you knew him. Good to see you. Three of Jake's teachers are here: Mr. Reyes, Jake's high school Spanish teacher; Ms Dugan, Jake's high school art teacher; Professor Tata, Jake's college advisor." Fred chuckled. "I swear Boulder teachers must be the fittest educators in America. You climbed this hill just as well as the kids." The teachers smiled and pretended to be winded. "Speaking on behalf of Jake's parents, Annie and Rob, again thank you for honoring a talented and loving young man."

He checked a 3x5 card. "You all know Jake was unpredictably funny. He could see humor in any situation. That rosy outlook is what made it so much fun to be near him. He ordered his cousins around like he was a king, only to meekly back off when they told him he was acting like a fool, not a monarch. He claimed he was the king when he played *Monopoly*. He said when he used the wheelbarrow token he never lost. I once told him if he had a hod to carry his loot, it would be a different story. The way I pronounced *hod* made him ask me if I grew up in Boston. He said it wouldn't be *hard* carrying cash on his shoulder. I reminded him Annie and I were from Pittsburgh, not Beantown." People chuckled.

"He learned a lot volunteering at Habitat. His activism pleased Annie. I think you know my sister's involved in the Boulder homeless crisis." Heads nodded.

"When Jake was younger, he considered studying earth science in college. But as it is with so many artists, he couldn't deny his calling. As it turned out, Jake was talented and inventive with a camera. His work was featured in the winter show at the Dairy Center. I recall seeing some of you there.

"Most of you don't know that when Jake was eighteen, he legally changed his family name from Canfeld to MacKenzie. That's when JC started. Jake's birth father died years ago. They were never close. He chose the name of his step-dad, Robert MacKenzie, a man he loved and honored.

"I know it's trite to say, but Jake died doing what he loved to do. He began rock climbing as a child at summer camp. Even as a preteen, he climbed many of Connecticut's crags. Often Rob was his belayer. It didn't surprise us, then, when he began combining climbing with photography.

"We're under the Boulder Star today because this is the place where Jake, Annie, and Rob truly became a nuclear family. It happened on Veteran's Day evening three months after the MacKenzies moved to Boulder. That was eight years ago. Am I right, Annie?"

She nodded yes.

"We're all headed back down to our cars, back to our routines, back to our own lives. All I ask is that when you see the Boulder Star alit this fall and every year thereafter, you remember my nephew, Jake MacKenzie. He was a star in my life."

The gathering was quiet. Some turned and hugged their

neighbors. Maryann kissed her brother, then spoke quietly with her sister-in-law, Lois, and her two nieces. Rob mingled and shook hands.

Finally, Fred spoke again. "Thanks for coming everybody. Be careful going down the slope. It's steep with loose gravel in places. Goodbye. Go in peace."

2028

Daily Boulder Reporter

BOULDER AT LARGE

First Tiny Home Community Opens for Business

Tuesday, July 18, 2028 $3.00

Ribbon cutting attended by dozens—MacKenzie honored—Boulder plan, a model for nation

By Steffi Dahl, Staff Writer

The first of four tiny home communities opened for business yesterday with eight newly minted owners moving in. Near the junction of 55th Street and Sioux Drive, the community sits on a ¾ acre parcel, recently "spot zoned" for tiny home siting. The developer, Boulder Association of Compassionate Conservatives, has options on three more parcels—one in South Boulder, two north of Valmont Avenue.

The East Boulder development is named "Jake's Place." That choice is in honor of Jacob MacKenzie, a Habitat for Humanity volunteer and son of Maryann Caton MacKenzie who was the driving force behind the rewrite of Boulder's homeless plan. Jacob's father is Professor Robert MacKenzie, a member of CU's science department. Jake lost his life more than a year ago in a rock climbing accident. Future tiny home communities will bear the name of deserving Boulder residents.

Jake's Place has access to sidewalks and paths leading to a variety of attractions. Nearby is the East Boulder Recreation Center, playgrounds for children, tennis courts, and a middle school. It connects with the rest of Boulder via a bus stop on 55th Street.

The eight homes were situated to insure privacy. Views of fields and meadows are to the east, the Front Range to the west. Three of the units are sized for a family of four, three are designed for couples, and two are for single persons. The units are mounted on concrete foundations and have access to city water and sewers. Heating and cooking is done by propane.

If employed, new owners must pay at least 5% of their monthly income toward mortgage satisfaction. They are also obligated to help keep the community pristine. Owners must refrain from harmful behaviors. Drug and tobacco use are prohibited, and excessive alcohol consumption can lead to eviction. The new owners were chosen through a lottery system.

Maryann Caton, 48 | Robt. MacKenzie, 60 | Jake MacKenzie, d. | World POP: 8.67 billion

---

Annie passed the regular cast of characters on her way to work. She said good morning to contortionist JeanPierre but was unsure he heard her. He was wrapped in a ball of knees and elbows. She dropped a bill into his bucket. She wondered how much longer he could tie his body into knots. He wasn't a young man.

JeanPierre earned his living busking on the mall, but did he have a permanent residence? She wondered about that. How could he afford to live in Boulder on the small amounts dropped into his bucket? He didn't appear to be homeless. Somehow he was getting by. Still, it had to be a struggle for him. He usually said good morning to her in return for her greeting and contribution. However, this morning he was bent in half, his head and shoulder girdle protruding through his legs in a way not intended for a human being.

Further down the mall, Annie saw and could hear the squeals of young children running through the water fountain. It was a "burper," shooting spurts into the air in a random pattern. Children and pets tried to guess where the next jet would pop out. They were having a grand time getting soaked. She stopped for a moment to enjoy their delight.

She pictured Jake at the same age on a Long Island beach. As waves receded, he tore into the salty foam, only to race back to the beach as a new wave formed. Like the children on the mall, he announced his joy with screeches and laughter.

That was the day, she recalled, when she hadn't diligently applied sunscreen to his tender skin. As a result, he suffered a nasty sunburn. Her penance was applying soothing and healing balm day and night, until he was cool to the touch. The incident taught her that loving and caring mothers sometimes dropped the ball when it came to their child's safety.

Had she dropped the ball with Jake regarding rock climbing? Had she been too trusting assuming he'd be safe? And even if she had forbidden him to climb, would he have followed her dictates?

Eighteen months later, the loss of her son was still a raw

wound. Her heart, once filled with love of family, now had a vacancy. She wondered if it would ever again be full.

Annie crossed the mall heading north on 13th Street. To her right was the massive art-deco Boulder County Courthouse. Across the street on the west side she saw a young man sitting on his backpack protected by a niche in a building's facade. He appeared to have an array of items displayed on a small table. She was curious. She crossed the street to see what he was selling. She was certain he was hawking something.

The vendor's table was draped by a black cloth. Arranged in a circle were wire figurines, some human-like, some like animals.

"Hi," she said, "may I look?" He nodded. She studied the display. "These are nice. You got the movement just right. The lion ready to pounce is especially good. Are they for sale?"

"Yes. The lion is five dollars. The others range from three to eight dollars."

"Did you make them?" She knew her question could be misconstrued, as if the young man had no talent. But there were plenty of cheap imports and knockoffs for sale on the mall.

"Yes, I made them," he said. He showed her the roll of wire, pliers, and tin snips he had stored out of sight.

"Well, as I said, they're excellent." Suddenly, her face brightened. "I know what they remind me of. They're similar to the wire sculptures made by the artist, Alexander Calder. He put together an ensemble called the *Circus*. Do you know it?"

He nodded. "I do. That's where I got these ideas."

Annie was compelled to relate her connection with Calder, despite having never met him.

"I moved to Boulder about ten years ago. Prior to that I lived in a small town in Connecticut. Calder had a home and studio in an adjacent town. By the time I moved there he was dead.

But friends kept finding small discarded wire sculptures in the landfill. You know the old story—one person's junk is another person's treasure. I also saw his *Circus* at the Whitney Museum in New York City."

The young man listened intently to her story. He nodded as if her facts corroborated with what he knew. "I've heard stories like that about him. Is there anything here you'd like to buy, ma'am? I'd appreciate your business."

She looked at the young man trying to memorize his features so she could describe him to Rob. "Yes, I'd like to buy the lion. I went to Columbia. The lion is Columbia's symbol." She handed him five dollars. "By the way, what's your name?"

"Sandy Callendar," he said, as if letting her in on a joke.

She stood quietly looking out her bedroom window. Morning light enhanced the fall colors of the field and meadow to the east. Yellowing grasses, ground level thorn tangles, dark brown buckwheat stalks, broom, wild parsley, reddening prairie grasses—the vegetation was shutting down for the winter. Today it was enjoying its last dance in beautiful earth-tone gowns.

Annie watched residents of Jake's Place come and go in the relaxed pace of a Saturday morning. A father and child were planting something—daffodil bulbs, probably—along the foundation of their new home. A few doors away a woman was washing windows. She saw that a new covered bicycle corral had been installed. It was nearly full. A door opened and a man walked to the bus stop while checking his watch. She wondered if his trip was to complete errands or head to work.

Her dream of a tiny home village for the homeless had come true. *I ought to visit these folks,* she thought. *They're my neighbors living in Jake's Place.* She took a deep breath trying to squeeze out her sadness. *I miss him. I'll always miss him.*

"Here you are, lass. I wondered where you went." Rob wrapped his arms around her waist and smelled her hair. He stared out the window. "It's a bonny morning."

"Yes, Rob, it's stunning." She hesitated enjoying the comfort of his embrace. "I think I'm going to visit our new neighbors after Halloween. It's time to introduce myself. Maybe I can convince some to join me out on the rec center field for the Boulder Star lighting."

"You don't want to go up there this year?"

"No, honey, probably never again. Down here's fine. When I see the star from this distance, I'll imagine my baby's an angel looking over us." She turned and rested her head on Rob's chest. "I miss him, Rob. I still feel the pain."

"Aye, love, I know you do. We both do." He thought for a moment measuring his words. "You're right. Seeing the star from down here's a good idea. Let's do it together. Maybe we'll be able to round up some folks from Jake's Place to join us."

2029

The Journal of the Spiritual Scientist

COPING WITH YOUR CHILD'S DEATH

Four Stages Of Bereavement

DEALING WITH SORROW IN 2029

by Dr. LEON GRAFF, Senior Fellow at the LAD Institute

Introduction: When we are born, we are destined to die. Our death is a certainty. This is true for every living organism on Earth. A typical house fly will survive for only twenty-eight days, a sequoia, 500 to 700 years. Under perfect conditions of light, climate, and nutrition a redwood might last 2000 years. But it too will eventually die. Knowing that death is certain, how do mindful species deal with loss and sorrow?

Human Life Expectancy: In 2029, U.S. life expectancy is 77.8 years, a slight decline from the high point of 79.84 in 2016. Presently, the U.S. ranks 65 out of 224 nations for which statistics are available. Average age at death worldwide is 68.7 years. Women live longer than men. As in the U.S., age at death is declining worldwide.

Coping with Death's Certainty: There are no meters or metrics to rate the levels of sorrow people suffer when a human dies. Some cultures mourn openly either in groups or individually. Other cultures retreat into privacy not willing to share grief's burden. When counselors try to measure levels of sorrow, they must rely on anecdotal evidence of mourner behavior, either verbally transmitted or through observed actions. Do mourners withdraw into a silent place, beat their chests and roll in ashes, or do they redirect their suffering to help others?

The Loss of a Child: Parents assume their children will outlive them. This is a reasonable assumption based on age differences and life expectancy. Unfortunately, all kinds of peril lie in wait for humans as they grow from birth to adulthood. Disease, accidents, drug abuse, suicide, and warfare are waiting to ensnare the unsuspecting. No matter how diligently parents try to shield their offspring from danger, children succumb to life-ending events. Therein lies the cause of humanity's greatest sorrow— death of a child.

The Four Stages of Bereavement: Knowing the four stages of bereavement can help mourners understand their actions and feelings as the suffering process begins then transitions into acceptance. Most people recover, but some never do. The stages have been identified and verified through the collective research of dozens of psychiatrists, psychologists, and grief counselors.

Stage One—Shock and Anger: Parents experience shock when a child dies unexpectedly. Even for those children who yield to a protracted illness, parental shock is common. Parents cling to the hope that modern medicine will heal their child.

When a child dies from an accident, however, shock is even greater as the sudden unexpected loss strikes home.

After shock comes anger, fueled by self-recrimination. Why did I let her ride a bicycle to school? Why didn't we recognize his drug problem? Why didn't I warn her school she was being bullied? Why did I let him climb trees? Why didn't I? Why didn't I? Why didn't I?

Stage Two—Crushing Sadness: When death's reality is finally acknowledged, anger abated, and all accept the fact that the deceased is gone forever, grief, sorrow, suffering, and loneliness take over. This is a normal human reaction. A similar behavior can be seen in other vertebrates as they pine for their dead offspring before accepting the truth and move on with the herd. Curiously, some canines appear to grieve for the rest of their lives over the death of their human owner, even more than the death of a puppy. Behaviorists think that's the result of litters being split up early before adult-child bonds are formed. In contrast, the bond between a dog and its owner is almost as strong as the human bond between parent and child.

Stage Three—Memory overload: Within months of a child's passing, a parent's memory bank is flooded with images and anecdotes of times long past. Occasionally, an unhappy memory will intrude, but it is usually quickly erased by the recollection of joyous events. In this stage, like the first, lingering questions persist. Why was I so busy I couldn't take him to the circus? Why didn't we lock up her bicycle so she wouldn't have been so upset when it was stolen? Why didn't we take him to see grandpa one last time? What was so important that we couldn't attend her ballet recital? Why didn't I hug him more often? Why didn't I say "I love you" more frequently?

Stage Four—Refocused Love: Nothing can ever replace a lost child. The parents of the children murdered seventeen years ago in Sandy Hook, Connecticut, still suffer from their grief of that day. They will never forget their murdered children. Happily, a few families have grown larger. A new child will never replace the deceased, of course, but a new child helps parents cope. They are able to direct affection toward a human rather than let their lingering love go unrequited.

Refocused love takes many forms. Grieving parents often direct their energies toward child advocacy causes, especially those that are combating the reason for their child's death. Drug prevention organizations, gun control groups, safe cycling proponents, and anti-bullying initiatives are examples.

Some bereft parents prefer to expend their efforts toward larger causes. They may support anti-discrimination efforts, become activists for the homeless, or fight for environmental protection.

Conclusion: A child's death is a life changing moment for parents. It can plunge a parent into a deep well of perpetual sorrow. Or the sorrow can be redirected toward a cause for the common good. The Life and Death (LAD) Institute stands ready to guide bereaved parents onto the road best travelled. Use your the passion from your loss to become part of society's effort to make the world a better place.

Maryann Caton, 49 | Robt. MacKenzie, 61 | Jake MacKenzie, d. | World POP: 8.78 billion

---

"Will I ever get over this sadness, Rob? Even after two years, it's tearing me apart. I'm afraid it's affecting my work and our relationship."

Rob unwound himself from his share of the comforter and slid next to her. He draped an arm over her waist and pushed his nose into the nape of her neck.

"I love you, Annie, you know that. It hurts me watching you suffer. I wish I could do something to help you."

"You're helping by sticking with me, love. I know I've been miserable to be around."

"Stick with you? How can I not? You're my life."

She rolled over and kissed him. "It's just been very hard. My baby was so young. No mother expects to outlive her child."

"Aye, and don't forget about me. Jake was my pride and joy."

"I know, honey. I'm sorry for thinking only about myself. I know you've suffered, too. Will our sorrow ever go away?"

"Nae, love. All we can wish for is that it will lessen. I'm hoping we'll begin to remember the happy Jake stories, not dwell on the last chapter."

Sandy Callendar didn't appear to Annie to be an itinerant wanderer. For more than a year she saw him in his 13th Street niche selling wire sculptures. Legally, he was entitled to do so. A municipal ordinance barring permitless street vendors had been overturned years earlier. In addition to animal and human figurines, Sandy had added a wire representation of JeanPierre to his line, a metal contortionist in a wire box. At least once a month Annie purchased one of his creations. She had a collection at home hidden in a spot Rob was unlikely to discover. She had never concealed anything from him. However, her compulsion to own Sandy's art wasn't behavior she could easily explain.

There was something about Sandy, some quality that defied explanation. For one thing, he was always immaculately clean.

Cleanliness was important to her. If he was as he appeared, she wondered, a street person, how did he bathe? He had only a small wardrobe, but what he wore was washed and in good repair. He was talented with wire, but was he also handy with a needle and thread?

She wasn't smitten by him in a visceral animal sense, but he did have the undeniable allure of a younger man. She knew nothing would come of her infatuation, but nonetheless, infatuation it was. When she thought about it, she understood his attraction was a combination of several qualities: he was a free spirit; he appeared to have no concern about a questionable future; he was young and polite with women; he lived a mysterious life in Boulder that was unimaginable to her. Where did he sleep at night?

Annie normally preferred men with closely cropped hair. That had been Rob's style since their wedding. Now at age 61, his top was thinning and turning from russet to grey. Sandy Callendar's mane, by comparison, was stylishly sloppy, overlapping his collar and curling behind his ears. Like the rest of him, his locks looked clean and soft, free of greasy strands flattened to his skull like so many of the homeless.

When he stood to stretch, she estimated he was about Jake's height. When he moved around to uncramp his legs, she saw he had a pronounced limp.

Later, thinking about Sandy while nursing coffee at Starbucks, she wondered about his lineage. Was it possible he was related to Alexander Calder, even though there was a slight difference in their family names? Calder was a Scot by heritage. In Scotland she had seen men with Sandy's coloring— dark hair, beard shadow, dark eyes—vestigial remnants from the Pictish tribes of an ancient wilderness. Where did he shave? And then there was his facial threesome—two dimples and a cleft chin. She could imagined him as an 18th Century highlander—swarthy, broad of chest and shoulder, with an eye for the most comely village lass. But in 21st Century Boulder, he was another aging urchin, adrift on the street. His vulnerability awakened maternal instincts in her.

"I found a whole zoo of wire critters, lass. You've been holding out on me. Why didn't you say something?"

"I was embarrassed. Now they look silly to me, like a collection of toys."

"Nae, love. They're better than toys. They're quite good. They remind me of something I saw years ago."

"Alexander Calder's *Circus*?"

"Aye, that's right! How did you know?"

"That's what I thought when I saw them. What were you doing in the storage closet?"

"Trying to snare a mouse. I was setting traps. Sometimes Colorado rodents are vectors for the plague, especially the bloody prairie dogs."

"I don't see any burrows in our lawn, so I guess we've escaped them."

"So far, so good."

For the first time in weeks, Annie had a full-throated laugh. "Jeepers! A mountain lion was photographed lounging on a deck in North Boulder, a bear and her cubs had to be tranquilized and removed from a tree down the road in East Boulder, and a moose was wandering around West Boulder. We're under attack." She wrapped her arms around Rob's neck. "At least we're only fighting with mice in this house." She kissed him.

"Aye, and I hope it's only one wee beastie and not a clan."

They descended to the kitchen where both pitched in

preparing dinner. "So tell me about your wire toys, lass. Where did you get them?"

"A young man sells them on the Pearl Street Mall. They reminded me of Calder's figures. So I'm collecting them."

"Calder's art is worth thousands. What did you pay for these?"

"They run from three to eight dollars."

"That's a Scottish bargain. Good going!"

"Do you remember that Calder lived for a time near Roxbridge?"

"Aye, I do. But that was before our time there." He thought for a moment. "One of his earliest mobiles is in the National Gallery in Edinburgh. It's called *The Spider*. I've seen it. Hanging high, it really resembles a bloody arachnid. If we head back to Scotia to see the military tattoo, we'll include a trip to the museum."

"I'd love that, sweetie." She began preparing a salad.

"Tell me about the lad on Pearl Street." He pulled a wine cork. They hadn't enjoyed a glass together in months. "Does he have a studio in Boulder?"

"I'm afraid not, honey. I'm pretty sure he's homeless. I don't know much about him. But I do know his name. You won't believe this . . . Sandy Callendar!"

"Och! Both Calder and Callendar are Scottish family names. I wonder whether he was telling you the truth."

"He seems honest. When we talk, I don't detect any pretenses."

"How long has he been on the mall?

"About a year, I guess. He's a lovely young man. He's so different from the other drifters downtown. He's clean and presentable. I don't know how he manages that."

She dumped the greens into a bowl. He handed her a stemmed glass with white wine.

"I have a favor to ask, Rob. Please don't hesitate to say, 'no.'"

He laughed. "Don't you worry about that, lass. I can crush hopes and dreams like a puffball in a lawn of rye grass. How can I help you?"

"I'd like to invite Sandy Callendar to dinner." She glanced at Rob's face. It gave no hint as to what he was thinking. "I know that's asking a lot. I have no ulterior motive other than I'd like to learn more about him. Truthfully, I'm not sure he'll accept."

Rob was quiet. He turned his back to her and topped off his glass. He sipped then faced her. "This isn't about Jake, is it? I know you've been hurting, but bringing another lad into the house might not be a good idea."

"It's not that . . .," she stammered.

"You know I'll do anything for you, Annie. You've been sad for so long. Sure. If you want to invite the lad for dinner, that's okay with me." He sipped again.

Her face softened. She smiled. "Thank you, my dear. I love you so much for agreeing."

He felt compelled to warn her. "I don't think I need to tell you, Annie, but someone else will never replace your son." She nodded seeming to accept his advice. "Be careful how you proceed." He was tempted to warn her of the danger of adopting a stray pet when one is lost. But he thought better of the idea and remained quiet.

Maryann and Rob waited for their guest to arrive for dinner. They confessed to each other they were unsure he'd actually show up. When Maryann invited him, she gave him directions—from the 14th Street bus depot, take #225 to the East

Boulder Rec Center. Number 1 Rim Rock Circle is a short walk west from the bus stop.

Through her conversations with Sandy, Annie learned that he was originally from New Orleans. She wondered if he had experienced Hurricane Katrina. He appeared to be about the right age.

While waiting for Sandy, she told Rob she had read *Children of Katrina*, a 2015 report published by the University of Texas. The facts troubled her. Mental problems among children spiked 9% after the storm. In a city of 455,000 there were 1,800 storm related deaths. Initially, population shrank by 60,000, stayed steady for ten years, then began increasing to 405,000 by 2029. Overall, it was a net loss of 50,000.

Rob listened to the details, occasionally nodding his head, as if his suspicions had been confirmed. "Aye, love. I'm not surprised by what you say. It was inevitable. It will happen again. No city should be located on a tidal floodplain two feet below sea level. No city should be sited at the mouth of the Mississippi River. It makes no sense. It's mass death waiting to happen. New Orleans is poorly protected by levees, dams, and pumps. Advice from the Dutch was totally ignored."

The doorbell rang. Annie felt a twinge of anticipation. Rob greeted the visitor. Sandy Callendar entered bearing a big smile and a bouquet of flowers. Rob closed the door and followed him in.

"You made it okay," said Annie, relieved. "I'm never sure my directions are accurate. Oh! And you brought flowers. How lovely! Before sitting down, I'll put them in a vase."

"Thank you for inviting me, Mrs. MacKenzie, and you, too,

sir. I've never been in someone's home in Boulder. You have a nice place."

"I'll hang your coat," said Rob, "then let's sit for a wee bit until Annie's ready to serve."

"Yes, sir."

"Forget, the 'sir.' Rob's plenty formal enough. May I get you a drink? Beer? Wine? Do you drink?"

"Rarely. I can't afford it."

"Well, you're not paying the tab tonight, lad. From what Annie's said, you have some Scottish blood. How 'bout a pint of wee heavy?"

Sandy chuckled. "I haven't heard that term in a long time. Ale would be good." He sat.

Rob entered the kitchen, uncapped two bottles, took out two mugs. He poured wine for Annie. She was fiddling with an oven thermometer and timer. As he assembled the drinks, he could see Sandy admiring the display of his wire art Annie had arranged on a sideboard.

Rob re-entered the living room. Annie joined him.

"The lasagna has a few more minutes to go," she said. "I want it to be piping hot before serving. Let's chat until it's ready."

"Again, thank you for inviting me," said Sandy.

They toasted. "Sláinthe!"

"The lad knows some Gaelic," said Rob, amused. "Now I'm sure he's Scottish. Nobody in Boulder says 'sláinthe' unless they're in Paddy Hogan's drinking Guinness Stout." They laughed, then raised their glasses again.

The whole time, Annie watched Sandy to see how he handled himself. As she predicted, he was immaculately clean. He had trimmed his hair. He appeared to be comfortable with them. She was certain he had been raised within the embrace of a family.

Rob was the first to broach Sandy's homelessness. Normally, Annie got right to the point. Tonight it was Rob. "So, lad, apparently you don't have a permanent home."

"Not here in Boulder, Rob, but I did have one in Florida."

"Why did you leave it? Why are you here?"

"I wanted to escape hurricane alley. I lived through three of them. Three's enough. I escaped, but my family continues to struggle."

"You said you were from New Orleans," said Annie. "Were you there in 2005 for Katrina?"

"Yes. I was only four at the time. Our ward was hit hard. My mother drowned. My father was a musician. He couldn't take care of me. So he shipped me to relatives in Florida."

"Is he still alive?"

"No. He was a victim of the opioid epidemic. He killed himself trying to numb the loss of my mother. Unfortunately, drugs are a big part of the music culture."

"That's so sad." Annie hesitated before posing another question. "Where in Florida did you live?"

"In a small town on the northwest coast—Dunedin."

Rob smiled. "Och! 'Fort Edin' or 'Edin City'. . . no matter how it's translated it means 'Edinburgh.'"

"That's right!" agreed Sandy. "I learned the town's history in elementary school."

The oven dinger went off. "Supper's ready," announced Annie.

While eating, they resumed their conversation. "So you were shipped off to a relative's house. Aunt and uncle?"

"Yes, the MacLeans. My aunt is my father's sister. They're all second generation Scottish-Americans. My grandparents emigrated to the U.S. after the Second World War. They said conditions in Glasgow were bad after the German bombing."

"Aye, that I know," said Rob. "Rebuilding was still going on when I left."

Maryann wanted to learn more about Sandy. "Why did you leave your aunt and uncle?"

"Hurricane Irma hit Florida's west coast hard in 2017. Then in 2018 Michael smashed into the panhandle, followed by Hurricane Lorenzo which flattened the center of the state in 2019. By then I had had enough. When I was eighteen, I hit the road. I've been wandering ever since trying out towns."

"And you landed in Boulder."

"Yep. I heard it was an accepting community. It makes an effort to help people."

Annie looked at Rob in a knowing way. She wondered whether Sandy knew the extent of her involvement in Boulder's homeless crisis.

Sandy continued. "When people see me, they think I'm a drifter without a future. That's not true. In a pinch I could return to Dunedin. But I want to make it on my own. I'm not looking for handouts. I don't beg."

"There are new homeless initiatives being implemented in Boulder," said Annie. "Do you know about them?"

"Very little. Oh, but I do know about the tiny home communities. They sound cool."

When Annie heard Sandy say 'cool,' she thought of Jake. "Do you know you passed a tiny home village on the way here?"

"I thought so."

"It's called Jake's Place. It's named in memory of my son."

Sandy looked up as if stunned. "What? Your son? I didn't know. I'm so very sorry."

He suddenly realized Annie was *the* Maryann Caton MacKenzie. He was talking to Boulder's main advocate for the homeless. How could he have not connected the dots?

"I loved my son as any mother would," she said. "His untimely death was an accident. Gradually, I'm coming to accept it. Now I have his memory living across the street in that little community."

They were silent for a moment, heads down concentrating on their food. Annie spoke once again. "Is your name on the list of tiny home applicants? From what you said, one of the units would be perfect for you."

"It never dawned on me that I'd be eligible. How do I sign up?"

"Before you leave, I'll give you an application. It contains information about eligibility, what proofs you need, and ownership obligations. Units aren't given away. You have to become an owner. Drop it off at city hall. Two more communities are nearing completion, but it may be awhile before we have certificates of occupancy."

"Aren't I too late to get in line?"

"No, there is no line. If applicants meet ownership criteria, they're eligible to enter the lottery. That's how it works."

After Sandy departed heading to his bed in the North Boulder shelter, Annie floated an idea to Rob. "I've never done this, honey, but I wonder if I could help Sandy land a tiny home? Would that be fair?"

"He's certainly an engaging young man," said Rob. "I don't have any misgivings about him." He thought, then addressed her fairness question. "Fairness is relative, love. As far as I'm concerned, helping a young man with a promising future is fine. I don't see any harm in talking to one of the committee members about him. You're not directly involved in the lottery."

Rob thought for a moment, then continued. "He doesn't qualify for one of the large units, so he wouldn't be taking a home away from a needy family. You've contributed years to the effort. A home for the lad would be a good reward. But the lottery is a kind of promise—a statement that selection is random. I wouldn't advocate breaking that promise."

He went on. "Think about the proactive form of the Golden Rule—treat others as you would want to be treated. You would hope someone would advocate for you, right? So speak up for Sandy. It all fits in with what I believe—ULAR, the Universal Law of Reciprocity."

2030

The NEW YORK MESSENGER

"THE SPIRIT OF PUBLIUS"

NEW ORLEANS DEMOLISHED!

September 10, 2030 $4.00

Cat 6 Hurricane Travis obliterates much of coastal Louisiana 13 years after Hurricane Harvey flattened Houston—Mississippi River channels need remapping, dredging—groundwater pollution covers thousands of square miles—crude oil contaminates fisheries in Gulf of Mexico—human health in jeopardy—deaths may reach quarter of a million—Louisiana economy teeters on edge of collapse

ANALYSIS: ❖ By Ronald Tobin, NYM Financial Staff Writer ❖

It's too early to know for sure what the cost will be for Louisiana to recover (if ever) from Hurricane Travis. The amount could approach one trillion dollars. The U.S. economy, already faced with a 23 trillion dollar debt, is burdened with the expense of massive regional rehabilitation and rebuilding. The U.S. is facing this bill only 13 years after absorbing the costs caused by hurricanes Harvey, Irma, Maria, and Nate in 2017. Is this any way to do business?

Is the U.S.A. writ large responsible for paying for the costs of regional rebuilding? Does even the idea of rebuilding in the floodplain of the Mississippi River make sense? What are the obligations of industry, local governments, and individual homeowners?

After Harvey, et. al., in 2017, it became crystal clear that the entire Gulf Coast and Louisiana in particular were terrible locations for millions of people to live. The same is true for most shoreline areas, as witnessed by the destruction wreaked by Hurricane Sandy in the northeast in 2012, Hurricane Irma in Puerto Rico in 2017, and 2018 Hurricane Michael in the Florida panhandle. Flooding, sea level rise, storm surges, and insane cyclonic activity are more apt to occur in southern regions close to the warm waters of the Gulf of Mexico.

Post Harvey, why didn't state governments heed the advice of Dutch hydrologists to relocate pedestrian neighborhoods further inland? Why were permits issued to rebuild along bayous and waterways using structural designs more suitable for Nebraska? Why weren't Dutch flood mitigation practices implemented? Can the so-called "cancer alley," the Bayou State's sprawling petrochemical landscape, be made safe from future storms? In Texas, can Houston's "oil patch" be protected, if it is to continue providing distillates to the nation?

These questions must be addressed and answered by state and federal policy planners. Uninformed politicians must stay out of the debate. Purveyors of blind faith need to disappear from the discussion. What happened to New Orleans was not God's will. It was the result of human negligence tangling with elemental forces.

Hidden among these questions is the issue of overpopulation. If people are forced or willingly agree to move inland, the nation's 337 million will be concentrated in a smaller useable land mass. If millions move away from coastal areas, how will infrastructure, food production, and social relationships adjust?

The U.S. government needs to convene a population summit which includes federal and state representatives, demographers, geographers, philosophers, and theologians. A federal population agency should be formed. The task will be difficult, but our nation must have a strategic plan in place for dealing with human migration now underway. It will swell to an exodus when Florida is permanently flooded by the end of the century or a Category 5 storm sweeps Cape Cod into the Atlantic.

News of Holland.nl 12 September 2030

Europe's Most Liberal News Source

Politics | Business | Society | Sport | Education
Environment | Health | International

New Orleans mortally wounded by Hurricane Travis—The Big Easy demolished by Category 6 storm thirteen years after Harvey swamped Houston—Deaths reach quarter million—U.S. declined Dutch expertise

ANALYSIS: ❖ By Hans Bechtel, NOH Environment Staff Writer ❖ Amsterdam

Since Hurricane Harvey in 2017, conservative American politicians and fundamentalist religious leaders have continued to refuse evidence embraced by the rest of the world—the global climate is changing. The earth is warming at a pace not seen since the Permian period—a time now known as "the great extinction."

Humans were not around 265 million years ago in the Permian, so people did not suffer. However, millions of other life forms disappeared. It is estimated that 98% of all species then in existence died. The causes of the great extinction are not fully understood, cloaked in the mystery of time past. But one factor is clear—due to methane emissions and increasing levels of CO_2 in the atmosphere, the earth overheated.

The "oven effect" is underway full steam in the 21st Century. Increasing amounts of Permian gases—methane, CO_2—as well as industrial pollutants are again filling the troposphere. The sun's rays (energy) are converted into heat and trapped by these gases. Heat is absorbed by land and sea. Oceans are particularly suited to hold surplus heat.

The increasing frequency of gigantic mega-storms is a direct link to the earth's warming and hotter oceans. Warm air holds more water vapor. Warm water expands exacerbating storm surges. Warm water fuels cyclonic winds. Melting land-based glaciers and Greenland's disappearing ice shields are lifting ocean levels by feet per decade.

The Netherlands has been dealing with these issues for hundreds of years. Weather generated dangers and water infiltration have been constant battles for the Dutch. As a result of storm-caused catastrophes, a country that is 25% below sea level and has half its landmass only one meter above sea level has been forced to learn to live with the sea's insatiable appetite to regain what it once owned.

No one can dispute that the Dutch are the world's foremost experts in ocean water management. Dikes, canals, storm surge barriers, computer models, reclaimed polders, and an instinctive understanding of how to live with rising water, enable the Dutch to enjoy life at the highest levels of civilized development.

Dutch hydro expertise is available to other nations. Low country engineers, hydrologists, and scientists are eagerly hired by coastal communities worldwide to advise and help authorities cope with rising sea levels.

After Hurricane Harvey tormented Houston in 2017, the Netherlands offered help to the city as well as other municipalities along the Gulf Coast. Sadly, not one town or county accepted the offer, continuing instead, to deny global warming and live deluded believing Harvey was a one-in-a-thousand year event. Not one jurisdiction agreed to invest in safety. The connection between ocean warming and Hurricanes Katrina, Sandy, Irma, Harvey, and Michael was ignored. Hurricane Travis appeared less than a decade after Harvey.

In the past, Holland ignored nature at its peril. So, too, will America's coasts experience what it's like to have salt-water property twenty miles inland from what was once the beach.

All of Florida will be underwater in 65 years. In 2030, Florida is in denial.

Until the United States government starts acting rationally and accepts the hard evidence of climate change, resultant sea level rise, and the reality of increasing numbers of mega-storms, millions of American people will be in harm's way. Millions of Americans will die.

Maryann Caton, 50 | Robt. MacKenzie, 62 | Jake MacKenzie, d.| World POP: 8.84 billion

---

Professor MacKenzie laid out his lesson plans. He nodded a welcome to the group, then began teaching his 8:00 a.m. class of undergraduates the art of clear, unambiguous scientific writing. Unexpectedly, he had lugged a globe with him to class. He placed it aside without telling its purpose.

"Good morning, class. Are you awake?" A few heads nodded "yes" although he also saw yawns. "Our intention today was to exchange papers and critique cach other's work. Did you all write your paragraphs describing the effects of the varicella-zoster virus? Nasty disease, that. I urge you all to get vaccinated."

Heads nodded, but faces looked perplexed wondering where he was going.

"I changed my mind about what we're going to do today. If you own a wee muc, you get to decide if it lives or dies. Since I'm the swineherd, that's my privilege. So put away your chicken-pox essays, we'll look at them next time."

MacKenzie saw questioning frowns. Someone asked, "What's a wee muc?"

"A piglet," he said with a crooked smile.

The class groaned, then laughed.

"Instead," MacKenzie went on, "I want to discuss the term 'cliche.' You've all been taught to avoid using them like the plague. *Like the plague* . . . that's a cliche. But as sure as hell's bells you know what *like the plague* means. So cliches can serve a useful purpose.

"Other parts of speech are usually frowned upon if overused, especially in science writing. They include similes. An example: 'The chicken-pox oozed like Niagra Falls.' And then there are metaphors. A metaphor is a word or phrase used to describe a noun or verb for which it is not applicable. An example: 'Her laugh was infectious.' Let's face it, nobody gets sick laughing unless you've overdone it with beer."

More heads bobbed understanding, especially when beer was mentioned.

"Throughout your schooling, you've been advised to limit these parts of speech in your writing. That's because in an attempt to make writing elegant, people overuse them. The thing is, in science writing we rarely use them, assuming dry, overly objective prose is preferable. Often that's the case. But there are exceptions. First, I'll show you a typical science description."

MacKenzie handed out a printed sheet containing one paragraph. It was the introduction to a medical diagnosis and cure.

After ingesting capsaicin ($C18H27NO3$) infused capsicun annuum with a basic secondary amine (pKe of 3), the subject, who presents Barrett's syndrome, suffered a bout of reflux esophagitis, precipitated by chronic regurgitation of gastric acid in the stomach lumen causing a temporary rise of ph in the blood known as 'alkaline tide.'

He hesitated allowing the class time to decipher the handout.

"Now, lads and lassies, that paragraph is perfectly fine for a gastroenterologist reading a lab report. But how does an everyday Joe—by the way, *everyday Joe* is a cliche—make sense of it?"

It was too early in the day for students to risk speaking out. MacKenzie knew they would wait for his explanation. Often the answers he wrote on a white board were hilariously simplistic.

"It's early, so I was sure no one would speak up. I'm going to write a simple sentence everyday Joes and Janes will understand." In cursive he wrote:

**After eating too many spicy tacos,
the subject had heartburn.**

His sentence resulted in loud laughter. The class was wide awake at last.

He continued. "I'm not advocating that my short version is what an internist needs to prescribe medication or offer a course of treatment. Clearly, doctors must have precise diagnoses to craft plans for healing. But for the general public, who long ago abandoned their chemistry sets for jogging and yoga, my sentence is understandable. In fact, it's so simple, it spells out a common sense action plan: don't eat spicy foods; use antacids for relief; limit alcohol consumption; don't recline supine after a meal; when in bed, use pillows to elevate your head to keep digestive acids in your gut, not in your esophagus.

"Now I'm going to contradict myself. Having advocated keeping things simple, here's a situation where details were important." Mac distributed another handout.

For a man the president's age, his overall health is excellent. His LDL was a bit elevated but manageable. I recommend that he lose ten or fifteen pounds and add a program of vigorous exercise to his daily schedule.

MacKenzie explained. "From what I've advocated, usually this would be a perfectly good statement to tell the general public about an average person's health. It's simple, easy to understand. But in this case, since we're talking about the man who was leader of the free world, in my opinion more information was necessary. The results of all the tests President Trump allegedly took did not need to be published. But a more complete statement seemed warranted.

"Here are tests that usually are given in a thorough physical exam." He wrote on the whiteboard:

Tests for Biomarkers of Arterial Inflammation

LP-PLA2   C-CRP   Fibrinogen   FERRITIN
GGTP   Microalbumin/ Creatinine ratio-urine random
H Pylori Ab IGG   F2-Isoprostanes   Oxidized LDL
Serum Myeloperoxidase   Uric Acid   TMAO
ADMA/SMA

"It would have been silly," he explained, "to bombard the public with the results of this battery of tests. But a more specific statement about the president's health would have been insightful. Incontrovertibly, he had heart disease, but the reality of his condition was glossed over. In my opinion, here's the statement that should have been issued." He distributed a second handout.

The president's health is what would be expected for a person his age, especially considering his dietary and exercise habits. He has coronary atherosclerosis—heart disease. His LDL is 131; a score of 100 or below is the goal. It is unknown if his carotid arteries, abdominal aorta, and peripheral vessels are affected. A regimen of exercise and a healthier diet have been prescribed.

"So, lads and lassies," MacKenzie wrapped up, "this is a case where more information, not less, would have been better. Not every test needs mentioning, but a more detailed statement was called for."

The class nodded their apparent understanding, although he was certain they didn't know where he was heading next.

He changed direction. "Has anyone heard the term 'canary in a coal mine'?" He called on a student who had raised her hand.

"Yes, I know. In the old days, miners had a caged canary with them in the tunnels. The bird was a CO_2 monitor. If the air was going bad from toxic gases, the bird died. They are very sensitive. When the canary dropped, the miners knew they'd better get out fast."

"Exactly. That's good," commended MacKenzie. "Even though it's a cliche, scientists have begun using the term 'canary in a coal mine' as a warning to let people know something bad is about to happen. It's a verbal signal everyone understands. And it applies to what's happening in the world every day, every hour, every minute. In my taco story, what's the 'canary in the coal mine'?"

Unexpectedly, this time many hands shot up. MacKenzie selected a student.

"Knowing you have Barrett's Disease. The disease itself is the warning. As a result of a canary in your esophagus, don't eat spicy food. Tacos are dangerous."

The class laughed again. The student correctly, if comically, identified the canary.

"There are signals," said MacKenzie, "let's call them

'canaries in a coal mine' that Earth systems are unravelling. I'll list a few. Average annual global temperatures have increased every year since 2014. As a result, arctic tundra is thawing faster than ever recorded. As the permafrost disappears, methane emissions accelerate. The large ice shields in Greenland and Antarctica are disappearing. They're being undercut by meltwater. Sea levels are rising at measurable rates; worldwide fresh water sources are disappearing as a result of salinization; drought is gaining a foothold on a wider swath of the Earth; drought leads to mega-fires; mega-fires add to air pollution; greenhouse gases are rising as fossil fuels continue to be burned. The list goes on and on."

A few students had been scribbling notes, others used machines to record his words.

"In the 'canary' category is a tiny mollusk called the sea butterfly. There are trillions of them. They are part of the ocean food chain. They're losing their shells due to ocean acidification. Lost shells mean death. If they disappear, so will scores of other species, including all large fishes, marine birds, and penguins. Sea butterflies are, figuratively, the ocean's 'canaries in the coal mine.'"

The silence in the classroom was loud. MacKenzie sensed his group was uneasy.

"You all know about the devastation Hurricane Travis inflicted on New Orleans. Never before in the last hundred years have so many lives been lost in a single natural event. And I think you know the number of named mega-storms has increased since 2017. These are all events, easy to catalogue, easy to understand. But by now, these events have become identifiable trends, also easy to understand. No longer should we ignore trends. You can see how climate is trending. It's not good. Climate trends are now 'canaries in a coal mine.'"

MacKenzie focused on the faces of his students. "In other years, in other schools, I've used my globe to begin a class. I think it's a dramatic prop to help get my point across." He retrieved the globe and held it over his head.

"Today I'm using it at the end of my lesson. I want to convey the fragility of our little blue-green marble. If we ruin the Earth, we end our existence."

MacKenzie saw grim faces staring at him. A male student appeared to be sniffling. A female had buried her face in her hands. It was deathly quiet. He wondered if he had been too graphic. It was time to bring the lesson to a close.

"This is my home," he said, indicating the Earth globe. "This is your home. This is the home of everyone who ever lived. This is the home of everyone who will live in the future. This is the only home we have."

2031

Economics Explained

WORLD MARKETS STRUGGLE TO REGAIN FOOTING
AFTER CRASH. GERMANY'S BERNHARD HONHOFF
WEIGHS IN ON FUTURE GLOBAL ECONOMIC PROSPECTS

February 15TH--21ST 2031

How Lessons From A Hollywood Movie Could Have Saved Wall Street

By Bernard Honhoff | bhonhoff.com

Sebastian Junger's 1997 nonfiction book, *The Perfect Storm,* chronicled the confluence of three North Atlantic meteorological anomalies that merged to form a killer hurricane in 1991. The ensuing maelstrom resulted in the tragic loss of a fishing vessel with all hands. Ignoring clear calls to retreat, the Gloucester trawler, Andrea Gail, plunged ahead and was swallowed by a monster wave.

World market manipulators would have been well served to have read the book or seen the movie and applied the story's three warning signs to the arcane science of economics. The first signal was a weather condition resulting in an atmospheric glut of humidity. Condition two was the merging of three low air pressure weather systems plunging barometers to millibars rarely seen. The third condition was human greed. Let's fish! Full speed ahead! Ignore common sense.

Global economies tanked following last year's crash of the United States markets which were glutted by the overproduction of fossil fuels. A deflationary trade war among the United States, China, Europe, and Russia resulted in wide fluctuations of the price of consumer goods and services coupled with stagnant or falling incomes. The economic storm was made perfect by the manipulation of currency markets by foolish hedge fund managers. Three risky speculative practices merged to plunge the world into a deep new recession. Millions of consumers forgot the lessons of the first Great Depression. Avoid risky investments and have cash on hand to weather a storm.

Maryann Caton, 51 | Robt. MacKenzie, 63 | Jake MacKenzie, d. | World POP: 8.87 billion

---

Maryann and Rob were dinner guests at her brother's home in Louisville. Fred frequently invited the MacKenzies to social gatherings in an effort to take their minds off the loss of Jake. He was especially solicitous about his sister's welfare. After the accident, she constantly questioned her own complicity in the tragedy. After all, she had allowed her son to be introduced to the sport as a child.

At camp in New Hampshire and at the Dalton School in New York City, Jake had learned climbing fundamentals by scaling indoor walls. But he was always safely attached to a rope by a counsellor or teacher. The gym floor was covered with crash pads—just in case. Maryann came to believe that Jake's death on the First Flatiron was the result of overconfidence built up over years of climbing, when little or no danger was lurking at the next move.

Four years after Jake's death, Maryann appeared to be on the mend. Fred noticed a brightening in her outlook, a bit more bounce to her step. She was playing tennis again, and despite her responsibilities as a principal at **Pearl 2 Pine**, she continued to be involved in Boulder's homeless campaign as a representative of the Boulder Association of Compassionate Conservatives. Four tiny home communities were now up and running. All were the result of his sister's vision and determined grit to make her idea a reality.

"It's too cold to grill the salmon outside," said Fred after the MacKenzies had arrived. "Instead Lois is poaching it in the oven." He uncorked a bottle of chardonnay.

"Nibbles are in the living room," added Lois. She hugged Annie and Rob then hung up their coats. "I'll be there in a minute. Fred's got the wine."

Annie and Rob settled into chairs. The gas fireplace radiated heat. Fred carried in the wine and glasses on a tray. "I'm practicing my wait-staff skills," he said, balancing the load. "I may get a job in a restaurant when I retire." He poured, chuckling at his hollow promise.

Abruptly, Annie set her glass down and stood. She circled the coffee table. Directly across the room was a bookcase. A familiar shape was posed on a shelf. It was a wire sculpture of a contortionist in a box. Unmistakably, it was wire art crafted by Sandy Callendar. She felt her pulse quicken.

"Fred," she asked, "where did this sculpture come from?"

"It's nice, isn't it? Jeannie brought it home a few weeks ago. She said an artist on Pearl Street gave it to her."

Annie's eyebrows raised when she heard Fred's explanation. "The artist gave it to her? She didn't buy it?"

"Apparently not. She has so little money she hasn't been able to afford a tattoo. In this case, poverty's been a blessing." He laughed.

Months earlier Annie learned that Callendar was not chosen through the lottery to be a tiny home owner. There were too few single person units to meet the demand. Nevertheless, she continue to see him on the mall selling his creations. As far as she could tell, he was doing well.

Lois joined them. "I heard what Fred told you. It might be my imagination, but that little toy seems to have some good karma. Jeannie's been smiling more—she's even been fun to be around."

"Did she say anything about the artist?" asked Annie.

"No . . . except that he's very talented. She compared him with Alexander Calder. I wouldn't know. I'm unfamiliar with Calder."

Annie acted surprised. "Really? Don't you remember the big mobile at the Pittsburgh airport? Hanging from the ceiling? That's a Calder."

"Oh, of course! You're right. But I didn't know he made tiny sculptures. I thought all of his were large."

"Remember the Botanical Gardens?" hinted Fred.

Lois thought for a moment. "How stupid of me. Excuse my memory. Yes. About ten years ago we saw his work in Denver."

Fred gently corrected her. "Fourteen years ago, honey."

"Cripes, you're right." She shook her head at the realization that years seemed to be passing at increasing speed. "Anyway," continued Lois, "that little toy is like a lucky talisman. Since it's been here, it seems like I have my daughter back."

❖

"It's a bloody dreck day. Be happy you're inside, warm and dry."

MacKenzie allowed his students to remove their wet parkas and settle in before beginning his lesson.

"It's raining here at 5,400 hundred feet, but I'm sure you saw it was snowing at the top of the Flatirons. That means the Continental Divide is getting a good blanketing. If Colorado high country doesn't get a thick snowpack, we're all going to starve."

"Why's that, Dr. Mac?" A student in the front row looked skeptical.

"Snow melt keeps the Colorado River flowing. River water irrigates the crops in the southwest—California, Arizona—even into Mexico. Those areas are vegetable and fruit producers. They're just as vital to our well being as the midwest breadbasket. We need vegetables as much as grain. So, thank the snow gods."

MacKenzie continued talking but headed in another direction. He surprised the class.

"Up to now, your writing assignments have focused on hard science issues. By that I mean science branches where measurements are made, trends are identified, and conclusions are drawn based on collected data. What we've done in this class is practice writing about discoveries in clear, unambiguous prose."

Heads nodded in agreement. MacKenzie sensed that some students were thinking . . . *yeah, okay . . . so now what?*

"Today we're going to discuss one of two fields of study I call 'soft sciences.' These are theories about why people behave the way they do. In both cases, collecting data is nearly impossible, because the subjects are fickle human beings willing to change their minds on any whim. As I said, these sciences are based on theories, nothing more."

Students who had wondered, *now what?* were about to have their curiosities quenched.

"One field is political science," explained MacKenzie. "The word 'politics' comes from Greek and means 'citizens of a community.' Another way of saying it is 'the affairs of the people.' Politics are influenced by the philosophies people hold. The philosophies have been written about by a diverse bunch of thinkers like Aristotle, Machiavelli, Karl Marx, Margaret Thatcher, and Barack Obama. Dozens of theorists have taken a stab at explaining how the affairs of people work, or don't work, or might work, or could work, if only the principles they espoused were applied. Am I clear, or has my babble put you back to sleep?"

He saw smiles and heard laughter, so continued.

"But today we're going to consider a different soft science— economics. The field of economics is as fraught with ambiguity and uncertainty as politics. Economics is often referenced as a science, especially by economists seeking legitimacy. However, unlike chemistry or molecular biology, evidence of economic certainty is impossible."

MacKenzie let his generality sink in before proceeding. "Who knows what the word 'economics' means?" he asked.

Four students thought they knew and raised their hands. One was chosen to respond. "Economics is about money, the stock market, interest rates."

"Okay, thank you. Any other ideas?"

"Buying and selling."

"Aye. Anyone else?"

"GNP—the Gross National Product."

MacKenzie nodded. "All your answers fit within the overarching umbrella of economics, but all are sub-categories. As with the word 'politics,' the word 'economics' has its root in the Greek language. It means the science of household management." The students looked doubtful.

"Years ago, high schools offered classes in home economics. Unfortunately, instruction often narrowly focused on specific skills like baking pies, sewing, setting a table, and managing children. In those days home economics was aimed at young women likely to become homemakers and mothers a few years down the road. How many of you had home economics in high school?"

No one raised a hand. Finally a student spoke out. "We had a course in nutrition. And there was cooking—if you were interested in the restaurant business. But nobody sewed. Everybody bought their clothes." The class laughed.

"Exactly," said MacKenzie. "How much more relevant instruction would have been back in the day, if students had learned the importance of saving, how to budget, how to invest, how to balance a checkbook." He hesitated checking their attention. "Then something came along that changed everything," he said with a snicker. "Care to guess what it was?" No response. MacKenzie filled in the blank.

"Credit Cards. All of a sudden hard cash melted away in favor of plastic. Once credit cards became universal, all the thoughtful planning home economics should have taught became moot. Now people spend more than their means. Card companies give detailed monthly reports. But despite transparent account knowledge and the burden of personal debt, credit card debt is a trillion and a half dollars. Households are overextended. People haven't saved for a rainy day—like this one, today." He chuckled.

"When you write about economic issues, you're going to be tempted to become verbose. You're going to be faced with the problem of explaining why people behave the way they do where money is concerned. And your explanation will only be plausible until some event occurs that requires people to change their behaviors.

"I want you to take ten minutes and write a definition of economics. Make it as concise as you can. Remember, our goal is to make science writing easy to understand. We'll share a few before we head out into the rain."

As the class worked, MacKenzie patrolled the aisles looking over shoulders. He saw they were having difficulty with the task.

"Okay, lads and lassies, time's up. Any volunteers?"

Hesitating, a few spoke out.

"Economics is the study of how humans behave when faced with competing choices."

MacKenzie nodded. "Not bad, lass. That's a good answer. Anyone else?"

"Economics is the science of human behavior when humans have abundant resources or are faced with scarcity."

"Excellent! Any more?" "Economics is a theory of world domination by nations competing for limited land and finite resources."

"Aye, they're all good responses, folks. But I'm going to write on my whiteboard the most simplistic definition I can think of that is the root of all your definitions. Your definitions are longer variations of mine." He turned to the whiteboard and wrote:

Economics is about supply and demand.

"That's it my friends," he explained. "All economic theory is about commodities that humans need or want. When humans face dwindling resources they need—like water, food, shelter, space to live and thrive—they compete for those needs. If possible, humans barter one need for another. But shortages often lead to war.

"More problematical are human 'wants.' This gets into theories about greed, domination, and what exactly is the difference between a 'need' and a 'want.' We may want a limousine, but we don't need one. We may want a large family, but we don't need one. In North America, for example, we no longer need big families to run farms or businesses or to care for us when we are elderly. Automation and social welfare programs have eliminated those needs. Now no reason exists to want them, either, other than greed.

"If someday you tackle a writing chore to explain an economic issue, think KISS—Keep it simple, stupid. Condense your essay into as few words as possible. Wrap your premise around one theory—human economic behavior is predicated on supply and demand."

The MacKenzies and Catons had a table waiting for them on a Saturday evening at Farmstand, a field to kitchen restaurant in Niwot, fifteen miles north of their homes in Boulder and Louisville. Vegetables were locally grown and meats were free from growth inducing hormones. Cattle and bison grazed on native grasses on the restaurant's pasturage. Poultry was raised free range. MacKenzie was always amused visualizing a cowboy in full regalia chasing un-cooped chickens with a lasso. He thought back to his childhood in Scotland where lads would try to invent the most ingenious trap to snare a haggis. There were no successes, of course. Everyone knew the joke that haggises were very shy and elusive.

They settled in, ordered drinks, and were given menus. Maryann noticed Lois fidgeting, an annoyed scowl on her face.

"Damn!" she said. "Where are my glasses? Fred, did I leave them at home?"

"No, honey. You put them in your purse. Remember?"

"Oh, yes," she said, finding them. "How forgetful of me."

"That's all right, dear. You've had other things on your mind. Now check out the menu. They have sea scallops, your favorite."

"Are they the little ones? I don't like the little ones."

"No, these are big."

"Oh, good."

It seemed to Maryann that her brother was patiently solicitous toward his wife, as if this scene had been played out before. She made a mental note to ask Rob if he noticed the incident.

"It's good getting together again," said Rob. "How are the girls?"

"We just got an email from Lindsay," said Fred. "Second year law school at Rutgers is going well."

Annie smiled her pleasure. *Another lawyer in the family,* she thought.

"And Jeannie is as happy as a hamster these days. Something's up with her, but we don't know what it is. Much of her life is a secret. It's amazing how twins can be so different."

"Jeannie has more of those wire toys," added Lois.

"They're art, honey," said Fred, "not toys."

They sipped their drinks. The waiter appeared and took their orders. Lois ordered the scallop special.

"So tell me, sister. How's your homeless crusade progressing? I know Jake's Place is up and running, but what about the other three?"

Annie smiled. She briefly thought of all the time and energy it had taken over many years to make her vision a reality.

"Everything's going well," she said. "Thirty-two tiny homes are now part of Boulder's homeless plan. And Erie, Lafayette, and Longmont have started their own projects. Each town has its own sponsor. Do you remember who was Boulder's sponsor?"

"The Boulder Association of Compassionate Conservatives?"

"Exactly. They underwrote the whole project."

"I don't know the details about how it works," admitted Fred.

"Annie can fill you in on that," said Rob. "She knows every detail down to page number, paragraph, and sentence." He chuckled and touched her hand.

"What do you want to know?" she asked.

Fred considered for a moment. "I know units are initially awarded based on a lottery. I know residents take a mortgage. And I know owners are obliged to pay off the mortgage with a percentage of their income."

Maryann nodded. "Yes, they pay five percent of their monthly earnings."

"How many years does the mortgage run? Twenty years? Thirty years?"

"It's open ended. There's no time limit for repayment."

"Really? That ought to take some pressure off," said Fred. "How are the units priced? I assume valuation is based on size."

"Correct. A set value was established by the BACC. It's separate from market pressures. BACC owns the land and acts, de facto, as the mortgagee. Prices range from fifty thousand for a single person unit to one hundred thousand for the largest."

"It's a clever manipulation of supply and demand," added Rob.

Annie agreed. "There's a demand for the little beauties, but at this time supply is limited. BACC is planning to add more."

Salads were served. Fred shared his with Lois.

"One thing I don't understand," said Fred, "is what happens if an owner moves? What happens to his or her equity? Does BACC broker the deal? How does it work?"

Annie nodded her head understanding Fred's puzzlement. "If someone decides to move, they can list their unit for the amount of equity they've built up, plus one percent to cover maintenance and any upgrades.

"So, for example, if a couple wants to sell their two-person unit valued at seventy-five thousand, they can list it for the yearly amount they paid times the number of years of occupancy plus one percent of the unit's worth. If the couple had a combined income of forty thousand, each year they are obligated to pay two thousand. In three years six thousand would have accumulated. Then add one percent of the unit's value—seven hundred fifty dollars. It all adds up to an asking price of six thousand seven hundred fifty dollars."

Fred listened intently, Lois looked lost. Rob sat back admiring his wife's business acumen.

"Buyers have the option to pay the seller outright or finance a new mortgage through BACC. If they pay the owners directly, the mortgage is reduced by that amount. In the scenario I described, a seventy-five thousand dollar mortgage becomes a sixty-eight thousand, two hundred fifty dollar loan.

"It's a bit complicated, but the plan insures that owners of good faith have a chance to recoup their investment. BACC makes no money on the transaction, except interest generated by holding mortgage payments in escrow."

Fred's brow furrowed as he tried to follow Annie's explanation. "Complicated," he mumbled.

Rob laughed. "It's the science of economics. It all follows a predictable pattern, except when it doesn't."

Annie nodded. "It's an unusual arrangement, but one

that evolved out of good intentions. BACC is helping needy folks without worrying about getting a direct return on their investment."

Meals were served. Lois looked puzzled. "I thought I ordered little scallops."

"No, honey," Fred reassured her, "only big ones were on the menu."

She suddenly became anxious. "Where are my glasses?"

"On the top of your head, dear. You pushed them up after reading the menu."

She relaxed and smiled. "Of course. How silly of me. These scallops look delicious."

Maryann sighed. "I felt like Harriet yesterday, trying to solve a mystery." She was sitting on the edge of the bed watching Rob button his plaid shirt.

"Who's Harriet?" he asked. He was talking to her reflection in the mirror. At the age of fifty-one she retained her pixie-like beauty. Her eyes had regained their sparkle after years mourning Jake's death. She was on the mend, he sensed, with a renewed purpose to her life shepherding homeless initiatives through Boulder County politics. Jake's memory would always be in her heart, he knew, but now there was room for other passions.

"Who's Harriet?" she echoed. "You've never heard of *Harriet the Spy*? It was one of my favorite kid books."

"For me, it was *Rob Roy* and *Ivanhoe*," said Rob.

She laughed. "Of course, Scottish classics. I should have known. Anyway, Harriet was made into a movie. It's about an eleven year old girl in New York City who's curious about everything and writes convoluted stories. Her stories remind me of what Jake wrote when he was about Harriet's age. Remember the one about Pop Ular and Ann Knee?" She laughed. "It had so many twists and turns, I couldn't follow it."

Rob smiled and nodded. "Aye. He wrote that when we were in Scotland. He could barely wait until we got home, so he could read it." Rob fiddled with his cuffs trying to button them. "So, you were sleuthing like Mata Hari. What were you investigating?" He turned to Annie and held out his arms. "I can't get these bloody things done. Help . . . please!"

She loved the fact that her husband the scientist could act like a helpless boy at times. "Loose or tight cuff?" she asked.

"Loose cuff. It's easier to see my watch."

"Do you have to be somewhere?"

He nodded. "After you button me up, I'm going to lie down and pull you with me. We need a morning cuddle."

"Rob!" she giggled with mock annoyance. "I've got chores to do."

"They can wait, Harriet. Tell me about your spying."

They flopped back on the bed. Maryann stared upward, as if her story was written on the ceiling. "On my way to work yesterday, I saw Jeannie and Sandy Callendar walking west on the Pearl Street Mall. They were holding hands. They didn't see me—they were heading toward 12th Street. I was a block away behind them going to my office."

Rob turned and faced her. He propped his head up. "Really? Are you sure it was them?"

"Yep, without a doubt."

"Och! That is big news."

She continued. "He didn't have a backpack. He was carrying a small duffle— presumably with his art. They looked like all the other tourists. I was amazed."

"Did you tail them, Harriet?" Rob was amused but curious.

"I did. I'm embarrassed to admit it." She thought for a moment arranging the details. "They crossed 12th, then turned right on 11th. There's an out-of-the-way coffee shop near Pine. He kissed her goodbye then continued north toward Mapleton Hill. I went up to the store. I've never been inside. It's called Joe n' Mo. They sell exotic coffees and teas. You know what those shops are like—a little bit of everything. Apparently, Jeannie works there."

"Lass! What a discovery! Your brother's child has been hiding in plain sight. Should we tell Fred?"

"I don't think so. Let's invite Fred and Lois to lunch on the Mall, our treat. Afterwards, we'll stroll around and check out the businesses on the side streets. We'll tell them there are always surprises waiting to be discovered in Boulder. Finding Jeannie at work ought to be the biggest surprise of all."

2032

Naturally

THE MONTHLY JOURNAL OF SCIENCE AND NATURE

AGRICULTURE

Failure of 2031 Apple Crop Linked to Collapse of Bee Colonies

April, 2032

BY JEFF ZHANG

The Attorneys General in Washington, New York, Michigan, Pennsylvania, and California have filed class action lawsuits against the Bayer and Dow Chemical Companies in the U.S. and Mitsui Chemicals and Nippon Soda in Japan. This is the result of the catastrophic nationwide apple crop failure in 2031, due to the use of the pesticide neonicotinoid, sold under various product names. The suit alleges the companies knew the pesticide was harmful to crop pollinators such as honeybees (Apis mellifera) and bumblebees (Bombus). As a result of bee colony collapses, 2031 apple production was off 83% from normal annual yields.

Neonicotinoids are not used to combat apple tree diseases like apple scab and apple canker. These conditions can often be ameliorated through chemical-free green practices such as thinning, pruning, and soil amendment. Using a dormant spray is recommended, but any chemical spray is potentially a human carcinogen. Daminozide (Alar), a plant growth regulator, was banned in 1989 on food crops, but is still legal for use on non-food plants. Since then, apple tree sprays have been formulated to not affect humans, if apples are thoroughly washed before consumption. But, like Alar, neonicotinoids are used to combat insect depredation of shade trees and ornamentals. Ambient environmental neonicotinoids are the cause of pollinator colony collapses.

Two years ago in Batavia, New York, shoppers at a Walmart Supercenter were astounded to find an estimated forty thousand bumblebees dead or dying in the parking lot. It turns out the collapse was due to neonicotinoid poisoning after the city sprayed linden trees (Tilia), also known as basswood, to control aphids. Targeted spraying proved impossible. The effects of the poison reached a much larger sector of the insect community including pollinators. After years of chemical assault, bee colonies finally died en masse.

State economies will be hard hit. Many producers face bankruptcy. The price of apples is expected to soar as supply will not be able to meet demand. Apples are the basis of many commercial products including most fruit juices, sweeteners, packaged goods, and fruit preserves. Fresh fruit for consumption will be drastically limited.

"What did you think about that article I brought home—the one in *Naturally?*" Rob was slicing tomatoes for a caprese salad.

"It's sad. I read about the apple failure in the news. It's pretty scary." Annie arranged basil leaves on salad plates. "As I recall, there have been small bee colony collapses that go back fifteen years or so. Now the collapse is country-wide, and an important commodity has been affected—apples. Prices in the supermarket have skyrocketed."

"Aye, it was bound to happen sooner or later. Too many chemicals are going into the environment not to have an effect."

Annie shook her head trying not to appear discouraged, but nevertheless, sounded worried. "Is this another one of those 'canary in a coal mine' situations? Are we going to see more crop failures?"

"It's likely unless pesticides are reformulated to be safer. The industry has to be better regulated—get fossil fuel distillates out of pesticides, start using natural products like soap spray, onion and garlic spray, citrus oil and cayenne pepper, and introduce an ancient formula used by Indians—Neem. We need to kill and repulse destructive and disease carrying insects while not harming pollinators. You're familiar with all this. It'll be a challenge."

Rob cut pieces of feta cheese and layered them on the basil leaves in between the tomato slices. Meanwhile, Annie was preparing a sweet balsamic dressing.

"It reminds me of *Silent Spring*," she said, "Rachel Carson's exposé of the pesticide industry. Then it was about the harmful effects of DDT. Now the problem's neonicotinoids. Fortunately, DDT was banned in the 1970's, if I remember correctly. Thank goodness for the ban, or we wouldn't have magpies flying around squawking at us."

Rob laughed. "Sometimes those bloody corvids are too clever for their own good. Yesterday I saw one pick up a cigarette butt and fly away. If they start smoking, I'm going to take up hang gliding." He carried the assembled salads to the table. Annie dished out risotto.

"This year I'm planting squash and pole beans," he said. "I guess it's a gamble anything will produce without bees. But I know other pollinators are around—butterflies, moths, wasps, hornets—even common flies. I hope there'll be enough to do the trick."

"If other insects don't take over and fill the gap," she said, "we're sunk."

Rob agreed. "Aye. Maybe congress will get off their keisters and do some regulating. History shows that nature can bounce back, if given half a chance."

On the drive east to Louisville with Rob, Maryann saw bulldozed piles of soil, protruding utility boxes, and newly cut roads of sprawling housing developments under construction. Hay fields and pastures once filled with black angus cattle on either side of South Boulder Road had been erased. Denver's expansion coupled with Boulder's housing shortage resulted in the disappearance of rural scenes and small farms to accommodate Colorado's population explosion. The Front Range plains were being paved over.

Would there be enough potable water, she wondered, *to meet human demand in this semi-arid land?* And when climate change mega-storms unexpectedly dumped massive amounts of precipitation in the mountains and on the plains, where would the water go? Would Boulder's streets again become roaring rivers as torrents sluiced down the canyons tearing away roads and homes? That had happened in 2013 and again in 2023. "Once in every 500 year storms" were now predictable every ten years. All land in Boulder had been developed including marginal acreage on flood plains. Future storms promised widespread destruction.

South Boulder Road was always busy with rush hour traffic. When the MacKenzies moved to Boulder, Maryann remembered that usage slowed down in the middle of the day. Now, however, heavy traffic was constant except for the early hours of the morning. *Thank goodness for the time out*, she mused. *People had to sleep.*

Maryann recalled that Colorado's population was five million when they moved west. It was easy to remember because Rob was always talking about the dangers of unchecked population growth. Now it stood at over six million in the Centennial State with 8.5 million predicted by 2050. And in the City of Boulder, the number of full time residents had jumped to 130 thousand since the city had allowed buildings to grow taller than fifty-five feet high. When the university was in session, the number swelled to 180 thousand. No longer could one park downtown. Shuttles and bicycles became the dominant means of transportation in the city center. Views of the Flatirons from the Pearl Street Mall were blocked by sandstone faced, Italianate-style high-rises.

World population was about to hit nine billion, she knew. Where would it all end? She tried to swallow her pessimism by asking her husband a question about Lois.

"The last time we ate out with Fred and Lois, I noticed she was forgetful and repeating herself. Did you see it?"

Rob kept his eyes on the road as he approached the

McCaslin intersection, always a tricky spot with cars coming from the other direction turning left crossing the eastbound lane, while the marked bike lane edged toward the center of the road away from the shoulder. He checked his right side-view mirror, looking for a cyclist he had passed.

"Aye, lass, that I did. Every once in awhile it happened. It didn't seem to bother Fred, though. He was very patient with her."

Maryann nodded in agreement. "Yes, my brother's a good man." She stopped to consider for a moment. "But if something is going on, I wonder if he sees it. Sometimes living day to day with someone dulls your awareness of the problem. On the other hand, some people are astutely attuned to behavior changes in their mates . . . or anyone, for that matter. Do you know Cassie Pfister from my tennis group?"

Rob nodded. "Aye, she's the tall lady, right?"

"Yes. She notices everything—new clothes, if you look tired, a new sun spot on your cheek, a new hairdo. I wonder how she can keep her eye on the ball."

At 95th Street, Rob turned north, then almost immediately swung east into Louisville Commons. They wound through roads bordering the development's meandering golf course, finally reaching their destination. Fred and Lois's home had settled into its location with mature foundation plantings and columnar oaks lining the driveway. Rob figured development sidewalks probably led to a direct route out to the main road and bus service.

They entered the house through the garage. *Why didn't people use front doors?* Maryann wondered. They passed by a powder room and entered the kitchen. Maryann plunked down two bottles of wine—one red, one white. She was unsure what Lois was preparing. They hugged. Maryann related what she saw on the way up. They agreed traffic had gotten worse and was a continual problem.

Fred opened both bottles of wine knowing Rob preferred red, his sister, white. Long ago they discontinued matching wine color with menu offerings. If one liked pinot grigio with a hamburger, so be it. If red with chicken tenders fit one's taste, that was okay, too. They carried their glasses into the living room. On the way, Maryann noticed the table was set for six.

After sitting, they laughed at the futility of Colorado's football teams. Rob speculated the concussion issue may make football moot in a few years. Across the country, high schools were shutting down programs. "Why accelerate brain disfunction," he said, "before we have to deal with it as we age." Rob glanced at Lois, then at Maryann.

Lois mentioned a novel she was reading. For the moment she seemed to be in control of her memory, remembering the title and author.

"I love the book. It's been around for awhile, but it's still topical. It's called *Still Alice* by Lisa Genova. Fred bought it for me. The main character, Alice, and I are about the same age. But she's a professor. I'm a lowly housewife." She laughed at her self-inflicted disparagement.

"You're more than a housewife," said Fred, "you're my sweetheart."

Maryann and Rob looked at each other and smiled. Fred was his usual caring self. And his words of encouragement meant for Lois were equally applicable to the MacKenzies. They were each other's sweethearts and had been since their first date.

"The table's set for six," said Maryann. "Who else is coming? Do we know them?"

"Jeannie and a friend."

"Does her friend work in the same store? Three or four girls are always behind the counter."

Since discovering that Jeannie had a fulltime job at Joe 'n Mo, Fred and Lois had become closer to her, tolerating her breezy approach to life, happy their nonconforming daughter appeared to be maturing. But they still were in the dark about her private life, who were her friends, and where she stayed when she didn't come home at night.

"We don't know who she's bringing," said Fred. "They'll soon be here, and we'll find out."

Annie digested his words, then smiled. *I think I know who the mystery guest might be*, she thought. She looked at Rob. They traded nods. Apparently, both were on the same wavelength.

Maryann heard the hallway door open and the footsteps of the guests. Fred and Lois went into the kitchen to greet the arrivals. Now Maryann was one hundred percent sure who Jeannie's friend was. She heard the soft southern accent of a male voice. It was Sandy Callendar. She winked at Rob, who also had picked up on the clue.

The MacKenzies stood as Fred and Lois escorted Jeannie and Sandy into the living room. Lois was holding a bouquet. Her face was gleaming with happiness.

"Rob and Annie, this is Sandy Callendar," announced Fred.

Maryann grinned broadly. "Yes, we know Sandy. He had dinner with us a year or so ago. I was taken by his sculptures." She stepped forward and gave him a hug. As she expected, he smelled clean and fresh.

"Hi, Annie," said Sandy. "I figured you might be here after Jeannie told me about her family. It's great seeing you again."

Rob moved closer and extended his hand. "Good to see you again, laddie. What a nice surprise!"

Jeannie slipped her arm under Sandy's and looked at him with smiling eyes. "We've been seeing each other for some time," she said. "We have a lot in common. Sandy's become my best friend."

Rob couldn't contain his highland curiosity. "Are you sure you're only best friends? To my Scottish eye, you two look like a couple."

Maryann frowned at Rob's forwardness. He was as bad as she was—always coming straight to the point. She saw Sandy blush a Celtic pink. Jeannie kissed him on the cheek. "Yes, Uncle Rob. You could say we're a couple, and you'd be right."

Fred and Lois stood agape at the news. They were amazed that Rob and Annie seemed to know what was happening, while they were in the dark.

Lois was the first to speak. "Isn't Sandy a girl's name?" she asked, looking perplexed.

"It's a diminutive of Alexander," explained Rob.

"What does dimin . . . that word . . . mean?"

"Sandy's a shortened version of Alexander, honey. That's what it means." Fred gently squeezed her shoulder.

"Of course! I knew that!" She sounded relieved. "I'll check on dinner. Why don't you all sit at the table. There's a big bowl of mixed greens you can start with. I was going to make one of those . . ." she hesitated, thinking ". . . hotel salads. But apples are so damn expensive this year."

Annie tried to unravel the meaning of hotel salad, then understood. "That's a Waldorf salad, Lois. But I kinda like calling it a hotel salad." She chuckled.

Fred refreshed the MacKenzie's wine glasses. Sandy and Jeannie opted for water. Lois brought a platter of sliced pork tenderloin to the table. It was followed with a covered tureen of mashed sweet potatoes and a long bowl heaped with asparagus spears. The food was passed, plates loaded. Rob raised his glass.

"To my brother and sister in law . . . as usual the most bonny hosts. To the young lad and lassie . . . I'm happy you found each other. To my beautiful wife . . . I love you more than ever. Let's tip our glasses to a future filled with happiness. Sláinte."

"Sláinte!" everyone responded, respecting Rob's gaelic blessing.

Table small talk turned to the lives of the youngsters. "Are you two in love?" Lois asked bluntly.

Jeannie chuckled. "You're getting right to the point, aren't you, Mom?" She looked at Sandy. "Yes, we're in love."

"When are you getting married?" Lois persisted with her cross-examination.

"Whoa, slow down, honey," Fred scolded gently. "Don't be so forward. Jeannie admits they're a couple, but they need some room to breathe. It's a long way from dating to the altar. I'm sure if they get to the point of marriage, they'll let us know." He looked at his daughter for reassurance about his prediction. She nodded.

"I apologize for your mom's nosiness," he continued. He covered Lois's hand with his. "Recently she's become less inhibited about asking questions." He looked at Lois. "Am I right, dear?"

Lois frowned then brightened. "I suppose so. I just want to know. I'm nosey."

Maryann jumped in to give Lois support. "Are you living together?" she asked Sandy, much to Rob's surprise.

Sandy nodded. "Yes, on and off. We don't have permanent housing, so the only time we're under one roof together is when one of our friends is out of town and let's us stay at their place."

He looked at Fred to see if his confession had displeased

Jeannie's dad. Was their occasional cohabitation tolerated? Fred's face appeared soft and understanding.

"Sometimes I think living together before marriage ought to be the law," said Fred, nodding. "When Lois and I were dating, it was frowned upon. It even had an ugly name— 'shacking up.' Am I right, honey?"

"Yeah, I wanted to sleep with you."

Lois's blunt admission made everyone laugh. Maryann nodded but said nothing about the prenuptial eight months she and Rob had shared in her Connecticut home. Despite his insistence that they abstain from sex before they were married, she figured no one would believe her. Thinking back, their abstinence had been a miracle.

"What are your plans?" asked Maryann. *What a stupid open-ended question,* she thought.

Sandy looked at Jeannie as if seeking her permission to say more. She nodded. "We may get married someday," he said, "but first we have to find a home. That's where we are now— trying to decide what to do about housing."

Maryann spoke up. "If you're homeless, you still qualify for the tiny home lottery. When new communities open, you may be selected for a unit."

"That's what I thought," he said. "I'm still on the list, but something better has come along."

"What is it?" asked Annie. "Tell us."

Jeannie answered. "Two tiny homes are on the resale market. As you know, Aunt Annie, anyone considered homeless can buy them. Most homeless people haven't saved for a down payment. But we have."

"I hadn't heard units were opening up," Maryann said, looking surprised.

"We have a realtor looking out for us," explained Sandy.

"Yes, Aunt Annie. A two person unit is coming available at Frank's Field north of Valmont, and a three person unit is available now in Jake's Place. We're allowed to make an offer on both. Even though there's only two of us, we can buy a three person unit."

"You have enough money?" asked Lois. She looked both amazed and lost, as if the youngsters couldn't possibly have the necessary cash.

"Yes, Mom. If we combine our savings, we can buy either. We're leaning toward the larger unit to allow Sandy room to make his art. It has a bigger kitchen, too. Working at Joe 'n Mo, I've become a pretty good baker."

"Jeannie makes the best scones in Boulder," said Sandy, grinning at Rob.

"Wow! This really is exciting!" gushed Annie. She was brimming with happiness and anticipation at the thought her niece and Sandy might be living down the road at Jake's Place. It was the best news she had heard in years.

"If you need some extra cash, don't be afraid to ask us," said Rob. His Scottish frugalness had suddenly evaporated.

Maryann felt her heart swell with love for him. He had said exactly the right thing at exactly the right time.

"Same for us," agreed Fred. "We helped Lindsay with school—now's the time to help you." He stood and moved to Jeannie, kissing her on the cheek.

"Thanks, Dad, and you, too, Uncle Rob. But I think we can do it on our own." Her response surprised no one. It was typical for Jeannie. She had followed her own path since high school.

"Do we have enough money?" Lois asked Fred.

"Yes, dear. If they ask, we can help. No need to worry. We're rich." He patted her hand.

Relieved, Lois served dessert. Soon it was time for the youngsters to return to Boulder.

"Can we give you a ride?" asked Maryann.

"No, Aunt Annie. We'll take the bus. The next one's due out on 95th Street in thirty minutes."

"Are you sure, honey? It's getting dark."

"Yes, we're fine."

After Jeannie and Sandy departed, the Catons and MacKenzies sat around the table drinking coffee and reliving the meal conversation.

"It's hard to fathom," said Fred. "A romance has been blossoming under our noses all this time."

"They're in love," said Lois.

"Yes they are," agreed Annie. "I'm in happy shock to learn they might wind up as neighbors. The three person units in Jake's Place are really nice. There's more room inside than meets the eye."

"Much more," said Rob laughing. "Room for two adults and a bairn."

"What's a bairn," asked Lois, looking befuddled.

"A wee'un."

"Huh?"

"A baby, Lois. A bairn is a baby."

"Wouldn't that be nice," she said smiling, her face softening as if remembering a past memory. "I've always wanted to be a nana."

Traffic was less heavy on South Boulder Road when

the MacKenzies headed home. Maryann thought about the afternoon's events. She had mixed emotions about what she learned, although the news about her niece and Sandy Callendar outweighed her immediate concern for Lois. *Imagine*, she thought, *a relative and a lovely guy might become neighbors living in a tiny home community named in memory of my son.*

The tiny home community north of Valmont, Frank's Field, had been named for Frank Shorter, an Olympic marathon champion and long-time Boulder resident. Scott Carpenter Park on 30th Street honored the famous astronaut. It was Boulder's practice to honor residents who had contributed something to the city in action, deed, or spirit. She admitted to herself that the name Jake's Place was less about her young son and more about her. It was a "thank you" gesture for all the work she did championing the homeless.

Her thoughts returned to Lois. She was certain some sort of mental deterioration was at work, but exactly what, she wasn't sure. Lois was only two years older than she, not yet close to being considered elderly. Was *Still Alice*, the novel Fred gave her, the tip-off? Maryann knew the story was about early-onset Alzheimer's Disease. Had her sister-in-law been diagnosed with the condition or did her behavior show symptoms of something else?

"You must have seen the signs that something's up with Lois," she said to Rob.

"Aye, that I did. It was more pronounced today than the last time we were with her." Rob merged into the right lane preparing to turn north at 55th Street and begin the big sweep around the rec center heading toward Rim Rock Circle. "Without knowing what's going on," he continued, "we can't be sure." They crossed Ontario Place. "But to me it certainly looks like dementia of some sort."

Maryann nodded. "We must ask Fred. He may need help caring for her. And he needs to care for himself, too. He can be selfless to a fault."

"Aye, I agree."

They came to a stop behind the rec center to let a gaggle of Canada geese waddle across the road, heading to the center's pond. Horses no longer grazed around them behind pasture fences. The city had purchased the Hogan-Pancost property in 2018, implying it would not be developed because it was susceptible to flooding from the South Boulder Creek. Ten years later, however, mounting pressure for affordable housing resulted in the property turning into a development of mixed-use units on marginal land. Maryann saw lights in windows and wondered whether they'd go dark when the next so-called five hundred year flood inundated the area as predicted by engineers and hydrologists.

"Do you remember when Sandy came to our home for dinner, he had a noticeable limp?" Maryann brightened thinking about the young couple.

"Aye. I never asked him about it. But I didn't see it today. What do you think, love? Did the young man have a touch of gout?"

Maryann laughed. "Gout? I don't think so, Rob. That's an old man's disease. Today he barely touched his meat and had no wine. Those are triggers. I suspect he broke his toe. Maybe he kicked an ice block frozen to the ground." She chuckled remembering a Roxbridge incident. "That's what Jake did, remember?"

"Aye, he limped around for two months."

"He had that long middle toe—Morton's toe."

Rob nodded. "If Sandy and Jeannie move to Jake's Place,

you'll have a chance to ask him." He patted her leg, then they continued toward home, as the last bird cleared the road.

"I hope so," Maryann said wistfully. "I hope they buy that unit."

2033

Jeffersonian Jeffersonian Jeffersonian

AUTUMN 2033

World Population Reaches 9 Billion

| by Paul Baker | pbaker.com |

Defying demographic forecasts and trashing computer models, Earth's human population reached 9 billion in 2033, nine years earlier than predicted. As a result, behavioral scientists are rethinking theories associated with procreation. It was believed that birth rates would decline as living conditions grew harsher. Curiously, just the opposite occurred. After typhoon Anish flooded Bangladesh and large areas of coastal Sri Lanka, waters never receded. Coupled with worldwide sea level rise and mega-storm inundation, thousands of square miles of land are now permanently under water. Millions have been forced to move to higher ground. The largest mass migration in human history is underway.

Unless more catastrophes occur, experts believe human population will continue to grow, although at diminishing rates. Ten billion is predicted by 2050—11 billion by 2100. Much of the growth will take place in sub-saharan Africa. Kenya is growing by 2.7% annually compared with the world rate of 1.07%. But even though overall global rates are easing off, 96 million humans are added to the Earth's totals every year.

Maryann Caton, 53 | Robt. MacKenzie, 65 | World POP: 9.0 billion

---

"Here's a bloody sad article," said Rob. "But it confirms what we've known for a long time."

Maryann brought their filled coffee cups to the table. She sat down to dig into her Scottish breakfast staple—oatmeal. "Read it to me, honey. What does it say?"

Rob added raisins to his porridge. He began telling his wife the gist of the article rather than reading it. "Ever since the EPA reopened mines, coal extraction has continued in Colorado and Wyoming."

Maryann remembered when it happened. "It was the result of all that nonsense Trump promised years ago—clean coal—jobs for miners."

"Aye. But the industry replaced men with robots. No paychecks to issue—no benefits to worry about. Robots always show up on time for work."

Maryann nodded and thought about the road trip they had taken to see a surface mine in Montrose County. It was a huge black pit, a gaping maw, a scar on the landscape. And deep within the pit were Lego-like machines—drilling, scraping, loading, and transporting the product to the surface. At the time, she had counted one hundred fifty-one train cars on a siding, their hoppers filled with bituminous coal—soft, friable, sooty.

"Anyway," continued Rob, "Green Space has filed a new lawsuit against coal producers. They've joined forces with the ski industry."

Maryann interrupted, surprised. "What do you mean?"

"Ski resorts have been dealing with storms bearing much higher wind speeds than in the past. As a result, coal dust from distant mines is darkening snow slopes. It's ruining the state's premier industry. It's also affecting human health. The rate of asthma in mountain towns is skyrocketing."

"I've noticed that here in Boulder, too," said Maryann. "There are days when it's hard to breathe. Air particulates never seem to go back into the green healthy zone." She was referring to the Air Quality Index printed daily in the *Boulder Daily Reporter*. It rated the health danger from four pollutants: ground level ozone, particulates, carbon monoxide, and methane. The last pollutant, methane, had replaced sulfur dioxide and nitrogen oxide on the chart, when it was discovered that fracked wells were significant methane polluters as well as livestock flatulence.

"Be thankful you have your rescue inhaler," Rob reminded her. For eight months Maryann had been dealing with irritating lung congestion.

"I know. It's in the powder room." She hesitated, sipped her coffee. "So the slopes are turning black. How disgusting."

"Aye. And there's another twist to the story. Black snow absorbs the sun's heat. Vail can't make snow fast enough to replace what's melting. The industry's in jeopardy."

"What can be done, love?" She anticipated a technical answer from her husband, the scientist.

"It's simple, lass. No more fossil fuel extraction. Close the mines, plug the wells. We need to get to one hundred percent renewable energy. It's where Xcel is headed in Denver and along the Front Range."

"Also in Boulder?"

"You should know by now. That remains to be seen."

"Did you enjoy seeing the star turned on?" asked Maryann. "You said you've seen it once it was lit, but actually watching it come alive is, I think, a special treat—especially for Rob and me."

Sandy, Jeannie, and the MacKenzies were returning to Rim Rock Circle from the rec center soccer field where they had watched the Boulder Star switched on. It shone like a jewel gleaming in the bosom of the mountains. At 6:00 p.m. on Veterans Day their neighborhood was cold and dark. But a warm meal awaited at home. Annie had invited the Callendar-Catons to dinner after the lighting.

"I loved it, Aunt Annie," said Jeannie. "Knowing the history of the star within your family made it extra special. Sandy and I hiked up there this summer so he could see how difficult the climb is. I was up there when dad spoke at Jake's memorial service. The last stretch up from Flagstaff Road is a killer. I'm amazed you were able to do it in the dark."

Annie nodded, remembering. "Rob and I had flashlights. Jake wore his headlamp. We were younger then, too. I was thirty-seven. It seems like an eternity ago." She looked at Sandy. "You're not limping anymore. That's good."

"Limping? What do you mean?"

"When I first saw you downtown, you had a noticeable limp."

Sandy thought for a moment. "Oh, that's right. I haven't thought about it since then. I had an ingrown toenail."

"Ouch!" she said. "Well, that answers that. Rob thought you might have had a touch of gout. Did you see a podiatrist?"

"Couldn't afford it. I went to Emergency Care. They fixed it. It hurt like a copperhead bite."

"Really?" Maryann said, surprised. "You've been bitten by a snake?"

"Twice. I don't intend to make it three times."

Once inside, they warmed up with hot tea. Rob passed on oolong in favor of a wee dram of scotch. In twenty minutes they brought their drinks to the table where Crock Pot lamb stew was waiting.

Rob made his customary gaelic toast and then said the Selkirk Grace: *"Some hae meat and canna eat, and some wad eat that want it; but we hae meat, and we can eat, sae let the Lord be thankit."*

"It's one of the few times Rob acknowledges a higher authority," Annie explained, chuckling. She smiled at her guests. "I can't tell you how happy I am that you're living at Jake's Place. Imagine . . . my niece and her man are here in Keewaydin! Amazing!"

"What's Keewaydin, Aunt Annie?"

"That's this whole development, honey. Technically, Jake's Place isn't part of it since it's across the street. But for all intents and purposes, it is."

"What does the word mean?" asked Sandy. "It sounds Native American."

"Aye, you're right, lad," said Rob. "We didn't know what it meant, either. So I contacted my friend, Ursa Bent. It's an Ojibwa word. It means 'north wind.' The Ojibwas are mostly found in the northern tier of the midwestern states and into Canada. Sometimes they're known as the Chippewa. Whatever the name, their influence spreads far and wide. That's how Keewaydin made it to Boulder."

"And Longfellow used the word in his poem, *Song of Hiawatha*," added Annie.

"Aye, but it's too damn bloody long to read, let alone memorize it. We had to commit poems to memory when I was in school, but nothing that daunting." Rob took a sip of his drink.

Sandy laughed. "All I know are the first two lines: 'By the shore of Gitche Gumee / By the shining Big-Sea-Water.' I looked it up once. Gitche Gumee means Lake Superior."

"First Nation geography!" chuckled Maryann. "My, we're all so educated." She passed the rolls, then became serious.

"Have you seen the change in your mother, Jeannie? It has Rob and me worried."

"Yes, how could I not? I asked dad about it, and he confirmed my worst fears. She has Alzheimer's. It's sad, but there's nothing we can do about it except make her life as comfortable as possible and support my father."

"Aye, that's what we figured," said Rob.

"It's going to be up to me to help dad," said Jeannie. "Lindsay's staying in the east. She has a job lined up after law school."

"I'll help, too," said Maryann. She thought for a moment. "Have you considered being tested for a genetic link?"

"No . . . and I don't think I want to know."

Rob agreed. "It's a hard choice to make."

Jeannie smiled. "Sandy promised to stand by me no matter what. Right, dear?" She kissed him on the cheek.

"Forever, Jeannie."

"That's why I want to talk to you both," said Jeannie, looking serious. "Mom keeps asking me when I'm going to have a baby. She's desperate to become a grandmother. She still understands what that means. I don't know what to tell her. Dad tries to divert her attention, but she always returns to the baby question. What should I say?"

Maryann and Rob looked at each other, hoping the other

would have the answer. They were unable to immediately reply. Finally, Rob spoke.

"I think the answer's up to you, lass. If you think having a bairn is what you want, then tell her so. Say you're thinking about it, but you're not ready yet. Say you're saving money for a larger home. That may not be true, but a wee fib like that won't hurt her. But it gets more complicated, of course, if you don't want to bear a child."

"It sure does," said Maryann. "Telling Lois you don't want a baby could speed up her decline. It's fine to be undecided. It's fine to say 'someday.' But it's not fine to say 'someday' when you know it's never going to happen. Even dealing with a sick person, tell the truth. It's a matter of ethics."

"True," agreed Rob. "Always do the right thing. It can be difficult figuring out what the right thing is, but you can do it. I've seen you show great empathy toward your mum. That will help. All of us face thorny issues like this from time to time."

Rob left the table to get dessert. He had made a Scottish trifle, a deep bowl lined with sherry soaked sponge cake, the inside layered with whipped cream, strawberries, custard, and sliced almonds. Sometimes he used pistachios. It was a dessert fit for a . . . well . . . someone not concerned about his or her waist size.

"Having a baby, Uncle Rob . . . I have mixed feelings about it." Jeannie dug into her dessert. "All the things I've heard about climate change makes me wonder if bringing a child into the world is smart. What do you think?"

Rob looked at her sharply. "If you're asking me if you should have a child, I can't answer that. It's your decision alone . . . and Sandy's, too."

She nodded. "I know that. But you're the expert on these things. I need your opinion on what my baby might face."

Rob took a deep breath and slowly exhaled. He pushed his dessert bowl aside and turned to face her. He knew his news wouldn't be pleasant.

"First of all, a bairn will live among an ever increasing population. Know how congested it is downtown now?"

Jeannie nodded.

"It will only get worse. If you gave birth today, by the time your child is your age, there will be 10 billion earthlings." He tried to lighten the discussion. "But looking at you, lass, I don't think a wee bairn is imminent." He chuckled.

"Can't a bigger population thrive?" asked Sandy.

"Are societies thriving now?" asked Rob. He answered his own question. "There are some places where congestion is being dealt with. Most are in countries in the northern hemisphere. But in China, India, all of middle and central Asia, and Africa, human misery is mounting because of too many people. Let me try to be clear . . ."

"Being clear would be nice," said Annie, interrupting with a laugh.

"My wee wife wants me to get to the point." He sipped his drink. "People per se," he said, "are not the issue. It's what they need that's the problem. More people means a greater demand for resources. We need food. Arable land is being gobbled up by urbanization. We need water both to drink and quench crop appetites. Aquifers are drying up, and climate change has rendered rainfall unpredictable. Sometimes we have enough potable water. Then other times we're being flooded out, and not just from mega-storms, sea level rise is contributing, also."

He finished the last of his drink. "But perhaps the biggest modern day challenge is to supply the 21st Century with enough energy to run all its gadgets. That includes power for transportation, electricity for communication, heat and AC for our homes. The list is never ending. And here's the thing. The result of producing power is pollution, especially carbon dioxide. We've exceeded what earth scientists considered to be the tipping point—400 ppm. We're now at 415 ppm. Even if population rates were to drastically decline beginning next year, the snowball effect of global warming would continue to . . ." he hesitated, shaking his head, ". . . frankly, no one knows."

Sandy remained quiet digesting Rob's information. Jeannie turned to Maryann. "Aunt Annie, with what you know, would you have a child now?"

"No, honey, I would not. I loved my son, but like you, he was a product of another era when less was known about the future. Scientists had hunches, of course, but the average person went on their way largely ignorant. But don't let my answer tell you what to do. It's your choice. If you raise a child with love, educate him about the future and give him coping skills, it could work. At this point in my life, I'm too old to deal with it."

"Thanks for your honesty, Aunt Annie, but you're not that old. What about you, Uncle Rob?"

"From what I said, you ought to be able to guess my answer, lass. Annie thinks she's too old to mother another baby. If we had a child I'd be old enough to be its granddad. A wee'un needs a young daddy, not an old geezer." He chuckled. "But it's not age that's the determining factor for me. At this point, a new child will face a world where systems are in collapse. I wouldn't want that for any bairn."

2034

ID⊙DA

THE MAGAZINE OF THE INFECTIOUS
DISEASE DEFENSE ASSOCIATION®

WHO: Humans Are Being Consumed By Consumption

by Winslow Greenfield, MD, PhD

March 2034

Overview

Pandemics have been predicted for twenty-five years and are now here. Infectious and insect borne diseases are beginning to ravage the human species with the appetite of the Grim Reaper. Unless government funding for disease research is restored to 2020 levels, it is probable that millions of Americans will die from one of the more than 40 high mortality infections. A concentrated effort of nations led by the World Health Organization (WHO) is vital to prevent billions from perishing worldwide.

Mosquitos

Poisons and natural predators have been unable to stop the spread of mosquito borne illnesses. The Zika and West Nile viruses are at work on all continents. Global warming has rendered the Arctic and Antarctic regions perfect for mosquito breeding. The cool-climate *Culicidae* bonanza has joined swarms typically found in temperate zones. The genus *Aedes*, an especially insidious vector, is resistant to all forms of known poisons, but up to now, can be held at bay with mint infused DEET-based repellents.

Ticks and Fleas

As human populations grow, rodent populations multiply alongside. People generate mountains of plant and animal refuse, a feast for common rats, field mice, and giant Norwegian brown rats. Rodents transport ticks and fleas. Both insects attack humans. The result is a mounting number of Lyme Disease sufferers, widespread outbreaks of Spotted Fever, and small clusters of bubonic plague limited, so far, to the slums of third world cities and the American West, with most US cases clustered in Arizona, New Mexico, and Colorado.

Infectious Bacterial and Viral Diseases

While the spread of disease by insects is a cause of worldwide alarm, the explosion of human transmitted disease is apocalyptic. The threat of flu is more severe now than at any time in modern history. The Spanish Flu epidemic of 1918-1920 resulted in 50 million deaths. With humans more heavily concentrated inland due to coastal flooding, another flu epidemic would result in human loss by degrees of magnitude. Stanford University's

Carl Rutherford predicts another flu outbreak could cause 3 billion or more deaths, one-third the Earth's present population.

The list of bacteria and virus caused diseases reads like an epidemiology textbook.

- **Bacterial**: anthrax, tick borne infections, typhus, syphilis, legionellosis, bubonic plague, tuberculosis, MRSA
- **Viral**: hepatitis, encephalitis, herpes, HIV, MERS, smallpox, rubella, measles.

Sexually transmitted viral diseases are proving hard to cure due to the diminishing efficacy of drugs. Also, large scale parental resistance to preschool vaccinations has resulted in increased case severity and a more rapid transmission of illnesses through close communities. Herd immunity has proven to be a myth. Lasting effects of untreated viral diseases include blindness, loss of hearing, AIDS, ravaged derma, shingles, liver disease, and death.

On the bacterial disease front, the news is equally grim. Many diseases have mutated to become resistant to antibiotics. As humans are forced to live in closer proximity, the increase of insect borne infections grows. (See Mosquitos and Ticks above.) Human bodily wastes carry disease. Untreated water, sewerage, and human sputum either transmit infections or provide ideal breeding grounds for germs. Communities are surrounded with environmental petri dishes nurturing life threatening contagions.

Conclusion

Tuberculosis has regained a firm hold on humanity. It's resurgence began in the late 20th Century in the cramped slums of Southeast Asia, in the Russian penal system, and among the homeless everywhere. In 2034, TB is resistant to antibiotic therapy. In the early 19th Century, before antibiotics, patients spent time in the countryside resting and breathing clean air. This cure is no longer available due to shrinking rural areas and severe air pollution. Consumption is a pandemic now, gaining strength in its early stages. The WHO says it has the potential to consume the human species.

Maryann Caton, 54 | Robt. MacKenzie, 66 | World POP: 9.02 billion

---

"Once more, welcome to science at 8:00 in the morning," said MacKenzie smiling wryly. "It's such a bonny time of the day to begin using your noggins. Please put away your cell phones, iPads, and laptops. We're going to do some actual thinking before we turn to Wikipedia for help."

MacKenzie watched as the class sleepily closed their devices. A few yawned. "Let's go, lads and lassies," he urged, "it's time to wake up. This isn't the land of nod, it's the land of learning." He moved to his whiteboard.

"Today we're going to focus on medicine," he began. "To be more specific, we're going to consider a type of infection gaining a foothold all across the country. Your task this morning is to compose a two or three paragraph description of the disease, something you'd find in a pamphlet in a doctor's office. Some of you are going into medicine; some of you might end up working for drug companies. No matter what your path, concise, clear writing is essential.

"When we finish our discussion, you'll be able to use your devices to do some research about the disease. Your assignment will be to complete your pamphlet at home."

A hand raised. "I think I know what you mean, Dr. Mac," said a female student. "When I visited the dermatologist to have a mole removed, he gave me a pamphlet about squamous cell skin cancer and told me to limit my time in the sun. I'm Irish and burn easily."

"Aye, lass. You can see from my receding hairline, what's left is reddish. You and I are descendents from the Celts— light eyes, fair skin, ginger hair. We need to be cautious in the sun."

"May we see where your mole was removed?" asked a male student, grinning.

"No you may not!" snapped the woman angrily. "Mind your own business, or I'll report you for sexual harassment."

"Only kidding," he said, "only kidding." He held up his hands in surrender.

"Don't show me how immature you are," said MacKenzie, annoyed. "Let's get serious." It was the only time the class had heard their teacher scold them.

MacKenzie consulted his notes. "Who knows about *borrelia burgdorferi*?" He wrote it on the white board. No one responded. "It's a spirochete that causes Lyme Disease," he said. "Where did the disease name come from?"

A student responded. "I'm from Connecticut, Dr. Mac. I know the answer. It was named for Old Lyme, Connecticut, where it was first detected. Lyme, Old Lyme, and East Lyme are towns along the Connecticut River where it flows into Long Island Sound. It's very pretty and heavily wooded, at least inland. As I recall, the disease was diagnosed in 1975. At first people thought it was juvenile rheumatoid arthritis. But it turned out to be much more serious than that."

"Excellent, lass. Where did you learn all that?"

"Sophomore biology class in Old Lyme High School." She smiled.

"Och! Then you're from ground zero." MacKenzie nodded, remembering his own experience. "I lived in Connecticut, too, although seventy-five miles away in the western part of the state. By 2016, the disease was firmly entrenched in my town and up and down the eastern seaboard. I was bitten and infected. I'll tell you what happened in a minute."

"So it has nothing to do with citrus trees?" asked a student in the rear.

MacKenzie wasn't sure whether the lad was asking a legitimate question or joking. "Nae, it does not. The towns are spelled L-Y-M-E, not L-I-M-E," he said. "But linden trees in Connecticut are called lime trees in Scotland. That might be the reason for your confusion."

On the whiteboard, he made two columns, labeling them "bacterial" and "viral." "Diseases can be grouped by how they're transmitted," he continued, "or by their biological structure. Today we won't cover animal disease transmitters such as apes carrying ebola, but only consider the blacklegged tick, the vector for transmitting Lyme Disease. It's mostly helped along by rodents."

In the "viral" column he wrote: hepatitis, encephalitis, herpes, HIV, MERS, smallpox, rubella, and flu. Beneath the "bacterial" heading he listed: anthrax, Lyme Disease, typhus, legionellosis, bubonic plague, tuberculosis, and MRSA.

Viral	Bacterial
Hepatitis	Anthrax

Encephalitis	Lyme Disease
Herpes	Typhus
Smallpox	Legionellosis
HIV	Bubonic plague
MERS	Tuberculosis
Rubella	MRSA
Flu	

"As you might guess by looking at these lists, diseases caused by viruses generally are spread by humans. Diseases caused by bacteria have a broader range of transmitters. For example, through sputum, TB is spread from human to human. But Lyme Disease is not spread from one person to another, at least as far as we know."

"What's legionellosis?" someone asked.

"Legionnaires Disease. Often it contaminates closed water sources such as potable water tanks on ocean liners or air conditioned humidifying units in hotels."

"Tell us about your run-in with Lyme Disease, Dr. Mac."

"One weekend I felt really bum, like I had the flu. I ached, I ran a fever, I had no appetite. I spent the day in bed watching TV. All I could get were reports about Trump, and how he was nearing the Republican nomination. That made me even sicker." He heard chuckles.

"Then, while turning and tossing, I bumped the back of my knee. It felt like a bad bruise. It was hot to the touch. I got out of bed and looked in a mirror. Sure enough, I saw the tell-tale bullseye. It was Lyme Disease. My doc prescribed an antibiotic. That seems to have worked. It's been eighteen years, and so far, I have no symptoms. Not everyone is so lucky."

"How do you think you got bitten?"

"I was rebuilding a stone wall. It's the perfect place for mice to live. My guess is a tick jumped from a rodent onto me."

He erased the whiteboard. "Okay, laddies and lassies, it's time for you to get to work. Fire up your devices and begin writing a Lyme Disease pamphlet. There's time for you to get started before class is over. If you have a question or need help, raise your hand. I'll be right there.

"Remember, you're researching *ixodes scapularis*, the deer tick, and *borrelia burgdorferi*, Lyme Disease. *Dermacentor andersoni*, *variabilis*, and *rhipicephalus sanguineus*, dog ticks are the vectors for *Rickettsia rickettsii*, the bacteria that causes *ehrlichiosis* and *tularemia*, both Rocky Mountain spotted fevers.

"In keeping with the theme of this course to write simply and clearly, I challenge you to write your pamphlets without using latin names for the insects or the disease. Good luck."

Maryann knew it was silly to talk to Fred on the phone. They lived close enough that visiting each other at home made more sense. Yet Fred always was constrained in what he could say about Lois's condition with her in the same room listening to him. According to Fred, at first Lois would be smiling and nodding, then her demeanor changed to one of puzzlement. Finally she would scowl and become angry. Over the phone he could describe her condition and admit his worry while she was napping.

Fred told his sister about their recent trip to see a neurologist. Cognitive tests were performed and compared with previous baseline results, he related. Lois was deteriorating rapidly. She couldn't remember her own name, but did smile when asked about her husband. Fred said she had called him "that nice man." He admitted it broke his heart, but at least she knew he was a man. Her doctor told him that there was no set timetable for regression—only that death was inevitable.

Visits from Jeannie brightened Lois's day, he reported. But becoming a nana was fixated in Lois's mind with what little cognition remained. She badgered Jeannie to have a baby.

Jeannie had matured so much, he recognized. She remained calm and sweet under Lois's cross examination, knowing her mother had no control of her brain. She deflected Lois's urgency for a grandchild by saying she was considering it.

Maryann also learned from Fred that Sandy had a new job. He was hired as a trainee by Downtube Cycles, a manufacturer of custom titanium bicycles. He was being taught how to measure for tube cuts, and how to weld parts together to make bike frames. A benefit of employment was that after hours and on weekends, he could use the business's welding equipment to create life-size replicas of his wire art. He had to buy his own titanium, of course. But, to make their bikes ultra-lightweight, Downtube Cycles used only hollow tubing. It couldn't be bent without crimping or breaking. Solid bars, however, were more flexible. Fred said Sandy was experimenting with how much bend his rods could take before snapping. In the meantime, he was creating linear geometric art. Curve-like arcs could be fashioned by welding together tiny straight pieces cut at precise angles.

Responding to a question from his sister, Fred told Maryann that Sandy was also experimenting with color. The sculptures could remain titanium shiny, have a brushed chrome finish, or be painted any color. A full-size replica of his contortionist in a box was painted vivid red, green, yellow, and black—Rastafarian colors. Fred said he had seen a photograph.

Maryann reported she hadn't seen Sandy and Jeannie since

last November when the Boulder Star was lit. She told Fred about the child versus no child discussion they had had at dinner. She confessed she had no idea what the youngsters planned, but at least they were considering their options and the environmental scenario a newborn would face. She agreed with Fred that his daughter and Sandy had matured into thoughtful, productive Boulderites.

Maryann relied on her rescue inhaler more and more. Her Primary Care Physician, Dr. Lisa Jeffries, prescribed one after Annie showed signs of asthma. An article in the *Daily Boulder Reporter* described how air pollution was continuing to mount along Colorado's Front Range. Increasingly, pollutants measured by the Air Quality Index were permanently settling into the moderate and severe categories. Respiratory distress were becoming chronic in the state.

The culprits were obvious. Dust and emissions from fossil fuel extraction were causative factors. The drought being experienced on Colorado's eastern plains and in the San Luis Valley unleashed massive dust storms, a reprise of the Great Dust Bowl. Forest fires continued to rage unabated in California where twenty years of minimal precipitation had turned wood lots into tinder. Fire ash and soot drifted east over the Continental Divide spurred by La Niña gusts and westerly trade winds.

Colorado's mountain forests were ripe to explode. Pine bark beetles had killed hundreds of square miles of timber, leaving behind ever-brown national forests—firewood waiting for the next lightning strike, careless camper, or discarded cigarette butt.

Maryann learned to remain indoors on especially unhealthy

days. But even when the air was occasionally blown clear, she kept her medicine at the ready. It was no fun lying in bed with persistent chest tightness, working hard for the next breath. Her condition reminded her of the stories she read years ago about inner-city children suffering higher asthma rates than youngsters living in the country. Now everyone seemed to be affected.

2035

THE MARKET STREET GAZETTE

FRIDAY, APRIL 20, 2035 - VOL. CCLXXXII NUMBER 16
DJIA 19024 -0.17% NASDAQ 6145 - 0.15% STOXX 353.85 -
O.2% 10-YR. TREAS ⏶ 12/32, YIELD 1.024%

WORLD MARKET ANALYSIS

U.S. Markets Continue to Slide

U.S. markets continue to slide as world events portend a dark future. Economists have long agreed that real estate valuation is based on three factors: location, location, location. In like manner, market analysts now agree that capital asset valuations also ride on three human emotions: uncertainty, uncertainty, uncertainty. Unlike past periods of uncertainty where market volatility remained low, in the first quarter of 2035, worldwide markets have begun what appears to be a rapid and inexorable return to lows not seen in thirty years.

Ten key factors are at play:

1. East Asia environmental degradation due to continued coal burning in India as well as permanent ocean flooding of coastal areas

2. New York City: repeated flooding of lower Manhattan
3. Increased petrochemical pollution in Louisiana's "cancer alley," coupled with two new disasters at drilling rigs in the Gulf of Mexico
4. Chinese bellicosity in the South China Sea
5. U.S. trade imbalances across the globe resulting in the levying of import taxes and trade wars
6. U.S. national debt of twenty-five trillion dollars and climbing
7. Middle East wars over water rights in vast drought stricken areas
8. Sub-Saharan conflict over arable land
9. Mass migration from Africa to Europe
10. Russia's claim to Arctic Ocean and its vast reserves of oil and natural gas

In the past, market stability would sometimes be tested by only one or two factors. As problems were solved and new international agreements reached, equilibrium returned. However, since the Trump administration almost twenty years ago, nations have disregarded accepted market protocols and have turned economic theory upside down. Protectionism is the new norm. Trump's withdrawal from American and Pacific trade agreements (as well as his disavowal of the Paris Climate Accord) were contributing factors. They signaled America was no longer capable of being the world's economic powerhouse. American threats and demands were ignored or marginalized. China has ascended to economic superiority.

Where are the changes headed? Economists have been unable to formulate a new model. Too many variables are at play. Certainly, global warming and national hegemony are key factors. But perhaps the biggest question mark is what impact world population will have as the number of humans approaches ten billion. The Earth is running out of livable space and resources.

Maryann Caton, 55 | Robt. MacKenzie, 67 | World POP: 9.06 billion

---

Maryann fiddled with her hospital gown hoping to look presentable. She hated the damn things, unable to securely tie the strings behind her neck and back. Not that it mattered. The doctor would undo her wrap to examine her lungs. *How did these things get the name Johnnie?* she wondered. It was all so humiliating.

She heard a knock on the examination room door. "Come in," she barked, "I'm ready."

Dr. Jeffries entered. "Hi, Maryann," she said. "My nurse said you're still struggling with asthma."

"Yes, Lisa. I think it's getting worse. The medicine you prescribed doesn't seem to be working."

"Well, the air quality certainly hasn't been cooperating recently. I can smell smoke in the air. I'm going to undo your gown and listen to your chest."

Maryann's PCP asked her to breathe deeply. She listened from the rear, then from the front. She tapped on Maryann's chest cavity. "Okay, you can cover up," she said.

"What's going on, Lisa? Can you tell?"

"There's something rattling around in there, but I don't know what. I'm going to give you the name of a pulmonologist. I want you to see her. She's very good."

"Is it that serious?" asked Maryann, alarmed.

"I'm not sure, but probably not. Other than your asthma, you're in good health. You've never smoked. You do cardio when the air quality permits."

"When it doesn't, I get my cardio in the gym," she pointed out.

"Right. Although locker room humidity can cause problems."

"Like what?"

"Fungal infections. Things like that. I just don't know what's causing your discomfort, so I'd like Dr. Lin to take a look."

"Is Dr. Lin's a female?"

"Yes. You don't have to be examined with a witness present."

"All right, if that's what you advise."

"I do. Before you leave today let's take a chest x-ray. I'll send it to Dr. Lin so she'll be able to view it before you arrive. She may want to do more tests, but an x-ray is the place to start. I'll look it over, too. Maybe between the two of us we can figure out what's going on."

The MacKenzies had just returned from a late afternoon walk. Furious downslope winds the night before swept the Front Range clear of pollution. They had done their favorite loop— east past the rec center, north on the South Boulder Creek trail, under Baseline to Gapter Road, left at Dimmitt Drive to follow the multi-use path to the Centennial Trail behind the golf course out to 55th Street. They returned home via 55th. The walk was about four miles and promised sightings of red tail hawks, ospreys, an occasional golden eagle, and in the autumn, swarms of painted lady butterflies. At the Bobolink Trailhead there were dogs acting goofy chasing soggy tennis balls thrown by their owners. They reminded Maryann of Jake's pup, Nova, the dog who never turned left or right when she could walk straight ahead.

Maryann heard the doorbell. *Jeepers,* she thought, *someone's actually at the front door and not at the side entrance.* She heard Rob singing upstairs in the shower. She went to see who was calling.

She was gobsmacked by what she found. There stood Jeannie Caton with a baby! A carriage was off to the side. Maryann rapidly tried to do the math to make sense of what she saw, but came up with nothing.

"May we come in, Aunt Annie?" asked Jeannie, a mischievous grin lighting her face with happiness.

"Of course! Of course!" Maryann searched for words. "You have a baby!"

"Yes I do. That's what my little bundle is. May I present Alejandro."

"Oh, my gosh! He's beautiful." She yelled for Rob. "Laddie, get down here even if you're only wearing a robe. Be prepared to be surprised."

"What is it?" he called.

"No time for long distance questions, Rob. Come down and you'll find out." She remembered the baby. "I hope I didn't upset him with all my yelling. Oh, Jeannie, he's gorgeous." Maternal instincts stirred in her. "May I hold him?"

"Of course, Aunt Annie." She passed the baby over. "I may have to turn to you to get advice."

"Och! What have we here?" asked Rob entering the room, surprised. "It looks like a wee bairn."

"He's wee for sure," said Maryann. "And he's whole. I counted ten fingers and toes."

Jeannie laughed. "That's the first thing Sandy and I did when we picked him up—count digits . . . plus he has two eyes, two ears, a button nose, and the most beautiful rosebud mouth. He looks like an angel."

"And black hair," said Rob. "He's nae a Celt."

"No, Uncle Rob. He comes from an orphanage in Puerto Rico. He was abandoned after the last hurricane. As you know, the island's been totaled. We've been on a Denver agency's waiting list for a year. There was a hold up until Sandy got a full time job."

"What's the bairn's name?"

"Alejandro."

"Aye, I approve. That's a good strong name."

"Yes, that's the name he came with. Of course, we can change it to whatever we like."

Maryann held Alejandro close. She smelled the wonderful aroma of talcum powder and sweet milk. She nuzzled the baby's tummy. She blew a raspberry into his soft belly skin. Alejandro's eyes blinked open, he smiled, then burped. "You must have told Fred and Lois," she said, still grappling with the news.

"Yes. Sandy and I took him to Louisville yesterday. They know."

"I'll ask you about Lois's reaction later," said Maryann, "but why didn't Fred phone and give us the heads up?"

"We asked him not to. We wanted to spring the surprise."

"That you did, lass. For sure, that you did. C'mon Aunt Annie, let Uncle Robbie have a turn with the wee'un."

Maryann passed the baby to her husband. Her heart filled with love watching him cuddle the child. "Where's Sandy?" she asked. "Is he happy with all this?"

"He's finishing up a project at work. And yes, he's as thrilled as I am."

"Alejandro's a mouthful," said Rob. "Does he have a middle name?"

"Yes . . . Caton."

"Oh, then you're using your family name as a middle name. That's very European, you know. Some Scottish ghillies use two surnames. Makes them think they're lairds of an estate when they're only a generation removed from being a crofter." He shook his head at the very idea. "What will be the wee'un's family name?"

"Callendar, of course. He's Alejandro Caton Callendar—Alex for short."

"Sometimes unmarried couples hyphenate their last names," said Maryann taking Alex out of Rob's hands.

"There's no need for us to do that, Aunt Annie. Look." She held out her left hand. "Sandy gave me this. It's made of gold, not titanium." She laughed. "We're getting married."

"Good morning class, another fine day it is. I have some news to share with you. I think it's only fair to let you know in case you had any inclination to join me in class again next semester."

MacKenzie looked at the young people watching him closely, wondering what he was about to say. At 8:00 a.m., they often had sleepy faces, but nevertheless radiated expectancy knowing they were about to be challenged to think clearly about the world of science they hoped to enter. If asked, many would say Professor Robert MacKenzie, the Scot, was the best teacher they ever had.

MacKenzie moved to his trusty whiteboard, then made his announcement. "I have submitted a letter of resignation to the Chancellor." He saw frowns and heard someone say, "Oh, no!"

"Aye, it's true. It's time for me to move on and try some new things. Since moving to Colorado, I've climbed only one fourteen-thousand-footer." He laughed. "That's an embarrassment. And there are multi-day bike tours to experience, like Ride the Rockies and Pedal the Plains. I don't want to wait to do these things until I'm too old, or the environment becomes so spoiled that doing them becomes impossible. So, there you have it. I told you. With you lads and lassies knowing my plans, my decision is now official."

He saw frowns turn to smiles. Students began to speak out.

"Good luck, Dr. Mac. If you tackle climbing Longs Peak, remember to bring crampons."

"And a rope," someone else added.

"I wish . . .", a young woman looked around as if affirming everyone's sincerity, ". . . *we* all wish you a happy retirement."

MacKenzie saw nods, heard yesses, even detected an "aye."

"Thank you, my friends. I won't bore you with the contents of my resignation letter, other than to say it was traditional in tone and way too long. In keeping with the purpose of this class, here's all I needed to say." He wrote two words on the whiteboard: **I quit**.

The joke went over well. There was laughter and more smiles.

"I'm dismissing you early today, so you can work on your projects. But I want you to remember the most important lesson of this course, and it has nothing to do with language concision, although that is important."

MacKenzie raised his constant companion, a sixteen inch globe of the Earth. "This is my home," he said. "This is your home. This is the home of everyone who ever lived. This is the home of everyone who will live in the future. This is the only home we have. Please take care of it."

"What happened when your mom saw Alex?"

Maryann had just poured tea for Jeannie who held the baby to her shoulder. She was rocking back and forth as mothers do, looking as if she was on a bongo board.

Jeannie took a deep breath, then chuckled. "If she wasn't confused before, meeting Alex pushed her over the edge."

"I can imagine," nodded Maryann.

"She couldn't fathom how I could have a baby without getting fat. That's how she said it, 'getting fat.' I tried to explain the adoption process to her, but she didn't understand. 'Why are they giving away babies?' she asked."

Maryann nodded, imagining the conversation.

"She seemed happy when she held Alex, but the fact that he has different features than Lindsay and I had when we were his age—plus his darker complexion—befuddled her. I said he was adopted from Puerto Rico. She seemed to know about Puerto Rico, perhaps because of the continual news coverage the island is getting. She watches a lot of TV.

"Anyway, then I tried explaining his looks by saying he was mestizo. That was a mistake. She pulled back his blanket and studied him. She looked totally baffled. 'He's not a mosquito,' she said. 'Can't you tell the difference between an insect and a baby?"

By now Maryann was doubled over in laughter. Jeannie also was cracking up. Alex gurgled.

"I'm not making fun of her or getting jollies because of her condition," said Jeannie, breathing deeply to regain her composure. "I genuinely love my mom, Aunt Annie, and it's sad to see her this way. But her reaction was funny. Even dad was smiling."

"It's not going to get any better," reminded Annie. "She'll continue losing touch with reality until there's no more of her. I'm sure you know that."

"I do. I'm resigned to the fact. Fortunately, she has my dad. He's a saint."

"I agree," said Maryann. "He was kind even when he was a child. He always looked out for me, if I was being bullied. That's what big brothers are for."

Jeannie passed Alex to his great aunt. She sat and sipped her tea. She remembered a question she wanted to ask Annie. "What did you think of Sandy's sculpture? It was picked best in show."

Maryann looked stunned. "Damn! I forgot about the library! I never miss that show. I have a friend, Elizabeth, who always has needlepoint on display. How stupid of me! I should have checked the calendar."

"That's okay, Aunt Annie. You'll get to see Sandy's work permanently in place on Pearl Street. The Boulder Merchants' Association bought it. It'll be installed in front of the courthouse. The contortionist hasn't showed up for a few years, so the Association is erecting Sandy's art in his place."

"You're right," acknowledged Maryann. "I haven't seen JeanPierre in quite a while." She tickled Alex. He responded with a smile. "I assume Sandy's sculpture is a replica of the small ones you and I have."

"Not exactly. It's a figure standing behind a box ready to squeeze in. It's constructed so little kids can climb in and pretend they're contortionists. It'll be near the water feature. Little tykes will have another attraction, besides getting wet."

"That's nice for the children," said Maryann. "Pearl Street's become quite a draw for them."

Jeannie nodded. "The city needs to do more to keep the tourists entertained. Flatiron eye candy is now hidden behind office buildings." She stopped to think. "Oh well, I suppose that's the price of progress."

Or the price of too many people, thought Maryann.

"Hello, Mrs. MacKenzie. I'm Dr. Lin. Dr. Jeffries sent you to see me because you're having recurrent bouts of asthma. Am I right?"

"Yes, I just can't shake it. There are good days when I can be outdoors and everything's fine. But then there are days I suffer. As the air quality worsens in Colorado, there are more days like that."

"Are you feeling the effects indoors?"

"No. In the summer when ozone levels are high, I stay inside, and we keep the air conditioner on. I'm okay then. In the winter, when we're apt to have atmospheric inversions, I stay indoors. I'm fine in the rec center gym. But the whole thing is a damned nuisance."

"I understand, Mrs. MacKenzie. Struggling to breath is no fun." Dr. Lin retrieved an laptop from her desk. She began asking Maryann questions and entering her answers in a data bank. "I know you've been asked some of these questions before, Mrs. MacKenzie, so I apologize for repeating them and beg for your patience. Please bear with me as we go over them again."

"No problem, doctor. I'm ready for the inquisition." She smiled trying to lighten the moment, then took a deep breath to show she was feeling fine.

"My records say you were born in 1980."

"That's right."

"Where did you grow up?"

"In Mars, Pennsylvania, outside Pittsburgh."

"How many years did you live there?"

"Eighteen, until I left for college."

"Were the steel mills still operating when you were a child?"

"Yes . . . I think so. A few."

"Do you have any idea when they closed?"

"No, I don't remember."

"Were there any large industries near Mars?"

"Yes, one. Woodings Industrial."

"What did they do?"

"They manufactured components for blast furnaces. I had to do a report about them when I was in elementary school. The Pittsburgh area was filled with industry, still is—Heinz, PPG, and so on."

"Where is Mars in relation to Pittsburgh?"

"Northwest. Mostly north."

"So most of the big plants would have been southeast of Mars."

"Yes . . . I guess so with the exception of Woodings."

"Was there any industry to the west of Mars?"

"Let me think." Maryann laughed. "Yes, there was a cement mill in Wampum."

Dr. Lin chuckled. "Wampum? Isn't that Indian money?"

"Yep. Crazy name. That's how I remember the factory."

"How far away from Mars is Wampum?"

"It's just a guess . . . I'd say about twenty-five miles."

"Do you know there's a cement plant north of Boulder in Lyons?"

"That's right. Rob and I have driven past it. Why are you asking me about cement plants?"

"Big operations that use fire to manufacture their products spew pollution, even with smokestack scrubbers. As I'm sure you know, blast furnaces render iron ore into molten steel. In the cement industry, furnaces are used to chemically alter limestone. The new material is called clinker. Then clinker is ground to a fine powder to become cement. We're not talking concrete here, this is about concrete's basic ingredient—cement."

"Why do you know this stuff?"

"Because pollution emitting industries are the cause of many lung diseases. I need to know about them—I'm a pulmonologist. You don't have to see black smoke belching out of a plant, like the College of Cardinals signaling an unsuccessful vote for the Pope. Most pollutants are microscopic or in gas form."

"They lead to COPD. Right?"

"Yes, although COPD is an umbrella term covering a variety of lung ailments."

"Do you think that's what's affecting me?"

"Perhaps. Did you have asthma as a child?"

"No."

"And you had your full range of childhood inoculations, including DPT?"

"Yep. It left a little scar." Maryann showed her left arm.

"So, no whooping cough—pertussis?"

"No. As I said, I was vaccinated." As an attorney, Maryann understood the doctor's need to ask repetitive questions.

"Just double checking." Dr. Lin looked at her laptop. "You have a brother, I see."

"Right, he lives in Louisville."

"Did he have asthma as a child?"

"No, not that I recall."

"Any sign of it now?

"No."

"Were there smokers in your family."

"Sort of. In those days it seemed as if everyone smoked. But my parents quit when Fred was born. I had an uncle who smoked cigars, but he was banished to the outdoors when he lighted up."

"Did you ever smoke?"

"No . . . oh, like other kids I tried it in high school, but I was a swimmer and ran cross country, so it never became a habit—not even close."

"Where did you go to college?"

"Columbia, in New York City."

"Ahh, fine school. Did you smoke there?"

"No. I was getting financial aid as a diver on the swim team. I didn't want anything to jeopardize that. So . . . no . . . other than my silly attempts to look cool in high school, I've never smoked."

"Were you living in New York during 9/11?"

"Yes. I graduated college in 2002. Then I went to Columbia Law School."

"After law school, where did you go?"

"I got a job with a New York law firm and stayed in Manhattan."

"Have you ever been out of the country?"

"Yes, when I was in college."

"Tell me about it."

"I went to Peru as a member of an archaeological dig."

"Were you in Lima?"

"Only for a short time. Mostly, we were at a dig site in the mountains."

"What was the climate like? Were you in the eastern rainforest or above tree line on the altiplano?"

Maryann laughed. "You know Andean geography."

Dr. Lin nodded. "Just enough so that I can appear to look smart. Tell me about the conditions."

"We were in an exposed area above tree line. It was dry. I remember there was an open pit copper mine a few kilometers north of us. There was also gold mining in the area."

"Was it windy?"

"Yes, every day."

"What about dust. Did the wind blow up dust storms?"

"Yes, frequently. In fact, it was always good to get back to Lima, so we could get clean."

"How long were you there?"

"As I recall, about six weeks."

"Hmm . . . thank you, Mrs. MacKenzie."

"Is that all?"

"For now, yes."

"Do you have any idea what's going on, Dr. Lin?"

"I'm not absolutely sure, but from what you said and your x-ray, I have an idea."

"Can you tell me? I want to know. Am I dying?"

Dr. Lin laughed. "No, you're not dying. That's not going to happen for many years. You're still young. But you do have a condition that could worsen unless you're careful."

Maryann gulped. "Okay, what is it and how do I get rid of it?"

"Looking at your chest x-ray and from what you've told me, you have *silicosis*. Yours is a very mild case and shouldn't cause you any trouble, if you follow my advice."

"Wait a minute, doctor! What's silicosis?"

"You have tiny nodule lesions of silica dust in the upper lobes of your lungs. Sometimes it's called potter's rot or grinder's asthma. Normally, it's an occupational disease. But not always. Many New York City firemen suffered from it after 9/11. Twin Tower concrete was pulverized. Some men had to retire on disability."

"Hold on. I didn't work in any permanent job in a dusty environment."

"Yes, that's true. But throughout your life you were exposed to occasional bouts of dust emissions and other airborne pollutants. Usually, silica's a component of dust, but dust can also be composed of asbestos, fertilizers, loess, funguses, and industrial chemicals. Long-term exposure is usually a causative factor, not infrequent exposures the way you were. But everyone reacts differently to disease factors. Some potters never show signs of silicosis. Others are ravaged by it. In your case, for whatever reason, silica particles made a home in your lungs, and are causing you problems."

"Damn! That stinks. Can you take them out of me?"

"No, they're in there for the rest of your life."

"Will they grow and get worse?"

"No, they're inert. Fortunately, the nodules are very small."

"What about medicine?"

"There is no medicine that can cure silicosis. You have to learn to manage it. When breathing is hard, get indoors. Use a bronchodilator—I'll give you a new prescription. Cough medicine can help. If you get a respiratory infection, I'll give you antibiotics. But stay away from sick people. You don't want to get their illnesses. Antibiotics are losing their efficacy."

"Efficacy?"

"The ability to cure disease."

"Oh, I see. Is silicosis contagious?"

"No, your family and friends are safe. But you are more susceptible to certain things."

"Like what?

"Pulmonary infections, tuberculosis, lung cancer, chronic bronchitis."

"Wow! This is really bad news."

"Don't look at it that way, Mrs. MacKenzie. People live and thrive with all sorts of problems. At least you know what you're dealing with, and I'll teach you how to manage it."

Maryann took another deep breath. She didn't feel any differently knowing her diagnosis. "Of all the specialities to get into, Dr. Lin, why did you pick pulmonology?"

"My parents are from Beijing. I still have family there. It pains me to see them living their whole lives wearing surgical masks."

She narrowed her eyes in anger. "It's rumored China plans to build a hundred new coal burning power plants every year. In addition, six percent of southeastern Asia atmospheric pollution comes from India's coal burning plants. There are days in Delhi when breathing the air is like smoking fifty cigarettes." She set her jaw. "It's got to stop. We're killing ourselves."

2036

Dear Annie,

It's been so long since I've written to you, I'm ashamed of myself. I could have emailed or posted a hello on Facebook, but I've been remiss. Part of my problem is that I like to write full letters, not communicate in tidbits. But, alas, I too often put it off. In the old days I would have been hunched over a desk scratching with a quill pen by candlelight. At least now I use a computer and printer. My friends say I'm not a total troglodyte.

How are you? I learned about Jake from his Roxbridge pals. What a shock! I admit it now, he was one of my favorite childhood friends. It must be hard for a mother to lose a child. Please accept my condolences, as late as they may be.

Is Rob still at CU? I think of you two often, how kind you were to me, and your clever tactic to rid my speech of the word "like."

Mom is still stamping books at the Roxbridge library. Sometimes I wonder when they're going to get a machine to replace her. But in Roxbridge things progress slowly. Antique machinery is revered—not that Mom is an antique.

Dad's plumbing business has grown quite large. It pretty much covers all of the Roxbridge-New Milford-Kent area. Occasionally, I see his trucks passing along Kent's Main Street.

When I graduated from Columbia, I was unsure what I wanted to do. I received a good education in environmental science, so I hoped to get out in the field and put my learning to use. Someday I may return to school for an advanced degree, but not right now. In truth, it may become too expensive to do so.

I've had a few serious male friends, but nothing's lasted. I'm so involved with my work, I don't give guys the attention they want. I'm sure you know about male egos.

For the past five years, I've been Executive Director of the St. John's Cliffs-Kent Heritage Land Trust. There's a mouthful! Growing up in Roxbridge and watching you work with the Conservation Trust spurred me to do something similar. I won't spell out all that has happened this past year. That's in the lede I've enclosed from the 11/12/36 edition of *The Hartford Courier*. I thought you'd like to know that your crusade against radioactive waste in western Connecticut made an impression on a young girl. I like to think I'm following in your footsteps.

Have a wonderful Thanksgiving. Give my love to Rob. Write, if you have time.

Love,
Taylor

The Hartford Courier

"Connecticut's Historic Broadsheet"

November 12, 2036

Special Election RESULTS AND ANALYSIS: 2036

Padnam Shaw, Politics Editor

Taylor Peters, 32, Wins Seat in Connecticut's
108th Assembly District

A new face has emerged on the Connecticut political landscape. Taylor Peters, 32, has won a seat in the General Assembly representing Kent, New Fairfield, New Milford, and Sherman. Running as a Green Party candidate, she easily out-polled developer Ziggy Horst by 547 votes in a special election.

The central issue in the campaign involved siting a slots casino on Route 7 in Kent. Horst reportedly had formed a partnership with Kent's Schaghticoke Tribe to annex land presently owned by Kent Flower and Tree Farm on the east side of the Housatonic River. For years the Schaghticoke have been trying to reclaim land on the river's west side to construct a large comprehensive casino. Their efforts were thwarted by powerful trustee groups representing Kent Academy and Litchfield Hills Preparatory, two private schools that have been in existence for over 100 years.

Topography and transportation issues have also been roadblocks. Access to any casino from New York State's Route 22 would have to pass over the steep and impenetrable Kent Cliffs. The

Appalachian Trail Society owns land along that corridor. On the Connecticut side, narrow two-lane Route 7 would have to be widened to four lanes to accommodate traffic from downstate.

Peters is the Executive Director of Kent's land trust. She ran a positive campaign. Dozens of volunteers knocked on doors urging citizens to vote for her. She rallied people who wanted to keep the district pristine. She spoke in schools asking students to urge their parents to vote for her. She argued that a vote for her was a vote to keep western Connecticut forested and rural. She pointed out the economics involved—residential land values would plummet. A few people would get rich at the expense of the community.

She cycled to rallies. She challenged Horst to debates which he boycotted. Joined by 200 cyclists for her final campaign event, she pedaled 17 miles to New Milford High School. Connecticut State Police escorted the peloton. Horst was unavailable for comments on the outcome.

Maryann Caton, 56 | Robt. MacKenzie, 68 | World POP: 9.077 billion

---

"I'm happy Jeannie was able to stay with Lois so you could get away," said Rob, tasting his NA ale at Beer Barrel Growler, a new restaurant and brewery in Gunbarrel. "You need to get out of the house more often."

"I know," said Fred, "but it's hard to do with her end drawing near." He had ordered a stout with ten percent alcohol content. "This drink may knock me off the stool, but I need it."

"Don't worry," said Rob gripping his brother-in-law's elbow. "I'll pick you up. Let's get something to eat to go with our drink."

"Good idea," said Fred. "Then I can have more than one. Besides, you're driving."

They placed their order for bison burgers and asked for a second round of drinks.

"She's fully bedridden, now," said Rob, commiserating with Fred. "That must be hard to deal with. Does she have any recollection of anything?"

"She knows what to do when she's on a bedpan. I can't get her to the bathroom anymore."

"What about her side of the family . . . the Murphys. Are they of any help?"

"Yes. There's nothing they can do about Lois, but they spell me from time to time. They also do grocery shopping for me when I ask."

"Aye, that's what families are for." For a second, Rob's long-ago absentee father came to mind.

"And Jeannie and Sandy have been my anchors," continued Fred. "My daughter's turned out to be the most devoted child, as well as a devoted mother."

"You love wee Alex?"

"Aye, that I do," said Fred trying to mimic Rob's Scottish dialect. "He's the most bonny bairn."

Rob laughed. "That's good Scot-speak, lad. You'd be understood in Dundee. What about Lindsay? Is she coming home?"

"Yes, she's flying in for Christmas. I hope Lois lasts long enough for Lindsay to say goodbye."

The food arrived. As they ate, they continued to discuss Lois's outlook.

"What's in store for the lass?" asked Rob. "I apologize for asking a delicate question, but what will do her in?"

"That's okay, I understand." Fred considered Rob's question

between bites. "Her doctor says she's susceptible to anything—pneumonia, stroke, heart attack, blood clots. It could happen any time. It's unpredictable, undetectable, untreatable. All I wish is for her to pass gently."

"Aye, that's what we all want."

They finished their meals. Rob suggested a capper. "I see this place is enlightened enough to have some bottles of spirits on their shelves. Let's toast friendship, family ties, and life with a wee taste of Scotch."

Fred nodded. "I hope it's mellow. I don't think Islay whisky would sit well in my stomach right now."

"I saw the brand, my brother. It's a blend. You'll be fine."

The bartender poured two fingers for Fred and a splash over ice for Rob. They touched glasses.

"Cheers," said Fred warmly. "Thanks for listening."

"Sláinte!" answered Rob.

"It's time to trade this old clunker in for a new car," said Rob, on the return trip to Louisville.

"How long have you had it?"

"About twenty years. It was a year old when I bought it."

"Where did you get it?"

"In Connecticut. I needed wheels when I moved in with your sister." Rob worked up the courage to ask Fred a thorny question. "How did you feel about your sister taking in a total stranger—someone from Scotland at that?"

Fred laughed. "That's Annie, for sure. She always had a soft heart for stray puppies. She made up her mind you were the one. You should know by now, when she gets an idea, you can't dissuade her. The bigger surprise was when she married her first husband. Ever meet him?" Rob nodded. "We all thought he was a poor choice. It was all about him. He was puffed up with self-importance. You were a breath of fresh air."

"Speaking of breathing," said Rob, "her asthma is giving her trouble. In addition to her bronchodilator, her PCP prescribed an antihistamine thinking an allergy might be contributing to her discomfort. Did she have allergies growing up?"

Fred thought back to their childhood. "As I recollect—no hay fever, cat allergies, or skin rashes. But she appeared to have a reaction to chlorinated water. And, of course, she was in the pool all the time. Her eyes became red and her nose ran. I remember her telling me once that the inside of her mouth itched."

"Did your parents do anything about it?"

"What could they do? They weren't going to stop her from swimming. Basically, they said, 'tough it out.' She used eye drops at the end of practice. That's all I remember."

"She said you didn't have allergies."

"Not like hers, but I was highly susceptible to poison ivy. In Mars, open burning of tree branches, shrubbery prunings, vines, dead stumps, and even construction debris was allowed on certain days. Once I was bedridden by a case of poison ivy I got from the smoke of a trash fire. Not only did I have a rash on my arms and torso, I got it in my eyes. Fortunately, I didn't breathe it in."

"Och! That sounds terrible! I got small patches of it on my wrists working in the field behind Annie's house. I couldn't play the pipes for two weeks. As soon as I learned what it looked like, I gave it a wide berth. It didn't grow in Scotland. But we had other nasty plants waiting to grab us—stinging nettles, foxglove, wolfsbane, hogweed." Rob laughed. "It's a dangerous world beyond the front door."

"Rear door, too," said Fred, chuckling. He sat back enjoying riding as a passenger. He remembered a bit of information he planned to tell Rob. "Good news about Sandy. His show at the Dairy Center resulted in a sale."

"Aye, that is good news. What did he sell?"

"One of his giant figurines. The Denver Botanical Gardens bought it as a permanent installation. Sandy said it reminded the trustees of a piece from the Calder exhibition years ago. It will be sited near the Dale Chihuly glass sculpture. His work will be keeping good company living next door to a Chihuly."

"Aye. That's absolutely brilliant!"

2037

Recharge Electric Vehicles Gazette

ISSUE 52 | NOVEMBER-DECEMBER 2037 | RECHARGE.EVG.COM

Product Review

The 2037 IMPEL Bullet has upended the automotive world. It far surpasses the 400 mile "distance barrier" that has challenged EV manufacturers for years. The stakes are high for all EV companies to match IMPEL's performance or quickly become redundant.

The keys to the IMPEL breakthrough are two: a new proprietary two cell ultra-light battery system, and a sleek design that looks more like a fighter jet than a two-person vehicle.

The vehicle is powered by one cell at a time. As the Bullet moves, kinetic and brake friction energies are transformed into electricity that recharges the off-line battery. The process is repeated as battery one is depleted. Although the system is self-charging, IMPEL recommends plug-in recharging every 600 miles. Recharge time at a conventional electric outlet is two hours.

The car's motor, frame, and shell are made of welded and molded titanium resulting in a lightweight vehicle of incredible strength. Curb weight is 1050 pounds. Accessories (radio, GPS system, cooling canisters, padded seats) push the vehicle's maximum weight to 1300 pounds. Performance is not affected by the extra weight. Gross weight is 500 pounds less than the Dynamo Two X Two.

The Bullet is a low rider. Since it is low slung and narrow, vehicles within a 200 foot radius are warned of its presence by a radar activated yellow strobe light on its roof.

The Bullet's coefficient of wind and road friction is small. The vehicle cuts through the air like the projectile for which it is named. Seating is in-line, back to back, one passenger behind the operator. The seat configuration allows for a low cockpit cover. Standard seats are webbed slings, but can be upgraded with closed cell foam padding. Room for groceries is beyond the passenger footwell.

Color is limited to brushed titanium with either hazard orange or neon green accenting. Delivery to customers is expected to take two months.

Price: $36,000 plus tax. A 7% federal rebate program is available for qualified customers.

Maryann Caton, 57 | Robt. MacKenzie, 69 | World POP: 9.12 billion

"It's against my philosophy," said Rob, "but I had to trade-in the Prius after twenty-three years. Batteries are warranted for only ten years. In California they're covered for 150,000 miles, 100,00 miles elsewhere. We were over 125,000 miles. Replacing a battery now costs $3,500. The car needed new brakes, too. It just didn't make sense for me to put more money into Phil. But that's a Scotsman's opinion."

Maryann coughed. "You don't have to convince me, honey. It was time." She sat back and enjoyed the quiet ride of their new Ampere, an electric car manufactured in Boulder by FourTrack, a successful newcomer to the high stakes world of automotive engineering. They were on Baseline Road heading east toward Erie, the Wednesday office location of her pulmonologist, Dr. Lin.

"I'm glad you asked me to come along today, lass," continued Rob. "Having another set of ears hear what the doctor says is smart. Normally, you prefer to do these things alone. You can be as stubborn as a bulldog."

"I agree. (cough) That reputation goes back to high school." She took a deep breath. "I knew they wouldn't give you any information about me over the phone." She hesitated for a second, smiled broadly, then changed subjects. "The Prius was named 'Phil.' Let's call the Ampere, 'Andy.' It can be in honor of St. Andrew, Scotland's patron saint of the highway." She chuckled, then coughed again.

"Aye, a fine name it is. But Andrew was more like the patron saint of Scots being slaughtered by the Red Coats. Och! Never mind! I'll envision Andy as a fierce road warrior."

"And another thing," added Maryann. (cough) "Andy will be our Christmas present to each other this year. I don't have the energy to go out and battle the holiday shoppers, even with a saint at my side."

"I'll go with you, if you like."

"No, Rob. It's all commercial nonsense. (cough) I'd prefer to stay home with you and play *Scrabble*."

Rob turned off Baseline Road into a mixed use shopping

center and parked. They found Dr. Lin's office on the second floor of a building filled with professional offices. After checking in, they waited to be called. Finally, they were shown to an examining room and were met by the doctor.

"Dr. Lin, this is my husband, Rob. (cough) I asked him to sit in today. I hope that's okay with you."

Lin shook hands with Rob. "Welcome, Mr. MacKenzie."

"I'm more comfortable with Rob."

Lin nodded. "Okay, sir. Rob it is. No problem for me having your husband in here, Maryann. But won't you be embarrassed having me check your lungs while he's in the room?"

Maryann chuckled, then coughed. "Are you kidding? He's seen me naked for almost twenty-five years. We have no secrets."

"Since you aren't changing into a gown," said Rob, "I'll turn my back when Dr. Lin removes your blouse. You may be fine with it, lass, but I don't want to be a voyeur."

The examination began. Rob watched Dr. Lin take Annie's blood pressure and record her pulse rate. Then Rob turned away. He heard the rustle of clothing, the doctor's requests, Annie's cough.

"Sit up straight, Maryann, and take deep breaths. The stethoscope may be cold on your back. That's good . . . deep breath . . . exhale slowly. Again. Again. One more time. Now the front. Has the stethoscope warmed up?"

"Yes." (cough)

"Good. Same routine on this side . . . deep breaths, then exhale slowly. Again. Again. Last time. Now I'm going to tap on your back."

Rob heard the dull sound of Dr. Lin's fingers beating on his wife's thorax.

"Okay, Maryann," said the doctor. "Final thing, then you

can button up. I want to listen to your heart." There was silence. "That's it. We're through for today."

"What did you find out?" asked Maryann. "My cough hasn't gone away, and it's harder to breathe sometimes."

"Bad air days?"

"Yes, but it can happen other times, too."

The doctor described what she heard. "You definitely have congestion. I can hear the rattles. And your cough is consistent with adult asthma."

"Is it going to get better?" asked Rob.

"Not appreciably. Maryann has silicosis. I explained it to her. I'm sure she told you. It's incurable, but treatable. I'm going to try another medicine. It's also dosed by a bronchodilator."

She wrote a prescription and handed it to Maryann. "Take it three times a day or as needed. Don't exceed six doses in twenty-four hours. Do you still use the same pharmacy?"

"Yes, Walgreens, in the Meadows Shopping Center."

"I know that one. The pharmacist is very thorough. She'll go over the dosage with you again."

"I've followed your orders about avoiding air pollution," said Maryann. "Can I still serve meals at the homeless shelter? (cough) That project has been a big part of my life."

"You're in the kitchen?"

"Yes."

"Do you wear gloves?"

"Yes, we all do."

"What about surgical masks?"

"They're not required."

Dr. Lin thought for a moment, considering her words. "Tuberculosis is found in places where sanitation is lacking, and people live close together. The test we did last time you were here shows you're not infected. But I've heard there are cases of TB at that facility. Getting TB would be the worse thing you could do, Maryann. In the past TB was curable, but antibiotic resistant strains are now rampant. If you continue to volunteer, wear a mask."

"Won't that make the clients think I'm offended by them?"

"It doesn't matter what they think, girl. Your health is at stake." She turned to Rob. "You make sure she wears one. And having some handy at home for bad air days is a good idea. The Chinese are faced with this all the time. This is not the time for her to be self-conscious. It's time to be smart."

The MacKenzies stood and thanked Dr. Lin. "Do you want to see me again in another month?" asked Maryann.

"Yes, once a month from now on."

"Okay, doctor. Thank you."

Dr. Lin heard Maryann cough as she pushed through the door. She noticed a look of concern on Rob's face.

"Where will you be while I work, dear?" The car's chronometer said 5 p.m. Rob was dropping off Maryann at the homeless shelter for her two hour shift in the kitchen.

"At the North End Pub. I can get a meal and a glass of beer at the bar."

"Two hours is a long time to hang around a restaurant."

"Aye, but it'll be less time than that. I'll be circling the neighborhood looking for a place to park. You know North Boulder. Do you have your mask?"

"Yes, it's in my pocket." She pulled it out and showed him.

"Good lass. Have fun. I'll see you at seven."

Rob returned to the shelter at 6:40. He was early but went inside. An attendant recognized him and walked him to the cafeteria. The clients were finishing their meals. Some were in the kitchen washing dishes. Others had buckets of soapy water and were wiping tables. Rob filled a cup with coffee, then sat to wait for Annie's exit.

He saw her inside the kitchen. She was animated and happy, chatting away with fellow volunteers, occasionally lugging pots to the dishwashers. Then he blinked in disbelief. Maryann was maskless. He fought the urge to barge into the kitchen and scream at her.

Just then, he saw she was finished for the night. She removed her apron, hung it on a peg, and headed for the door. He slid his cup through the dish-return window and met her as she exited. She still looked happy. She brightened even more when she saw him.

"It's so sweet of you to meet me inside," she said. "How was your meal?"

He stared at her with concern. "You're not wearing your mask," was all he said.

With Annie forgetting to wear a mask or, saints forbid, purposely ignoring it, Rob researched what symptoms she might exhibit if her disease worsened. Without knowing the full picture of the disease's ravages, he would be unable to monitor Annie's condition. He learned that many lung illnesses, including silicosis, presented similarly: shortness of breath made worse by intense exercise; a persistent cough (sometimes wet, sometimes dry); fatigue; labored breathing; chest pain; weight loss as a result of appetite decline; fever.

He didn't let on he was keeping a journal of his daily observations of her. Doing so, he reasoned, would only frighten her, as if he was recording a countdown to her death. But Rob was a scientist, and a scientist recorded observations. She had many symptoms of silicosis but not all. He trusted Dr. Lin's advice that his wife's condition could be managed, if she followed a protocol of healthy living and avoided unsanitary environments.

Seeing her maskless at the homeless shelter had angered him. But still, he understood her behavior. She wanted to converse, smile, tell jokes, brag on her niece and baby—all without being hidden behind a mask. Her behavior was written in her DNA. She was a people person. Such folks didn't cower behind masks and barriers. They lived out in the open. He remembered the old aphorism he applied to his wife: *People like Annie live with their hearts on their sleeves.*

2038

Choices & Decisions Magazine

HELPING ACHIEVE MORAL CLARITY
LEADING TO DEATH WITH DIGNITY

❖ SPRING 2038 ❖

**Three Choices for You: Optimism,
Pessimism or Pragmatism.
How Do You Fit In?**

**By
Cynthia Bell, PhD, D.Div**

At some point in a child's formative years, they undergo a transformation so subtle and nuanced it's often missed. Born with a *tabula rasa,* clear of predispositions and most expectations, they begin to form behavior patterns that will define them for the rest of their lives. Often these behaviors are influenced by the people around them, conditions of life, hardships faced, love received. Behavior scientists have been searching for the link between adult personalities and childhood nurturing.

Babies do have expectations, of course. They may be unspoken but are, nevertheless, expressed through body language, facial clues, and oral emanations such as crying and cooing. These behaviors are not driven by the people and events around them; they are products of the will to survive.

As personalities form, clues to a child's outlook as an adult are slowly revealed. But the clues may be false positives. People can change their behaviors by their own volition, or be forced to change by the conditions they face. For no apparent reason, a person may flip from happiness to sadness, passivity to aggressiveness, hope to despair. Therefore, defining a person's personality based on any one behavior at any one time is too simplistic. Personality is based on an accumulation of feelings, but with one behavior ascendant most of the time.

Diverse philosophical terms have evolved to label behaviors: existentialism, nihilism, Pavlovian, operant conditioned. These terms came about as scientists attempted to quantify human behavior. But fitting personalities into a measurable framework is like blowing air into a punctured balloon. It doesn't work.

I argue that only three words are needed to define human behavior: optimism, pessimism, pragmatism. None of these are hard to understand and can be explained by the glass of water meme.

An optimist sees a partially filled glass as half full. Things are good. We're getting by. If we already have some water, chances are we'll get more.

A pessimist sees the opposite—the glass is half empty. Things are tight. We're just eking by. Since we have so little water now, chances are we probably will have less tomorrow.

The pragmatist is an optimist waiting to bloom. The pragmatist sees the water glass and thinks everything is okay for now. Odds are 50-50 there eventually will be more. And if more water doesn't somehow materialize, the pragmatist will search for a new source.

How do you see yourself? Do you approach life with a positive outlook? Do you react to problems by working to solve them? Do you help others to see that solutions are possible? Do you refrain from shunning those who can't help or don't want to help find solutions?

Your answers to these questions tell much about your spiritual life. Has it been a life of noble ideas and ethical decisions? Or has it been one of capitulation to dark dreams and patronizing superiority? Has your hand always been out to take, or has your hand been extended to give?

Maryann Caton, 58 | Robt. MacKenzie, 70 | World POP: 9.23 billion

---

Maryann had a particularly hard time in bed breathing without coughing. Spring exploded in a riot of new blossoms. Yellow pollen from Colorado pines coated everything, plastered to surfaces by sharp winds. Cottonwood and willow fluff danced on the breezes. Ragweed and goldenrod bloomed in the fields. It was a spring one might expect and wish for—a rebirth of plant life—but not if you suffered from lung congestion. Air conditioning helped asthmatics when indoors, but no door or window seal was one hundred percent airtight.

Rob retrieved Annie's bronchodilator from the bathroom. She sat up and inhaled a heavy dose of mist. "You should keep it next to you on the nightstand, lass. When you first notice a bout of coughing coming on, immediately use it."

"You're right, honey." She took another dose. "I'm sorry for waking you up to get it."

Rob chuckled. "You didn't wake me up. I was lying here listening to you. I've gotten to the point when I can tell a bad bout is coming on."

"That doesn't make me feel any better," she said. "Whether I'm waking you up, or you're on medical alert, you're still not getting sleep."

"Don't worry, love. Once you take your medicine you calm down and nod off. So do I. If needed, I can sleep in Jake's room."

"That stinks, Rob. I want you in here with me. You keep me warm." She kissed him then rolled on her side, her coughing under control for the moment.

He listened to her breathing. Even though they were following Dr. Lin's instructions, Rob was worried. He knew she couldn't be cured of silicosis. Did that mean she would spend the rest of her life repeatedly fighting for breath? Did it make sense to go on a lung transplant waiting list? And if you were chosen to be a recipient, what were your odds of survival? Rob knew of people who had weathered the operation, but then they faced a lifetime taking anti-rejection drugs. They could have serious side effects, too.

She was quiet, but he knew she wasn't asleep. He moved closer and kissed her neck. It wasn't a sexual gesture, it was meant to be reassuring. He loved her more than he could ever express.

She stirred and spoke. "Rob, do you ever think about death?"

He wasn't prepared for the question. He felt a chill tumble down his spine. "Death? Why do you ask, love?"

"Oh, for no reason. I just wanted to know. I loved you for months before I asked you about your religion."

He laughed. "Aye, then you got a full discourse about ULAR. It's amazing you married me after hearing my philosophy."

She turned to her back and propped her head higher on her pillow. "Other than dealing with Jake's passing, we've never talked about the end of life. I really don't know what you believe. Does dying frighten you?"

Rob was silent for a minute thinking about how to respond. "When I was a lad, I had dreams about what happened after I died. Usually, my actual demise was never a part of the story. Then, one time I had an image. It woke me up."

"Tell me about it."

"My lifeless body was loaded onto a wooden barge. Dead branches were piled on top. Someone with a torch lighted the fire, and I was pushed out onto Loch Lomond to drift to Valhalla."

"Like the Vikings?"

"Aye, exactly. Then it was followed by another dream about the Battle of Culloden, where again I died."

"You never mentioned that."

"Nae, after all they were just dreams, and I was but a wee'un. Besides in my imagination what happened to me in dreams was less bloody than sticking a muc in real life."

"Muc? . . . oh, that's right! A pig." She giggled.

"Aye, you remember. In my Culloden dream I was run through with a lance, but it didn't hurt. I wasn't afraid, and the dream didn't leave me hootin' and hollerin' in my sleep. I was a hero in my fantasy, not a corpse."

"Did you ever tell anyone about your dreams?"

"Nae. There are too many superstitions floating in Scotland. Many Scots believe there are people blessed or cursed with a 'second sight,' the ability to see the future, maybe interpret the past."

"Like fortune tellers?"

"Aye . . . or witches."

"There's so much about Scotland I still have to learn." She coughed.

"Aye, lass, me too. It's all hidden in the mist covered mountains among fairy rings and behind standing stones."

"You don't believe that stuff, do you?"

"Nae, love, by now you should know I don't. I'm a scientist. I observe things. I count things. I measure things. Then I make predictions. Witchery is about the occult. I don't believe in hocus-pocus, but still . . ." He chuckled.

Maryann snuggled closer. "Okay then, mister scientist, what is your philosophy about the process of dying?"

He held her hand. "All living things die, including us. You know that. It's inevitable. We're born to die. It's not sad nor tragic. It's the natural course of events. Death is hard on two groups—those that don't want to die and think their death is unfair, and those who are left living. The survivors feel the pain of losing someone. But there's nothing dying folks can do to help the living, except possibly pass away with dignity."

Both were quiet. Annie was digesting his words. He wondered if he had been too blunt, too objective. "What about you, lass? How do you face the inevitable? I want to know."

Now it was time for Maryann to put her thoughts in order. A variety of former beliefs and new ideas had to be integrated and catalogued. After all, she had lived with Rob for twenty-four years. He had mysteriously but fortuitously appeared in her life at a vulnerable time. Would those with second sight know that Rob and she would entwine to form a liana of incredible strength. She had seen such vines in Peru.

"I was raised in the Catholic faith," she said. "You remember. Maybe faith is the wrong word, because I never faithfully believed what I was urged to believe. A better way to say it is, I was raised under Catholic dogma. My religion amounted to rules and regulations imposed on me by a group of men living in Rome. I've always asked 'why?', even when I was little. And the stories and liturgy never made any sense to me. I was a freethinker. I continue to be. You have to deal me, so you know. In ancient times, I would have been labeled a heretic and burned at the stake."

Rob laughed at her allusion. "Oh, bonny lass, no man in his right mind would have done you in like that."

"No, you're wrong, Rob. History is full of powerful men out of their minds. You don't have to look any further than the Salem witch trials. And don't forget about Trump."

"Aye, I forgot about president bone spur. But it's true about Salem. Some of the women were accused of second sight."

"Correct. Then you came along in my life, a man with a practical outlook, a willingness to debunk superstition, and a well-formed ethical belief system. Your ideas changed me. It took me awhile to fully understand that what you were saying ought to be the guiding principle of human interaction—the Golden Rule in its many iterations. Your ideas have made me a better person."

"Thank you, lass. But it wasn't me. I only had ideas. You were the one who took those ideas and put them into practice.

The proof is what you've accomplished for the homeless folks in this town."

"I guess so, dear." She rolled left to face him. "I'm not afraid of dying. Like you, I know it's part of the master plan," she chuckled. "But I often wonder who the master planner is, and how he or she arrived at it."

"It's not me," said Rob. "I'm only along for the ride."

"I guess when I ask you about death, I'm asking if you think we have the right to end life on our own terms."

"Oh, I see. Am I master of my own domain? He laughed. "Aye, I'm master of me. Yes, I want to control what happens to me. If I want to die, healthy or not, I believe that's my choice. In fact, I can take care of that with a noose, gunshot to the head, or a bottle of sleeping pills and a bottle of whisky. If I reach the point where I want to die, I don't want some psychologist asking me to rethink it, some priest saying it's a sin, or some doctor saying they can't help me because of the hippocratic oath to do no harm. I'll never be convinced allowing someone to suffer end of life mental or physical pain is doing no harm."

"I felt the same way about abortion," confided Annie. "We were always careful, but if I had become pregnant after Jake died, I think I would have ended it. At the time, I was deeply involved with environmental law and homeless issues. Besides, forty-seven is pushing things."

"Aye. As far as I'm concerned, either way lass, it was your decision to make."

"That's why I'm so annoyed Colorado can't finally implement it's 'right to die law.' It's been twenty-three years since the act was passed, and three years since it was reauthorized. For pity's sake, the legislature can't agree on the drug concoction, and who controls the dosage. If I decide on voluntary euthanasia, I don't want some unknown physician controlling my fate. I want it to be up to me."

"Sweetie, I totally agree. But I'll take it a step further. I want the kit to be readily available in every pharmacy. Condoms are displayed. Products for hemorrhoids are front and center. There are rows of douche concoctions. Euthanasia kits should be available for sale."

"I think politicians believe there would be a rash of suicides," said Annie, "if kits were easy to get and administered unsupervised."

Rob harrumphed. "That's nonsense! We give ourselves enemas before colonoscopies. Certainly we can swallow a pill. And so what if there are unexpected suicides? There are too many people as it is. People who want to end their lives at an early age likely are not happy nor productive citizens." She nestled closer and held his hand. He continued. "Conservatives say they want the government out of our lives. At the same time, they allow the government make laws interfering in our personal affairs. It's all misguided stupidity fueled by evangelical fervor. It's mass confusion, and impinges on virtually every facet of the way we live. What is freedom, if we're not free to choose both how we live and how we die?"

"When are you moving?" asked Annie. She inched through the throng of children and adults on Pearl Street dressed in costumes for Halloween. She grasped Fred's elbow.

"The closing is on Monday, so as soon as papers are exchanged, I'm off to Strathmore Gardens. I think Lois would have approved of my unit. Rob's volunteered to help me with my mattress and sleeping bag. Everything else has been moved."

Fred turned and watched Jeannie and Alex pick candy out

of a cardboard pumpkin. Store employees dressed as ghosts and goblins stood on the sidewalk doling out treats. There was no way to count the number of Halloween celebrants. The crowd eased down one side of the mall, then returned on the other side.

"How many people do you think are here, Rob?" asked Fred. "C'mon, you're the scientist, figure it out."

"Don't get him started," said Annie, shaking her head. "He'll pace off the length of the mall and multiply it by the width to get the area. Then he'll divide the total area by one hundred to arrive at a smaller, more manageable space. Finally he'll sit on a bench and count the number of people who pass through that small space every minute. I've seen it before." She laughed, then cleared her throat.

"You've done that?" Fred asked Rob, amused by his sister's allegation.

"Aye, sort of. I once tried to figure out how many cubic yards of snow I shoveled after a big winter storm in Connecticut. The local lads with pickups and plows said they wouldn't be able to get to us for two days. I needed to get out of the house and get the stink blown off, so I went to work."

Fred laughed and winked at Maryann. "Get the stink blown off, huh? Lad, you've certainly picked up some Pittsburgh jargon."

Rob nodded. "It's true. I've lived with the wee lass for twenty-five years."

"So how many cubic yards did you shovel?" pressed Fred.

"Eight thousand."

"Not nine?" Fred chuckled.

"No, eight."

"And what's your estimate of the number of people on the mall?"

"I have no idea."

They all laughed at Rob's honesty.

"I love Jeannie's and Alex's costumes," said Maryann. Her niece was dressed as a beehive, and three year old Alex was a honeybee.

"Alex's antennae are a nice touch," said Fred. "That little guy is as sweet as they come."

"Thanks for returning so soon," said Dr. Lin. "It's a bit inconvenient, but after taking the test on Monday you needed to get the results checked within two days, three days on the outside, or you would have to take it again."

"No problem," said Annie. Rob stood at the side waiting to hear the results.

"Please roll up your sleeve, and we'll have a look." Annie unbuttoned her cuff. Dr. Lin examined the TB skin test. "Good news, Mrs. MacKenzie, you're not infected."

Annie's face softened from a frown of concern into a broad smile. "That's great news!"

"It was the prudent thing to do," said Lin. "After you said you occasionally forgot to wear your mask at the homeless shelter, this test was essential. You don't have any signs of TB, but I want you to promise me you'll always wear a mask when you're helping." She looked at Rob. "And you keep on your wife's case about it. No backsliding for her."

"Aye, doctor. I'll keep after her." He looked at Annie with a face that said, "I told you so."

2039

What Happened Then?

Historical Events of Some Importance or Little Significance

June, 1980

6/1 First transmission of CNN

6/3 Jimmy Carter (POTUS #39) is renominated by Dems

6/8 French Open Tennis, men:

Björn Borg defeats former Columbia University star Vitas Gerulaitis

6/8 French Open Tennis, women:

Chris Evert defeats Virginia Ruzici

6/10 Provisional IRA prisoners escape Crumlin Road Gaol in Belfast

6/12 Ronald Reagan promises to submit to medical tests if nominated by GOP

6/13 UN calls for South Africa to free Nelson Mandela

6/15 Maryann Caton born in Pittsburgh, Pennsylvania

6/16 New forms of life created in lab can be patented, US Supreme Court rules

6/22 Katri Tekakwitha, indigenous Mohawk woman, beatified to Sainthood

6/23 First solar powered coast-to-coast two-way radio conversation

6/27 US revives draft registration

Maryann Caton, 59 | Robt. MacKenzie, 71 | World POP: 9.29 billion

---

The harsh Colorado winter of 2039 was described in the state's newspapers. The air was drier than usual, magnifying the atmospheric inversions that had become more frequent. A forest fire burned north of Vail, unaffected by winter snows. Too many dead trees were left standing ready to ignite at any moment. Pine bark beetles had done their cruel deed.

Along the Front Range, controlled burns took place to rid counties of ash tree cuttings. Millions of trees had been killed by the emerald ash tree borer. Although saplings of hardier species were planted to replace them, the landscape reverted to what it had looked like in 1900: brown, treeless, a high plain, a semi-arid prairie. The difference between then and now, said the reports, was the sprawl of homes and highways covering terrain meant for grasslands and bison herds.

The air quality index rarely signaled a day when one of the pollutants was in the "moderate" range. Gone were days when "good" air existed. "Unhealthy" became the norm. Often particulates registered in the "dangerous" zone. On those days, warnings to stay indoors were issued for the elderly, children, and asthmatics. But even healthy people were aware of the bad air. Drug company stocks escalated in price, as lung soothing medicines found a large market.

Maryann now spent much of her life indoors. She ended her service in the homeless shelter. For her dedication, she received accolades from the City Council. She was pleased to learn a sixth tiny home community had been approved by planning and zoning.

The Compassionate Conservatives continued as tiny home sponsors. A few pundits began writing that the group was hardly conservative anymore. Liberal causes and good deeds had cleansed their souls of narrow thinking and social inertia.

Maryann was happy watching her grand nephew grow up. At four years old, he was no longer a toddler. Rob referred to him as "the wee lad." The wee lad had a broad vocabulary that included some four letter swear words and a decent Scottish, "Och!" His parents excused his behavior. They said he swore with a smile on his face, not in anger. They claimed he was doing it to make them laugh.

Rob knew Maryann's silicosis would never disappear. He was saddened to see her suffer with it, especially as environmental conditions deteriorated. There was nothing he could do to ease her symptoms except to make sure she got to her monthly check-ups with Dr. Lin. Some days she hacked incessantly, unhelped by the various combinations of medicines that were prescribed. Exercising at the rec center was no longer an option. She tried relearning how to knit, now with a child as the beneficiary of her work. Rob kept her stocked with books from the Meadows Branch Library. She grew to enjoy the old novels from the deceased Scottish writer, Alexander McCall Smith.

Newspapers said it had been the hottest June ever recorded in Denver. The pattern of heat intensity continued into July. Dry conditions along the Front Range resulted in a permanent halt to brush burning and open camp fires. Independence Day fireworks were cancelled in every town throughout the region. Nevertheless, air quality indicators remained within dangerous levels despite Colorado's effort at fire suppression. Pollution, especially smoke laden particulates from West Coast fires, blanketed the state.

The state's EPA office issued cease and desist orders to fracking companies drilling new wells. They also ordered the capping of many existing wells. The danger was methane gas. However, the head of the EPA, Bobby Smyth, an evangelical libertarian and former Tea Party activist from Louisiana, withdrew funding from the Denver office. It was money needed to inspect well sites and police enforcement of the cease and desist order.

Smyth was quoted as saying, "If Cajuns learned to live with chemicals and petroleum muckin' up their bayous, Colorado cowboys ought to be able to deal with smoke. It's nothin' more than sittin' around a campfire sippin' chuck wagon coffee." The head administrator of the Colorado's EPA office, Richard Clayton, resigned.

Maryann was coughing heavily trying to clear her lungs.

She propped her head up with two pillows. She worked to clear her throat, hacked, then gagged with the effort.

"Use your inhaler, lass!" Rob was in bed at her side watching her struggle to breathe. He saw her try to inflate her chest, searching for more oxygen.

"Rob, I can't breathe." There was fear in her voice. "The inhaler (cough) isn't working."

He heard panic amid her wheezing and rattling.

"Please phone Dr. Lin," she begged.

"Aye, love. I'll be back in a minute."

Rob knew the situation was dire. Annie had had bad spells before, but this was unlike any he had seen. He raced to the first floor, found Dr. Lin's number, and phoned. It seemed like an eternity before his call was received. It was the answering service.

"My name's Rob MacKenzie," he said with urgency. "My wife's a patient of Dr. Lin. She's having extreme distress trying to breath. Can you put me through to the doctor?"

"I'm afraid not, sir. The doctor is out of town for the holiday. But in off-hour situations when doctors are unavailable, we're authorized to to tell patients to go the the emergency room. That's my advice, sir. I'll leave a message for Dr. Lin."

"Och! Okay then. I'll get her to the hospital. Thank you."

Bounding back upstairs Rob thought: *It's three in the morning on the Fourth of July—of course Lin wouldn't be available.*

He rushed into the bedroom and turned on a lamp. He heard gasping. "Annie, get up, lass," he urged. "Put on your robe. I'm taking you to the hospital."

He disappeared into the dressing room, pulled on shorts and slipped his feet into sandals. He made sure he had his watch, wallet, and car keys. He returned to the bedroom. "C'mon, lass. I said get up. Let's get you some help."

No sound or movement came from his wife. Instantly, he knew she had died. He was stunned. He stood still for a moment in disbelief, then went to her and held her in his arms. She was still warm. He tried to revive her by blowing into her airways. She didn't respond. Then he kissed her and wept.

Her illness had taken its toll. She was frail. She had lost weight. He could feel bones where he should have felt muscle. She had lost her appetite. Blindly, he had attributed her withering to the aging process. In reflection, he was sure Dr. Lin saw Annie's downward spiral. But what doctor wanted to tell an ambulatory patient she was dying? Lin had said repeatedly there was no cure for silicosis. It could only be managed. But managing a serious pulmonary disease in an environment that was progressively unhealthy was impossible.

Robert MacKenzie held the love of his life in his arms. He gently rocked back and forth as if reassuring a child. He smelled the perfume of her he had known for twenty-five years. He nuzzled her neck. Tears cascaded down his cheeks.

He couldn't remember crying in all his seventy-one years. Annie once told him he was too much of a stoic. "Give it up, Rob," she had urged. "Let your emotions flow free." But until now, he never had. He didn't cry when his father died. He hadn't cried when Uncle Willie passed. The death of his first wife didn't elicit tears, although he was terribly sad. His mother's death was accepted as normal because of her age. And he locked away his own grief when Jake died to allow Annie her full measure of sorrow.

Now he wept and rocked. He felt utterly alone.

OBITUARY
Mayann Caton MacKenzie
June 15, 1980 - July 4, 2039

Maryann MacKenzie died at her home in the early morning hours of July 4, 2039. She succumbed to the lung disease, silicosis. She was born in Pittsburgh but lived her childhood in Mars, Pennsylvania, along with a sibling, Fred Caton, a resident of Strathmore Gardens in Boulder. She graduated fifth in her class from Mars High School before attending college in New York City. She was a nationally ranked springboard diver.

Maryann received her BA from Columbia College and JD from Columbia Law School. Upon graduating, she worked for a New York law firm specializing in environmental litigation. She was instrumental in defending Roxbridge, Connecticut, from the siting of a radioactive waste facility within its borders.

After her first marriage to Zachary Canfeld ended in divorce, she met the love of her life, retired CU Professor Robert MacKenzie, at Manhattan's Guggenheim Museum. They had a short but spirited courtship before marrying on Hogmanay, the Scottish name for New Year's Eve, on December 31, 2015. Dr. MacKenzie was raised in Balmaha, a small clachan on the shore of Loch Lomond in Scotland.

Maryann was a partner in the Boulder law firm **Pearl 2 Pine.** She spent years fighting fracking efforts at Colorado's Rocky Flats, a manufacturing site of nuclear weapons triggers from 1952 to 1992.

Annie MacKenzie was loved by both Boulder conservatives and progressives alike, citizens concerned with the city's homeless situation. She was a loyal volunteer at the North Boulder homeless shelter. After years of lobbying the City Council to amend its homeless plan and loosen zoning restrictions, she was instrumental in the establishment of six tiny home communities. Residences were available for ownership by needy families and individuals meeting application requirements. The first settlement in East Boulder was Jake's Place, named in memory of Annie's son, Jacob Canfeld MacKenzie, who died in a mountaineering accident in 2027.

Maryann is survived by her husband, Robert MacKenzie, her brother Fred Caton, two great nieces, Lindsay Caton, an attorney in New Jersey, Boulder resident Jeannie Callendar and her husband the sculptor Sandy Callendar, and their child Alejandro.

In lieu of flowers, contributions can be made to the Boulder Association of Compassionate Conservatives, P.O. Box 3131, Boulder 80306. A service of remembrance will be held at the Sunrise Amphitheater on Flagstaff Road on Sunday, July 31 at 5:59 a.m.

2040

The Clarion Call of the Mountains
THE DENVER HITCHIN' POST

TUESDAY, JULY 3, 2040 ☁ CLEARING IN
THE PM ▲ 97° ▼ 85° ● © TDHP $3.50

❖ Highlights of the Week in Review ❖

Compiled by John Mahaffey, Senior Editor
@ jmahaffey.com
THE DENVER HITCHIN' POST

Death with Dignity Regulations Eased

Twenty-four years after Colorado voters overwhelmingly
approved Proposition 106, the End of Life Options Act, the
General Assembly made sweeping changes to the law. The
biggest revision eliminated the restriction that terminally ill
patients had to have six or less months to live as diagnosed by a
team of physicians. The new law allows "death with dignity" at
any time in an adult's life. Consultation with a licensed, board
certified, mental health professional is advised. The vote was
93 ayes to 7 nays.

A joint statement was issued by Governor Tad Metcoff, Senate President Elise Calderon, and Speaker or the House Lyle Hastings:

The challenging increase in the state's population, coupled with growing water shortages, crop failures, and fracking disasters, have resulted in a spike of Colorado suicides. Clearly, many citizens no longer can cope with our coarsening environment and are taking their own lives as an escape. Suicide by firearms is the main factor. The new law will make access to life ending drugs possible without physicians' prescriptions as required in the old law.

During the next year, the impact of this law will be studied. Data will be collected. Law enforcement agencies will be required to submit statistics regarding firearm deaths. A comprehensive report will be the first agenda item of the 2041 General Assembly.

Second Gross Reservoir Expansion Planned

Twenty years after enlarging Denver's primary water source, Gross Reservoir in Nederland, work is about to get underway for a second enlargement. A burgeoning population along the Front Range is causing water shortages. Climate change factors have resulted in average daily temperature increases, regional droughts, and the drawdown of the state's aquifers. Residential and commercial water restrictions are now in effect from March 15 to December 15.

Gross Reservoir was last expanded in 2020 to provide a reliable water source for 1.4 million residents with more people projected to follow. The original project raised the existing dam by 131 feet to a height of 471 feet expanding the reservoir by 25 billion gallons. Six hundred thousand trees were clear cut. The dam was altered by buttressing the downslope side and working upwards.

The project added to the region's deteriorating air quality. The burning of forest waste, construction traffic, and concrete production added to particulate pollution. Shoreline picnic areas and parking lots were flooded. Even with an enlarged collection basin, a summer mega-storm in 2022 dumped so much rain in the mountains, the new dam was topped causing massive water damage along Boulder Creek and into Boulder City.

The second enlargement is projected to be completed in 2045. This time the expansion will require the condemnation of homes and businesses near downtown Nederland. The local government fears the project will result in the eventual disappearance of the city adding it to the list of Colorado ghost towns.

Barron Trump Donates 500 Acres to US Forest Service

Reclusive Barron Trump, the 33 year old fifth child of deceased President Donald J. Trump, has donated 500 acres to the US Forest Service. The land is adjacent to the Maroon Bells-Snowmass Wilderness area of the White River National Forest. The parcel was to be developed into a Trump branded golf course: "Trump Heaven: God's highest 36 Holes in the Rockies."

When his father's will was probated, it was learned the estate was valued considerably less than what the deceased president claimed. Nevertheless, it's estimated each child received a sizeable sum. Sources say the three oldest children, Ivanka, Eric, and Donald. Jr., each received between 200 and 300 million dollars. Tiffany Trump, daughter of the former actress Marla Maples, received 10 million dollars. It is unknown what Barron, son of third wife Melania, inherited. Trump's three wives, now all deceased, did not factor into the distribution of his estate.

Barron Trump has been giving away his fortune since his emancipation at the age of 21. Forensic accountants have identified the major beneficiaries of young Trump's largess: United Negro College Fund; American Indian College Fund; Conservation Colorado; Colorado Coalition for the Homeless; the National Trust for Scotland.

Trump lives on Eigg, an island in the Inner Hebrides,17.5 miles from the port of Mallaig on the Scottish coast. It's population in 2039 was estimated at 195. Eigg claims to have the cleanest air in the northern hemisphere. Its economy is based on sheep farming and daily tourism.

CO2 Sequestration Schemes Prove Too Little Too Late

Environmental scientists have been frantically searching for ways to reduce carbon dioxide presence in the atmosphere. Fifty years ago, it was predicted that topping 400 ppm of atmospheric carbon dioxide would begin the process of raising the planet's average temperature three to five degrees Celsius by 2050. In 2040, carbon dioxide is at 425 ppm with no leveling off or reduction in sight. As forecast, average planetary temperatures (up two degrees) have increased as carbon dioxide has mounted.

Global heating and climate alteration are now impacting large swathes of the planet. Worldwide food production is not meeting demand. There has been a spike in regional conflicts over potable water access and arable land.

A variety of schemes have been proposed and processes invented all aimed at reducing atmospheric carbon dioxide. In Iceland it was discovered that pumping dissolved carbon dioxide into the subsoil resulted in conversion of gas into rock. Elsewhere, smokestack scrubbers at power plants reduce carbon dioxide emissions, but do not reduce carbon dioxide already in the atmosphere. Other processes, including bioengineering, have proven effective on a small scale. The problem with all efforts up to now is what to do with captured carbon dioxide. The gas is a tangible product of the burning of fossil fuels. As such it has mass and volume. Where can it be sequestered? How might it be chemically altered to become a financial asset?

As the dilemma is debated among the world's geo-physical experts, and entrepreneurs search for an evasive "perpetual motion" solution, one realization remains unchallenged. The only way to rein in carbon dioxide emissions is to totally eliminate the burning of fossil fuels.

Broncos End Season Early—Concussions Take Toll

The Denver Broncos are the second professional football franchise to close shop this year. Following the Pittsburgh Steelers who ended their season in June, the Broncos shut down operations on July 1.

The decision was the result of five factors: 1. A roster ravaged by head injuries and knee damage. 2. The unwillingness of replacement players to risk losing their mental abilities as they age. 3. The shortage of new players as many high school and college programs are eliminated. 4. The decrease in interest among college graduates to join a league where salaries are tanking. 5. The over-saturation of markets with teams no longer playing at 2020 standards. The era of the 21st Century gladiator is over.

In comparison, the Ivy League continues to thrive. The decision in 2015 to prohibit live tackling at practices has resulted in the league's success. Whenever contact is required to learn blocking assignments, run pass routes, or smother an opposing team's offense, it happens against robot dummies that can scoot across the gridiron at human-like speed. The league that's arguably the most historic and venerable is alive and well. The 2040 football season in the northeast promises to attract national attention.

Tribal Nations Win: "Mt. Arapaho" Erases "Mt. Evans"

Following years of sit-ins, road blockages, and lobbying, Colorado's tribal alliance, **The People**, has succeeded in having Mount Evans erased from maps and replaced with a new title: Mount Arapaho. This follows similar peak renamings in other Colorado ranges. Indigenous peoples are finally being recognized as the rightful heirs to Colorado's legacy, not miners, not land speculators, not the Federal army, nor federal appointees. Tribal elders have sworn their campaign won't end until every label signaling white domination is gone.

The sixteen year effort to rename Mount Evans was attributed to a geopolitical coincidence of intention. On clear days the massif can be seen in the mountains west of Denver, thirty-six miles from the golden dome of the Colorado State Capitol. History suggests that influential white city fathers stood on the dome's balcony wallowing in the power they manipulated, as they watched Mt. Evans glow in alpenlite. After the official renaming decree ceremony, **The People** marched out of the assembly and reformed on the dome's balcony. For the first time in weeks they enjoyed clear air which offered an unblurred vision of Mount Arapaho. Most were silent in reverence. A few cried at what had been lost. Some cried at what had been regained. Mt. Arapaho is now a totem of a proud past.

Boulder Muni Dead, City Joins Denver in Regional Power Grid; Xcel Reaches 95% Renewables; Millions Wasted in Ill-conceived Effort

---

After thirty years of indecision, arrogance, truculence, political manipulation, mismanagement, and poor planning, Boulder's City Council has heeded the will of the people. A municipal power company will not be organized. The idea is dead.

In 2019, the Council tabled muni discussions when it became clear a 2020 referendum would scuttle the project. Citizens were tired of seeing tax monies disappear down the proverbial prairie dog hole. But the council refused to admit their incompetence and tucked the idea away within the pages of *Robert's Rules of Order.* As it turned out, the council's feet dragging killed municipalization. Inevitably, Xcel, the city's power provider reached 95 percent renewables with a plan for 100 percent renewables in three more years.

**Maryann Caton, d. July 4, 2039 | Robt.
MacKenzie, 72 | World POP: 9.34 billion**

"We're all set for the Fourth, Uncle Rob. We're picking up dad. What time would you like us?"

"How about one? That will give me some time in the morning to weed the garden."

"Perfect!" Jeannie's voice pitched up a notch. "Uncle Rob, good news! Sandy's got a commission from the Parks Department to create a sculpture for the Evert Pierson Kids' Fishing Pond along Boulder Creek."

"Och! That is good news. I know where it is. What's he making?"

"A weathervane, five feet in length. It's in the shape of a Colorado trout. The Park Department's going to bolt it to a large rock in the middle of the pond. It will show children which direction to cast their lines."

Rob laughed. "To be sure they'll be casting eastward most of the time, as they do now. The wind is always coming down Boulder Canyon from the west. Will the vane have directional cardinals?"

"Sort of." Jeannie chuckled. "Instead of N, S, E, and W, compass points are going to be mounted as fish names: Northern pike, Southern catfish. Eastern codfish, Western salmon. Clever, huh?"

"Aye, bloody good idea. That lad of yours is a keeper. Don't let him off the hook. If you have a drawing of the project, bring it along with you."

"Will do, Uncle Rob. See you tomorrow."

MacKenzie entered the house before noon and stripped off his shirt. It was soaked with sweat. Weeding and cultivating the raised beds in ninety-six degree heat was brutal. He put on a dry t-shirt and returned to the kitchen to get some ice water.

The items he needed to complete his project were in the living room on the coffee table: the unfinished scrapbook, scissors, a copy of his poem, three ring sheet protectors, and a photo of Annie at their wedding reception. It was time to bring a late chapter of his life to a close before the final one was written.

It had been a year since the passing of his wife. The grief he had suffered in the ensuing months gave away to inevitable acceptance. Annie once accused him of being a stoic where human life was concerned. He knew she was right. Other than the immense loss and lonliness he felt at her passing, he was ambivalent about death. He couldn't ignore his scientific objectivity in favor of the subjectivity needed to feel deep loss for others. "We're born to die," he often said, as if that excused his matter-of-factness about the final adieu.

He looked at his watch. Fred, Jeannie, Sandy, and wee Alex would be arriving in an hour for their July Fourth picnic. He had hot dogs and shrimp for the grill. Fred was bringing a six-pack of Old Chub Scottish Ale. Jeannie had promised potato salad and coleslaw. Sandy was in charge of Alex, and was bringing a scale drawing of his fish weathervane. Rob wondered what toys the wee'un would have.

After drinking water, he poured himself two ounces of

Aberfeldy single malt scotch whisky, added three ice cubes, then headed to the living room. He sat and sipped his drink. Images of the West Highland Way flashed in his memory. The aroma of the scotch was as much a mental stimulant as was its taste.

He opened the album and added a new insert for page one. He picked up Annie's photo, kissed it, then slid it into the sleeve. He stared at it for some minutes, his head clear of sad thoughts, then remembered the struggle to breathe she had endured the night she died. Always in the back of his mind was the question—how could someone who had lived such a vital life succumb to a vocational disease? Was it written in her DNA? Or was it a stroke of fate? Would Scots with second sight have predicted it? If so, could she have been warned?

"My lass, you always took my breath away," he whispered, staring at her image.

He added his poem to page two. Earlier he found it in his file of verse. He had written it in Connecticut when inspired by a dogwood tree shedding its petals into the Berkshire River. He gave it to Annie early in their relationship to show his love for her. Together they had titled it.

Love's Confetti

Delicate oval floating down / Updrafts tickle from below
Above on bank he sees it spin / Steady landing on the flow
Dimly lit he sees it drifting / Stay he must to see it go
Stop to think about the question / Answer he does love her so

The July third edition of *The Denver Hitchin' Post* was ready to undergo surgery. MacKenzie carefully cut out the "Week in Review" section. He trimmed it to fit the album. He turned the book over, flipping open the back cover. In the final empty sleeve he inserted his cutout.

"Here it is, lass. It's done. Twenty-five years of memories," he said aloud. "I love you." He closed the book and went to greet his guests.

❖ Benediction ❖

"A life well lived is a life shared with a lover."

"You can drain scotch out of a bottle, but you
can't drain Scotland out of a Scot."

"Height is of little consequence. The size
of the heart is what matters."

"There's wisdom to be learned from a wee'un, but
it may take years for it to become understood."

"Dogs are imperfectly perfect."

It's impossible to imagine what the second half of my life would have been like without Annie. Twenty-five years as a couple—astounding! We probably never would have seen our golden wedding anniversary together. By then, I'd be ninety-seven, Annie, eighty five. But I have no regrets. A quarter century union is a big achievement itself.

When first married, my thinking ahead five years was nigh impossible. The days, months, and years flew bye, often leaving me without time for reflection. A lot happened between our vows and old age. Tangled together were silly events and serious decisions, calamities and successes, medical problems and healthy pursuits, life and death. For me, the glue that kept our adventure alive was Maryann Caton, my wife.

I miss her more than I can describe. I miss our son, Jake. I miss Jake's pup, Nova. I miss no longer being part of a nuclear family. But what we were then, in my memory is still what we are now. We'll always be together—the three of us.

My life will continue as a writer. Scientific articles and books of poetry are in the past for me. But essays, criticism, and fiction will, hopefully, continue to flow from my pen.

An old friend from Roxbridge, Connecticut, Mo Klein, once said, "You die twice. The first time is when you take your last breath. The second time is when your name is never again spoken."

Although in the sundown of my life, enough light remains for me to see. Through my writings, I hope to keep my family alive, after I've taken my last gasp.

With apologies, I remind you our name is MacKenzie. We are the MacKenzie Clan of Boulder, Colorado, the "high place." *Tulach Ard!* Don't forget us.

Printed in the United States
By Bookmasters